praise for psychics of oracle bay

<u>Not in the Cards</u>

An Exciting Introduction: Amy's books immediately go to the top of my queue when they are released and they never disappoint. This was an exciting introduction to Oracle Bay and I'm looking forward to getting to know the rest of the inhabitants in future books.

Found Another Great Author!: I didn't know what to expect when I went into this book. The premise of the book sounded like something I would enjoy. At first, as I started reading the book, I wasn't sure I was going to like it. However, after a few pages, I was drawn into the book and it never let me go. In fact, by the end of the book, I was so ready to find out what was going to happen next from all the hints that were given, I wanted the next book right then. This book was well-written, had a great plot (both romance and intrigue), and I loved the characters, even the villain who I loved to hate. Can't wait to read more and I highly recommend!

Fantastic: A well written story with great characters and the location of Oracle Bay was inspired. The heroine in this story is a tribute to enduring heartache and finding a new life and love.

· · · ★ ★ ★ ★ ★ ★ · · ·

First Hand Knowledge

The author does a bang up job of making this mythical place not only enchanting, but a place I'd want to go. To live, even if I were the only mundane in the lot. She also expands characters from her previous book 'Not in the Cards' and keeps the story arc alive and moving forward. There's something to be said for a series that continues with the lives of all the characters, even when the focus is on only two at a time.

· · · ★ ★ ★ ★ ★ ★ · · ·

Wing and a Prayer

I have this terrible problem with Amy Cissell's books. I get hooked within the first few sentences, and want to read the whole thing in one sitting. They're addictive, fun, clever stories about people you wish you knew.

· · · ★ ★ ★ ★ ★ ★ · · ·

Belle of the Ball

This is the third book in the series, and I think this series is getting better each book. I love how silly, fun, and interesting this book is. Drew and Bill's romance was great, touching, and romantic. And, the mystery was great, too. Add to that, there were some revelations that were hilarious. There was a also point at the very end of the book that made me laugh out loud because when Drew couldn't see Bill, I thought he'd been turned into a toad. What really happened and why? You'll have to read this and find out. If you love a fun, cozy, romantic mystery, give this book and series a try; you'll love it! Highly recommend! I was provided a copy which I voluntarily reviewed.

Hell and High Water

I throughly enjoyed this book. It touches on so many possibilities of paranormal people. It has a good lead in, full rich characters with quirks and an unexpected ending.

Tempest in a Teapot

The ending got me! I have really enjoyed this series, and I was so darn excited to see another one in the series.I was extremely happy with this book as I couldn't figure out who the villain was. I had ideas, but the author was skillful at red herrings. Then the end hit...I was so darn angry! LOL! Highly recommend.

There are curses and bonds, mystery and mild romance, friends and family-both related and found. I do love Oracle Bay. I'm excited for the next story for Morgana

Psychics of Oracle Bay

Not in the Cards
First Hand Knowledge
Wing and a Prayer
Belle of the Ball
Hell and High Water
Tempest in a Teapot
Elements of Surprise
Dead Giveaway*
Bad to the Bones*
Shoot for the Stars*
Fun and Prophet*

Box Sets (ebook only)
Seeing is Believing in Oracle Bay (Books 1-4)

* forthcoming

belle of the ball

PSYCHICS OF ORACLE BAY
BOOK 4

AMY CISSELL

BROKEN WORLD PUBLISHING

BELLE OF THE BALL
Amy Cissell

A Broken World Publication
13820 NE Airport Way, Suite K395495
Portland, OR 97251-1158

one

Drew walked up to his front door, tipsy from both the celebratory post-apocalypse beers he'd downed with the other oracles at The Pour House and the hint of a flirtation he'd shared with his ex-boyfriend. A silly grin spread across his face; he tipped his head back to take in the night air.

A fog was rolling in off the ocean, and the moist air was saturated with the scent of brine. Drew closed his eyes and breathed it in. He loved the coast. Hearing the sound of the waves from his bed at night, tasting salt on his lips when the wind kicked up, and living in a town where he didn't feel like he had to constantly hide who he was—even if he was occasionally cagey about the literal realities of his job—was more than enough to make up for the long, gray rainy season.

The Pour House was on the other side of town from where he lived, but it hadn't been too far to walk, especially since it wasn't raining. The walk—and the lingering effect of the beers he'd consumed—had eased the tension from his shoulders he hadn't realized he was carrying until it had vanished. Opening his eyes, he strode up his front steps and fumbled with his keyring, looking for the right one.

He grabbed the key, took a step forward to insert it in the lock, and tripped, stumbling into the front door and narrowly avoiding falling on his ass.

"What the—" He looked down at the unexpected obstacle. A large cardboard box that hadn't been there when he'd left for the bar was perfectly placed to both block his path to the door and hide in the shadows.

The box mewed.

Drew took a step backwards, teetering on the edge of the stairs before regaining his balance. He crouched down and regarded the box with less-than-sober suspicion. "Did you say 'mew?'"

"Mew!"

Drew pulled out his cell phone and scrolled through his contacts. Who did one consult about a middle of the night mewing box? His finger hovered over Ceri's number; she was usually his go-to for weird, but from the way she and Andy had been looking at each other, he suspected she might be busy. Before Drew could decide to press the call button, the box mewed a third time.

Maybe Misty? She and Joseph were an item now, and they had experience with supernatural goats.

Something rustled in the box. Drew groaned. He was standing on his doorstep, acting like a scaredy-cat, over a box. There was no one he could call who would make him feel any less foolish than he felt right now.

"Everything all right?" a voice called.

Drew jumped again, although this time he didn't lose his balance. He turned around. His across-the-street neighbors were striding towards him. He waved. "Everything's fine," Drew said. "Just dropped my keys."

"How many drinks did you have?" Sandy laughed. She and her fiancé, Vincent, were stopped in the middle of the street. The pair were clearly torn between making sure Drew was okay and heading off to do whatever it was newly engaged people did after midnight.

"Not as many as you, Sandy," Drew retorted. They'd wandered away from the main group and ensconced themselves in a shadowy corner.

She laughed again. Vincent looked down at her and smiled. Even in the relative dark, Drew could see the affection in Vincent's eyes as he gazed at the olive-skinned beauty that was Cassandra Franklin, Oracle Bay's resident tarot card reader.

"You're sure you're okay?" Vincent asked, tearing his gaze away from Sandy and looking back at Drew.

Drew tried to ignore the ache growing in the center of his chest. It definitely wasn't jealousy that Sandy and Vincent had found each other and fallen in love. It wasn't regret that he'd blown his chance with the only man he'd ever loved, tonight's almost flirtation aside. It was exhaustion and concern over his—*MEW!*—mysterious box.

"Drew?" Sandy prompted, worry lacing her voice. She didn't seem to have heard the box.

Drew forced a smile. "I'm fine. Just tired. Go home and get some sleep."

"If you're sure..." Vincent said.

Drew flapped his hand in dismissal. "Gooooo!"

"See you later this week," Sandy said. "I heard there's going to be a post-apocalypse wrap-up. You know, so we can discuss best practices or something."

This time Drew's laugh was genuine. "Nothing like the end of the world to bring people and ideas together."

Sandy waved. She and Vincent turned around and walked hand-in-hand back to their house. Drew watched them disappear, then turned back to the box. He steeled himself, grabbed the tucked in flaps, and pulled them open.

"Mew! Mew!" the box erupted in frantic noises that seemed too loud to be made by the creatures inside.

Two tiny kittens, wearing matching green collars decorated with a leafy design, were sitting at attention in a sea of patchwork quilt and scattered kibble. One of the kittens looked up at him. The left side of its face was black with a blue-gray eye, almost exactly the same color as Drew's eyes. The other side of its face was orange and punctuated with a bright green eye. The dividing line between the colors ran directly down the center of its face and disappeared into a more uneven distribution of black and orange.

"Oh my god, you're fabulous!" Drew gasped. The orange and black kitten wiggled its butt.

"Mew!" The other kitten demanded attention. This one was entirely black, and its body disappeared into the dark corners of the box. Its eyes were identical to the first kitten's.

Drew picked up the box and headed inside. He didn't know what he was going to do with two kittens. He had no food and no litter of any sort, but he wasn't about to leave them in a box on his front steps. He placed them in the downstairs bathroom, filled up a bowl with water, and covered the floor with old towels, then tipped the box gently to let the kittens out. They scrambled out, and with them, a small, dark bag fell on the floor. Inside was a gallon Ziploc bag of kitten kibble, and a note.

Merry Christmas Drew. I hope you like these kittens. They reminded me of you. xoxo.

It wasn't signed, but it did come with a certificate good for one spay and one neuter at Live Long and Pawspurr, the local veterinary clinic and pet supply store.

"Mew!" the orange and black one said, pawing at the bag of food.

Drew shook himself, poured out some food, then backed out of the bathroom and closed the door. It was late. There would be plenty of time tomorrow to deal with mysterious kittens.

Drew startled awake and sat up in bed. His breath came in deep, gasping pants, and he could feel sweat beading over his face and chest. He glanced at the bedside clock; it was four am. Something had awoken him.

He slowed his breathing. It was probably nothing. Maybe Tuppence Beresfurred or Hercule Purrot had broken out of the bathroom and found something in the kitchen to knock down.

Drew rolled over, content in the knowledge that whatever it was that had startled him awake had been caused by cats behaving badly. He stretched out an arm and hit fur. The fur shifted and started purring; a second set of purrs almost immediately joined in. He sat up and switched on the light.

Tuppence and Hercule were curled up in a giant orange and black fluff ball on the other pillow. They should've been shut in the downstairs bathroom, not on the bed with a solid, fluffy alibi. It was impressive they'd found him and hopped on the bed without waking him, but they clearly weren't the perpetrators. This time.

"It's probably nothing," he told himself as he got out of bed and found his slippers and a robe. Drew stifled a yawn, opened the door, and flicked on the hall light. Footsteps echoed on the floor behind him, deceptively heavy for such small kittens.

When he walked into the living room, nothing was out of place. However, the air was far colder than the fifty-nine degrees he kept the thermostat set to at night. A breeze caught Drew's robe, lifting the corners, and sending frigid tendrils over his bare legs.

His stomach clenched. He'd doubled checked the windows and doors, making sure everything was closed and locked, just as he did every night before bed. But he'd left his cell phone upstairs. Drew was torn between running to grab it or doing a quick check to find out where the breeze was coming from. He paused, closed his eyes, and concentrated. Other than the periodic thumps and mews from the kittens still shadowing him, his home was still and quiet.

Drew opened his eyes and looked around. Nothing was out of place. The front door was closed, as were the windows. He flipped on the lights as he reached the far side of the room and stepped into the dining room. Nothing weird here, either. Everything looked just as he'd left it, down to the discarded napkins from his dinner that hadn't made it to the laundry room.

Another light switch and a few more steps brought him to the kitchen. The curtain over the sink was blowing in the wind, but the back door was closed and—he checked to make sure—locked. Drew cranked the window shut and looked around. Other than the window, everything looked normal. Nothing was out of place. None of the plants on the windowsill were moved. The cabinets were undisturbed.

Drew shivered. No matter how put together everything else seemed, the open window was wrong—he just didn't know how. He sighed, scooping up the kittens to deposit one in each robe pocket, and headed upstairs to call the police.

· · · · · ★ ★ ★ ★ ★ · · · ·

DREW PACED BACK AND FORTH IN THE LIVING ROOM, EVERY FIFTH STEP AN awkward hop over a kitten chasing the dragging ties of his robe. The cops were on the way. It was the night officers that Oracle Bay PD had recently hired to give Roger and Daniel a break. He activated his phone again, scrolling until he found Roger's number. He was probably asleep, Drew reasoned. Besides, recent events had put a little distance between them. Roger's and Daniel's terrible behavior during the recent supernatural goat crisis had been caused by an ancient goddess, but Drew knew both cops blamed themselves.

He put the phone down, then picked it up again, dialing before he could second-guess his motivations.

"What do you want?" Ceri grumped at him. She was not a middle of the night person.

"Something weird happened."

"Weirder than goddesses disguised as goats? Weirder than the impending apocalypse spearheaded by my...Andy?"

"Your Andy?" Drew asked. They'd been circumspect, but it was hard to hide a relationship in a town full of psychics.

"My favorite brewer," she replied, saccharine dripping from her words. "But he's not why you called. What's weird? It's the middle of the night and I'm exhausted, so if this isn't weirder than anything else we've dealt with in the last few weeks, I'm hanging up on you."

"Someone left a box of kittens on my porch and then I was woken up by a loud sound and found my kitchen window open."

There was a long silence on the other end. "Kittens?"

"And a bang and an open window," Drew said.

"Why would anyone give you middle of the night kittens?" she asked.

"Almost as excellent a question as who would break into my house through a tiny window full of obstacles and leave without stealing anything," Drew said.

"I'm on my way over. Did you call the cops?"

He sighed. "I did. I wasn't going to, not after the whole goat fiasco, but I didn't know what else to do."

"No, it's good." Her voice trailed off, and the line went silent.

Drew knew better than to interrupt her—this was the silence that only came with scrying. He took a deep breath in, held it for a count of four, then exhaled. After ten rounds of breathing, he was beginning to consider dropping his robe and doing a full sun salutation or two. There wouldn't be any more sleep this night; anything that would contribute to his calm would be welcome.

"Sorry, Drew," she said, breathless.

"Are you okay?" Her visions didn't come as easily as they had before. Whatever she'd seen when she looked into Andy and seen millennia of history as well as the impending apocalypse had damaged her abilities. She hadn't been prepared for so much pain and suffering and hadn't been able to break free. Diving into Andy's memories without barriers in place on either side to keep her safe and sane had unraveled her mind before she caught hold of herself and wound things back up again. Since then, her sight was taxing. Yet no matter how many times Drew told Ceri to take a break, she kept on keeping on.

"It's only temporary," Ceri said. "I was stripped bare because I didn't anticipate what would happen, but I'm already rebuilding. I'd be back to normal already if it hadn't been for that pesky apocalypse."

"If you say so," he said, one hundred percent sarcastically.

"I might be damaged, but that doesn't mean I'm missing your barbed points," she said. "Don't tell me you weren't affected by our activities last week. Channeling psychic power into gods and demigods is hard." In the background, he heard a car starting. "I'll be there in ten." *Click*.

Drew paced. And squatted down to offer scritches. And paced. And drank a La Croix, pamplemousse, of course. He checked his watch. It'd been seven minutes since Ceri'd hung up and twenty minutes since 911 dispatch had promised to send someone over. He dropped into a chair, huffing dramatically on the way down.

Before he could engage the lever to raise the footrest, the doorbell rang.

Two officers stood at the door, smiling politely in that way that indicated they had no intention of taking Drew seriously.

"Thank you for coming," Drew said. He tried to squash down the last interaction he'd had with the cops. Roger—who'd always been a friend—and Daniel had committed terrible miscarriages of justice. Sure, they'd been possessed. And sure, there'd been goddesses disguised as goats and other goddesses gumming up the works, but it was hard to remember his friend's—the cop's—douchiness had external causes.

"Can you tell us what happened?" Cop number one asked.

Cop two, who looked like an extra from Reno 911, gazed around the living room until he spotted the orange and black kitten. "Who's this little monster?" he crooned.

Drew immediately reevaluated his opinion of Officer Handlebar Mustache and Too-Tight Pants.

"That's Hercule Purrot," he said. "The all black one is Tuppence Beresfurred."

Cop one, tall, dark, and handsome, stopped glaring suspiciously at everyone and looked Drew in the eye. "You have a beautiful black lady cat, and you named her Tuppence Beresfurred? She's definitely more of a Michelle Opawma or Zora Neale Purrston."

"I just got them tonight," Drew said, more defensively than he'd meant to. "They were left on my steps."

"Who left them?" TDH asked.

"I don't know. There was a note and a gift certificate good for one spay and one neuter, but it wasn't signed," Drew replied. He rubbed his hand over his eyes and regretted calling the cops. "Nothing was amiss in my house when I got home, though. The window was closed."

"What time did you return home?" Reno asked, not bothering to look up from the floor where he was trying to get some belly rubs in without losing any skin to the kittens' claws.

"Just after one o'clock. I got the cats situated and shut into the bathroom over there—" he waved towards the downstairs half bath "—and was in bed and asleep well before two."

"And you woke up when?" Reno asked in a sing-song tone, following up his question with another: "Who's the cutest little monster? Who's the sweetest, sharpest boy?"

Drew held back a sigh, forced amiability into his voice, and said, "About forty minutes ago. Around four-thirty. I called nine-one-one about ten minutes after I woke up."

"But nothing was disturbed?" Tall, Dark, and Handsome asked. "There was no reason to call this in?"

Drew forced a smile. "I heard a loud noise that wasn't caused by the cats. When I got downstairs, the kitchen window was wide open —far more open than I ever open it; I don't want to blow over any of my herbs—even though I always close it before bed."

"But if you'd been drinking..." TDH suggested.

"If he'd been drinking, what?" Ceri demanded as she strode into the house, her red hair streaming behind her.

Both officers stood at attention; Drew took a moment to appreciate that Ceri could do what so few other of his close friends could… challenge police officers without fear.

"If he'd been drinking," TDH said, taking a few steps forward, attempting to force her to give up ground. "He might've forgotten to close the window or opened it more instead of closing it. The wind could've made the noise that startled him."

Ceri stood steady, ignoring the larger man who'd invaded her space until he took a half-step back. She looked at Drew. "Do you think that's possible?"

"Ordinarily, sure," Drew said. He took a deep breath, closed his eyes briefly, and pushed his shoulder blades down his back, forcing his shoulders to follow suit. The tension drained from Drew's shoulders, and he began to relax for the first time since he'd been startled awake. "But I closed the window and locked the backdoor before I headed out to The Pour House. I knew it'd be a late night and didn't want to take chances."

Ceri beamed up at TDH. "There you go! Couldn't have been due to drunkenness!"

TDH took another step back and nearly tripped when a kitten took the opportunity to twine herself around his legs. "Da—darn cats," he said, looking towards Ceri without meeting her eyes.

"What more do you need, officers?" Ceri asked, honey dripping from her tone in a way only a woman who's spent considerable time in the South can manage. "Are we good here?"

TDH nodded, but Reno interrupted. "I'm not clear on the sequence of events that led Mr. Hardy to call us. Seems to me that it's just a spooky noise in the night and an open window. Hardly nine-one-one material."

Drew sighed and found a chair so Reno and TDH could ask the same questions again. And again.

It was almost six-thirty before Reno and TDH stopped asking the same questions in new ways.

"Since nothing was stolen and there isn't any property damage, there's really no evidence of a crime," TDH said. "Next time you have a nightmare, phone a friend instead of wasting police time."

"You've been here for an hour and a half asking the same questions over and over," Drew said. "If anyone's wasting your time, it sure isn't me. That's all on you."

TDH scowled at Drew. "You need to show a little respect."

Drew bit back a retort and smiled at the officers. He didn't want to, but they were strangers, and he wasn't ready to get arrested for being a jerk. Yet. "Thank you for coming and taking my statement," he said without dropping his smile. From the glance at the hallway mirror, it looked more like a rictus than a natural grin.

The radios on the officers' belts buzzed to life. "Chad? Kyle? You guys done with the home invasion? We've got a situation on Main Street."

TDH grabbed his radio. "Just finishing up. No invasion. Probably just the wind or a cat or something. Owner was tipsy and doesn't quite know what happened."

"Hey!" Drew said. "The owner is right here, and that is not how we left things."

"Chad and I will be right there," TDH said, ignoring Drew.

The door slammed behind Chad and Kyle. Drew turned to Ceri, who was crouched on the floor and cuddling both kittens. "Am I completely off my rocker here?" Drew asked. "This is weird, right?"

Ceri looked up from the kittens in her lap; both cats followed her gaze to stare at him. She looked paler than usual, and her freckles stood out against her porcelain skin. "If you were anyone else, I'd tell you to get some sleep, lay off the gin, and find a nice man to make time with to relieve some of the hysteria. But you're you. If you say something is weird, then I believe you. I can't see it yet, and I'm not going to try again any time soon, but maybe you'll be able to see what's going on."

Drew stared at her until she sighed.

"Go get dressed," she said. "I'll make us coffee. Then we're heading to your shop to look at balls."

two

An hour later, Drew and Ceri were on Main Street in front of his shop.

"Something's wrong," Ceri said.

"But what?" Drew asked.

Nothing looked out of place. The door was closed, the windows intact, and the sign hand-painted on the picture window was...

"Look at the sign," Drew said.

"Behold, the Amazing Ramiro!" the text read, curving over a crystal ball. "No questions unanswered! No stone unturned. Your secrets revealed when Master Ramiro gazes into his mystical blue balls!"

Ceri started laughing. Drew glared at her for a few minutes before giving in.

"Fine. As far as vandalism goes, that's pretty funny," he admitted. "I think the previous text of 'Crystal ball reading—future, present, past—Love, Money, Destiny!' was more on brand."

"I rather preferred the original name of the shop, Amazing Ramiro," Ceri said. "Although if you don't start going by Mr. Amazing from now on, I will be disappointed."

"Ramiro was the name I used in the last town," Drew said. "Here, I'm just Drew."

"You're 'Have a Ball with Drew! Psychic Readings.' And the rest you said. This is weird."

Drew gritted his teeth and squared his shoulders. "We should go in."

It was dark in the shop. None of the lights came on when the switches were flipped.

"I am about ready to lose my mind," Drew said. His voice was thin, a quiet undertone to his loud, rapid respiration. "What is going on?"

"We should call the cops," Ceri said, the laughter gone from her voice.

"Not again. Not until I have something more than a professionally repainted sign and lights that don't work."

Ceri shined her cellphone flashlight up at the overhead fixture. "There aren't any lightbulbs."

"Everything is missing lightbulbs," Drew confirmed. He headed into the back of the shop where he stored the odds and ends that he didn't want on display, like brooms, his Halloween costume, a wine fridge for prosecco, and lightbulbs. On the table in the small make-shift kitchen was a large wooden bowl that reminded Drew of the salad bowls that'd been so popular in the seventies. The overhead light in the room was missing its globe, and the light was shining directly down into the bowl. In it were thirteen lightbulbs. "Found the light bulbs," he said, voice thin.

"Where were they—oh..." Ceri said, voice trailing off as she saw the spot-lit tableau. "That's really weird. But it's not as weird as what's going on in your shop."

"What do you mean?"

"After you came back here for bulbs, I shined the flashlight around. Granted, I haven't been in here in a bit, but things are different than I remember."

Drew grabbed a few lightbulbs from the utility closet, leaving the bulb bowl for the inevitable police investigation, and followed Ceri back into the main room. He screwed bulbs into the four mood lamps in the room—bright enough to see by, but dark enough to make customers squint a bit when they first came in from outside. Then he looked around.

"Oh my god," he said.

The table where he did his readings was in the center of the room, instead of further back. In Drew's chair was a figure in a purple wizard's robe wearing a pointy purply hat. Drew walked closer and pushed the hat back with one finger. A skull stared back at him.

"Oh my god!" he said. "It's a skeleton."

The robes were gaping open a bit near the chair, revealing a bony pelvis cradling wine in a straw-bottomed bottle. One hand was curled around the bottle. The other, hidden by the voluminous sleeves of the discount wizard's robes, rested on top of Drew's ball. He leaned in closer. "This isn't my ball. It's styrofoam!"

"What?" Ceri said, striding over and peering with him. She reached out and poked it. "Why would anyone leave a styrofoam ball?"

"Why would anyone do any of this?" Drew gesticulated wildly. "It took me ages to find a stone that resonated with me in that way. It might not have been worth much, but it was priceless to me. This has moved past weird and into scary."

"Agreed," Ceri said. "We need help. Someone familiar with scary weird."

"Morgana and Paska?" Drew asked.

"They're both extremely weird and more than a little scary," Ceri nodded. "I'll call Paska if you call Morgana?"

Five minutes later, they were back to square one. They'd left messages for Paska, Morgana, and Andy—the three Oracle Bay citizens most likely to understand the creepily weird events.

"Maybe we should ask Misty," Ceri said.

"She won't be home," Drew said. "She spends most of her time out at Joseph's now."

Ceri pulled out her phone, pushed a couple buttons, and held it to her ear. A few moments later, she ended the call. "She's not answering."

Drew looked around the shop and shuddered. "Let's go out there and talk to her. It's not too early to show up at a farm, right?"

"Definitely not."

* * * ★ ★ ★ ★ ★ ★ * * *

DREW KNOCKED ON JOSEPH'S DOOR AND TRIED NOT TO FIDGET. HE'D BEEN here a handful of times in the last few months—missing supernatural goats really did bring a community together—but before that, no one went in Joseph McEwen's home. They might stop at his farm to see the goats, or at the little farm store he operated closer to town, but no one ever saw the inside of his house. No one but—

Drew stopped that thought before it went too far down memory lane and paced back and forth in front of the door.

"I've never seen anyone pace in such a small area before," Ceri remarked.

"I'm tired and today has been really weird," Drew snapped. "I've earned the right to pace oddly." He closed his eyes and scrunched up his face before slowly opening one eye and grimacing at Ceri. "I am so sorry. I'm a little on edge and apparently, that makes me rude."

"It's okay. I shouldn't have teased you. I am often inappropriately humorous when it's uncalled for. I always think it'll diffuse the tension, but even after this many years of experience, I haven't learned it's just as likely to piss someone off as it is to make them laugh."

"Inappropriate humor, delightful cocktails, and boy-watching shenanigans are the hallmarks of our friendship," Drew said.

"I'm so glad you decided to cement your bff vows on my doorstep," Joseph said, pulling open the door and walking out onto the stoop, pushing Ceri and Drew back and down a couple of steps. "Have you finished what you came here for, or is there something you needed from me or Misty?"

"We came to talk to Misty," Drew said, leaning forward and taking the steps up, joining Joseph in front of the door. He put a hand on Joseph's arm and looked up at him pleadingly. "Is she here?"

"She's getting dressed," Joseph answered, standing back to let Drew and Ceri into the house. "You know, there's this new technology that allows you to contact a person without leaving the comfort of your home and then—this is the best part—you can talk to them without needing to drive anywhere!"

"It's rather an emergency," Ceri said. Her voice, usually relaxed with a hint of Irish brogue, was tight and brooked no nonsense.

"Of course it is," Joseph said. "Just promise me it's not my emergency this time. I still haven't fully recovered from being kidnapped by a vengeful goddess."

"As far as I know, it's completely goat and goddess free," Ceri promised. "There's been no evidence of either."

"Yet," Drew muttered, too low for Joseph to hear. Ceri shot him a chastising glance but didn't say anything.

"That's all right, then. Why don't you sit down? Misty will be out in a minute. Can I get you some coffee?"

"Yes, please," Drew said.

"No thank you," Ceri replied.

Drew was halfway through his coffee with cream when Misty walked into the room.

"What's up, guys?" Misty said, grabbing a mimosa off the counter. "Want one?"

"No, thank you," Drew said. "I know I should've called, but something weird happened, and I needed to tell someone."

"Why me?" Misty asked. "Not that I don't appreciate being the go-to for weird, but Morgana and Paska are better equipped if it's the same kind of supernatural happening we've been having lately."

"I couldn't reach them," Drew admitted. "Ceri has been with me most of the morning and can verify that everything is peculiar."

"I don't care that you didn't call me first. But I do care that you're talking about an oddness you haven't defined. What kind of strange goings on have you witnessed?"

"For starters, my ball is missing." Drew shook his head slowly as soon as the words were out of his mouth. Misty was fighting back a grin, Joseph was trying to cover his laughter with a snorting cough, and even Ceri looked like she was about to giggle.

"My crystal ball. My focus stone. It's missing." Drew glared at his friends. Maybe the wording was funny, but maybe this wasn't the best time to act like adolescents.

"That's terrible," Misty said. "I know how much it meant to you. Do you think it was a standard breaking and entering situation? Or something else?"

"Definitely something else," Ceri said. She drummed her fingers on the table one at a time. "There was nothing standard about this."

"Tell me everything." Misty leaned forward, words and posture indicating that she was devoting the entirety of her attention to Drew's problem.

"I spent the early part of the morning with the cops because I woke up to an open window I know was closed and a loud bang. It wasn't the kittens—"

"Kittens? Since when do you have kittens?" Misty squealed. "I know that's probably not the point, but maybe they're creepy kittens? Do you have pictures so I can verify whether or not your new kittens are the problem?"

Drew rolled his eyes. "You can come by later and personally examine them yourself. In fact, I'd welcome it. However, that was only the beginning. The cops decided that nothing had happened, except me being drunk and opening windows myself or something. We decided to head to my shop to do a little gazing to see what the problem was. When we got to Main Street, the first thing I noticed was that my sign was all wrong. It looked almost identical, but the words were completely different. The second thing we noticed is that all the lightbulbs had been removed from the lamps and piled neatly in a basket in the back room. And the third thing we saw was that there was a styrofoam ball the same size and shape as my focus stone, and a skeleton in a Halloween wizard's robes and pointy hat was sitting in my chair gazing at the ball."

"Oh," Misty said. "That is bizarre."

AN HOUR LATER, DREW WAS FORTIFIED WITH BREAKFAST AND COFFEE AND back in his shop talking to the police. It was Kyle and Chad again, and they didn't look much more interested in Drew's story than they had earlier. Once the cops had taken fingerprints and photos, confiscated the fake ball, skeleton, and wizardly garb, and left, everyone else arrived.

Drew had never figured out how word spread so fast in a small town, but within two hours of discovering Mr. Wizard in his emaciated state, everyone in Oracle Bay knew about the break-in—what exactly had happened, that he'd found kittens on his doorstep the night before, and that he hadn't gotten a *wink* of sleep, the poor dear. He grimaced as one more sweet old lady patted him gently and remonstrated him to take a nap, so he didn't ruin his youthful good looks.

"Drew!" a familiar voice called. Drew stood on his tiptoes, trying hard to see over the crowd, and spotted Sandy and Vincent, the former waving madly at him. He waved back and watched her weave through the crowd, stopping every couple seconds to greet someone. She'd only been in town about three months, but Sandy already knew almost everyone, and they all loved her.

Finally, she got to him. "Here," she said, thrusting a festive holiday gift bag at him.

"What could it be?" Drew asked, eyeing the tall, skinny bag.

"Duh," Sandy said. "Open it."

Drew pulled out a bottle of sparkling wine—one of his favorite Proseccos. "This is the best," he gasped. "Thank you! How did you know?"

Sandy rolled her eyes at him. "Drew. Are you serious? How did I know? I saw it in the cards. Obviously."

"Pfftt... That's not how it works." Drew stuck his tongue out at her.

Sandy rolled her eyes. "Fine, spoilsport. I asked around."

"However you found out, I don't care. It's my favorite, and it's impossible to find on the coast." Drew hugged the bottle to him and grinned at her over the top.

"Lucky for you, I'm still regularly making the trip to Portland," Vincent added.

"Regularly making the trip *and* he knows wine importers who can help find the good stuff," Sandy added.

"Isn't he...special."

Sandy and Drew spun to the right and came face to face with Adriana Covington's long face. Her mournful brown eyes were framed by wavy, tangled gray-black hair. She always reminded Drew of a particularly unkempt Afghan hound having an extremely disappointing day. Today, her sour expression, slightly pushed out lower lip, and gray tunic and trousers also made Drew think she'd be perfectly comfortable with a cat of her own. A white Persian, perhaps. Adriana had a fantastic Doctor Evil cosplay down, except for the hair, of course.

"Hi, Adriana!" Sandy said. "Are you going to be open later on? My wine cellar is running low."

Adriana looked pointedly at the bottle Drew was holding. "It must not be too low if you're giving away bottles you didn't buy from me."

Drew watched the confusion wash over Sandy's face and irritation gather in the corner of Vincent's eyes. Adriana ran The Covington Wine Shoppe a few storefronts down. Although she kept a great selection of wines—and in fact probably had one of the best wine shops on the Washington coast—she never managed to be a very popular spot. She was rude to almost everyone. Adriana mocked people who bought screw top wine, even if she did carry a few bottles capped that way and denigrated their taste in wine if they disagreed with her suggestions—even when they were choosing another wine she had in stock. But the sticking point for most of the locals was that she refused to rename her business to something more appropriate, something...punny. She also used her position on the City Council to actively campaign against punny entrepreneurs.

Sandy mustered a smile. "This was a specific special bottle that you didn't have in stock, and when I asked you about ordering it, you said it wasn't worth it. I buy most of my wine from you, Adriana, but this is Drew's favorite."

Adriana turned her glare on him. Drew smiled politely at her as Sandy mouthed, "Sorry," over Adriana's shoulder and started to back away.

Drew held out his hands. "Adriana, you're the only wine shop in town, but we're a small town and sometimes we go elsewhere for specialty items. It's not a slight against you. You know that we get all our regular meeting wine from you."

"You can forget about the discount I've been giving you," Adriana said. "If you don't value my store, I don't have to value your patronage."

She turned and flounced out of Drew's shop, narrowly missing a group of fellow Main Street business owners coming in, presumably to offer their condolences.

"Drew!" Ryan, owner of the Title Wave bookshop on the end of the block called out. "What the heck is going on in this town?" Ryan was closer to seventy than sixty but carried himself like a man in his early thirties. His impeccable posture always made Drew stand up straighter, and his white hair and blue-gray eyes were aging goals. "What happened? Your psychic gang better not be bringing in a bad element."

"Don't be ridiculous, Ryan," Antonia, proprietor of To a Tea said.

"You know what happened. Everyone knows what happened. There's no reason to think it has anything to do with any one type of business over another. I'm sure you'll manage to sell off your store and retire to the San Juan Islands."

Before Drew could reply, the door opened again, and he looked up to see which of his fellow business owners had shown up to scoop up the gossip under the pretext of offering condolences.

"Bill," he said, barely above a whisper. His hands dropped down to his sides and a wave of dizziness washed over him as the blood drained from his face. They'd reconnected lately and maybe flirted last night from across the room, but to see him here, in his shop... Bill had never set foot in here—he thought Drew's job was a silly affectation, little more than a diversion to make a few dollars and have a reason to stay in Oracle Bay. That's what they'd fought about most.

Bill stood in the doorway behind the small throng that had gathered, head turning as he searched the crowd. Drew saw Sandy and Vincent walk up to Bill, gesture in Drew's general direction, and then escort Bill towards the back of the shop.

Panic overwhelmed Drew for a second, and he backed away from Antonia and Ryan towards the door that led to the back room and the back exit, before telling himself it was ridiculous. He was an adult. He was not going to run away from his ex-boyfriend, no matter how tempting it was.

Bill broke through the crowd, a tray of coffee drinks in hand, and skidded to a stop in front of Drew. "Are you okay?" he blurted out.

"Yes. Yes. I'm...fine," Drew stammered. "Why..." His voice trailed off. There were too many whys.

"I had to see. I brought you coffee." Bill thrust one of the cups at Drew. "Caramel latte, extra foam."

"That's my favorite. Thank you." Drew took the cup, unable to pull his gaze away from Bill's. Their fingers brushed and Drew jumped, almost dumping his latte in the process.

"You're okay?" Bill asked again. "You're sure?"

"I'm okay," Drew said, more confidently this time. "I mean, I feel completely violated and more than a little nervous to go home and pretty pissed off that someone stole my crystal ball and vandalized my shop sign, but I am okay."

"You don't need to be alone tonight," Bill said.

Drew became suddenly and blushingly aware of Sandy, Vincent, Antonia, and Ryan watching the back-and-forth. Sandy was grinning like a fiend, and the other's eyes were wide. Ryan had his hands covering his mouth.

"I...uh..." Drew said, looking between Bill and their spectators. It was ridiculous that this one man, not even thirty years old, could throw Drew so off-balance. It'd been almost a hundred years since he'd been affected like this. *Nope, not walking down that path, either.*

"Drew! Darling!" A voice rang out over the crowd of people still milling about discussing safety and alarms and neighborhood watches.

Bill and Drew turned in unison, and Drew almost dropped his coffee for the second time in just a few minutes. A man, shorter than average with dark hair, light brown skin, and piercing blue eyes, strode towards Drew. He was wearing skinny jeans and a leopard-print button-up shirt with leather loafers. In one hand, he had a bottle of wine, unlabeled, and two glasses. A pair of sunglasses dangled from the other. A leaf-shaped pendant dipped behind the collar of his shirt.

Movement beside Drew caught his attention, and he turned in time to see Bill take a step away and set down the coffee carrier, stiffness masking the raw emotion that'd been showing moments before.

"Dio," Drew said flatly as the man pushed his way into Drew's personal space and kissed him on each cheek. When Dio went in for a third, Drew backed up, nearly running over Ryan. "What are you doing here?"

"I was passing through and knew I couldn't leave again without saying hello to my favorite former—"

"You can walk yourself right back out of town," Bill interrupted. "You're not welcome here."

Drew couldn't quite identify the surge of emotion that welled up. He was half swooning that Bill was being so commanding and protective, and half angry that Bill would take it on himself to banish Drew's rebound guy.

"I was invited," Dio said, giving Drew a very serious once-over.

"Invited?" Bill spat out, looking at Drew. "Really?"

"No!" Drew said, but it was too late. Bill was already out the door. "Dio! I didn't invite you."

"Never said you did." Dio shrugged. "Want some wine? It's an old family vintage."

"Why not?" Drew replied. Dio was a sore spot between Bill and Drew, as much as Bill's adamant refusal to believe that fortune telling was real. Regardless of recent events, there was no way to move past the obstacles Drew and Bill had placed between them. "Pour me some wine."

"Excellent." Dio uncorked the bottle with his teeth, spat the cork into the corner of the room, and started pouring. There were enough glasses for everyone in the shop to have wine, and most people had seconds and thirds.

three

"What are you doing here?" Drew hissed at Dio from across the table at the Sleeping Inn Restaurant and Bar. "And more to the point, what am I doing here...with you?" It'd taken at least an hour to get everyone out of his shop so he could lock it up. Dio kept trying to pour one more round. Drew'd finally gotten him to stop by promising to have lunch with him.

Dio grinned the slow, sly grin that had always turned up Drew's internal temperature. "I told you. I was passing through and didn't want to leave Oracle Bay without seeing you. I have some really good memories here."

Russell—the bar's manager, Misty's newfound cousin, and potential member of the Oracle Bay Psychic's Union—poured two more glasses of wine and lingered by the table.

"We're good for now," Dio said. "You can go eavesdrop on someone else."

"Dio!" Drew said. "There's no reason to be rude to anyone." He turned around and mouthed *Sorry* to Russell.

Russell grinned, made a rude gesture, and said, "Call me later. You owe me."

"What?" Dio asked, shrugging it off. "He is the waiter."

"He's not only the waiter, he's a friend. But even if he was the biggest jerk in town, him being a waiter is no reason to be rude, and it never has been."

"Whatever. I am not here to see him. I am here to see you." Dio said. He scooted his chair over, so his back was turned towards the bar where Russell was standing. "You had some excitement this morning, already?"

Drew looked around the restaurant, trying to figure out how he'd ended up here instead of chasing after Bill, or heading to The Pour House with Ceri and Sandy, or going home to check on his... "Kittens!"

"Your excitement was kittens?" Dio cocked his head and looked at Drew. "Did they do the damage in your shop? I didn't know kittens were that destructive."

"Yes. No. Argh!" Drew took a long drink from his wine glass and tried to settle his nerves and his thoughts. "Someone left kittens on my doorstep last night, and I forgot they were at home, alone. I need to go to Live Long and Pawspurr to get more food and a proper litter box for them. They'll need vet appointments to make sure they're healthy. And they are just *babies* and shouldn't be left alone this long."

Dio placed his elbows on the table, interlaced his fingers, and rested his chin on his fingers. "You're cute when you're flustered. Infuriatingly vague, but cute."

"Stop that, Dio. I don't want to flirt. What we had was fun, but it's been over for a long time now, and I'm not interested in rekindling anything with you."

"I'm not here to seduce you, silly man. Just to have a little fun."

"What kind of fun?"

Dio dropped his hands and leaned forward. "You'll see. I have a lot of surprises planned." He kissed Drew on the cheek, downed both glasses of wine, then skipped out the door. "See you later, lover boy!"

Drew stared after him, jaw unhinged. Dio had always been a bit of a wild card, a free spirit, but this seemed above and beyond, even for him. Drew turned back around, eyed the empty glasses, and realized that Dio had left him with the check.

"I really hate that guy," he said.

Russell handed over the bill. "Didn't look like it. You got a kiss out of it all."

Drew fished out his bank card and slapped it on the tray. "I hope no one else saw that."

"Look around. This place is packed with the lunch crowd. Everyone saw. Dio was loud and dramatic and made sure."

"What am I going to do, Russell?" Drew demanded. "I felt like things were definitely starting to look up between Bill and me, and now Dio's back in town?"

"Just because I'm your favorite bartender doesn't mean I have insight into your love life," Russell said.

"You're more than my favorite bartender," Drew declared. "You make the best French 75s I've ever had, you always know what I want to eat even before I do, and we've been friends for five years. That makes you uniquely qualified to have insight."

"If you don't want to see him, why are you here?" Russell asked. "You're not usually a pushover."

"That's a great point, and the answer is, I have no idea." Drew shrugged. "One minute he's making a scene in my shop, and the next, I'm following him out of the shop for lunch and drinks."

"Is he your kryptonite?" Russell struck a pose. He put his hands on his hips and straightened up, looking off into the distance. You could almost see his cape fluttering behind him.

"No! At least, I don't think so. Maybe? I never made very good decisions when he was around, but I didn't think I was the kind of person who'd let Bill walk away and have drinks with my ex." Drew took a breath and held it, afraid that if he let it go, he'd start talking again, and that if he started talking, he'd cry.

"Go home. Take care of the kittens. Get some rest. The day's barely half over. A lot more could happen." Russell picked up a glass and polished it with the towel he kept on his person at all times. It was so cliché bartender that it made Drew grin, which was probably exactly what Russell had intended.

"Wise words," Drew said. "I'll take that advice as soon as you run my card."

"Done."

· · · ★ ★ ★ ★ ★ ★ · ·

DREW RETURNED HOME TO CHAOS. DIRT AND LEAVES WERE EVERYWHERE— ground into the carpeted stairs, mashed into the hardwood floors, and tracked across the cream-colored furniture. For a moment, he was positive the intruder had returned to finish the job. Then Hercule tore down the stairs, Tuppence fast on his heels. Hercule was wrapped in a leafy green vine from one of Drew's purple spiderwort plants, and Tuppence was doing her best to catch the runaway plant.

Drew glanced at the bathroom. The door was all the way open, and the evidence of a toilet paper ticker tape parade was clearly visible.

"You two are monsters!" he said, scooping Hercule up and unwinding the vine from around his body—a task made even more difficult by Tuppence's passionate but pathetic leaps to catch the dangly leaves Drew kept just out of reach. He deposited them back in the bathroom, but not without a shudder at the mess.

Taking a deep breath, Drew headed to the kitchen. A large, picture window overlooking the backyard took up most of one wall. Around that window, both on plant stands and hangers, were over a dozen well-cared-for houseplants. The hanging plants were still there, and mostly unscathed unless their vines hung low or had a plant stand beneath them. But everything else was on the ground.

Nine broken pots, piles of rich potting soil, and shredded leaves everywhere.

Drew whipped out his phone and Googled every single plant he owned. He headed back to the bathroom with a broom and slipped inside. "You terrors are lucky that I don't own any toxic plants."

Neither kitten looked at him; they were curled up on a large pillow that had come from the guest room.

"How'd you get that in here?" he asked, then sighed. After sweeping up the toilet paper confetti, Drew did a quick check of the rest of the house. Although there were dirt and leaves everywhere, there were no other major centers of disaster. They'd left the rest of the house alone. For now.

He shook his head. There'd be time enough to clean the house later. Now that his shop had been cleared, it was time to get that back in shape. He walked downstairs and nearly tripped over Tuppence Beresfurred.

"How are you guys opening the bathroom door?"

"Mew!" she said.

"I guess you'll have to come with me. And we're going to need to make a stop."

Drew pulled into the parking lot at Live Long and Pawspurr, scooped the kittens into a paper grocery sack, and took a moment to settle his nerves. Driving the one and a half miles to the vet clinic and pet shop had been a harrowing experience with two enthusiastic kittens stuck on Warp Nine.

Drew power walked into the shop with his noisy, wiggling paper bag and headed straight for the vet reception desk.

"Drew!" Jeremiah said, looking up from the computer. "What can I do for you?"

"MEW!" the bag wailed.

Jeremiah looked over the counter. "Your sack has legs," he observed.

Two corners were chewed through and each corner sported a different colored leg.

"How many are in there?" Jeremiah asked.

"Two," Drew groaned. "But if you told me it was two hundred, I wouldn't argue."

"Where did you find them?"

Drew handed over the note and gift certificate. "They were left on my porch last night. I locked them in the bathroom, but they keep getting out, and they're destroying everything."

"Why don't you hand them over, and I'll have Marni do an exam to make sure everything's good. We can get started on a vaccine schedule and book them for their alterations. You go talk to Dara and they'll get you set up with everything you need. You are keeping them, right?"

"Of course I'm keeping them! The black one is Tuppence Beres-furred and the orange and black is Hercule Purrot. Be gentle with them."

Jeremiah laughed. "They're in good hands. Go. Shop. And might I recommend a couple cat carriers?"

It was well after dark by the time Drew finally walked back into his shop to clean it up. He was hoping he'd be able to open tomorrow—even if he'd have to do so with his backup ball.

He set down the cat carriers in the corner, set up a temporary litter box nearby, and got to work. Both kittens were drowsing after their veterinary adventures, and Drew was crossing his fingers that it'd last long enough for him to finish up. He started by screwing in all the lightbulbs and turning everything on. He didn't feel like being alone in the dark tonight. He started to prop the front door open to grab the late December breeze, then looked back at the snoozing felines, locked away securely in their carriers, and closed the door.

He turned up the volume on his Prince playlist and started picking up the detritus left from the break-in, the police presence, the throngs of well-wishers, and the chaos of Dio. He was belting out the lyrics of Kiss into the end of the broom when the front door banged open. Drew dropped the broom, looked around to locate the kittens—still in their carriers, but no longer asleep—and finally turned his attention to the door.

Ryan stood in the doorway. He was wearing a dripping trench coat, a tweed flat cap, and a scowl. "You! You did this!"

Drew picked up the broom, leaned it against the wall, and walked towards the book seller. "What do you mean? I did what?"

"You and your band of play psychics," Ryan snapped. "Every day there are more of you. I don't know how Misty tricked poor Vincent Bryson out of his real estate holdings, but she shouldn't own the whole town. It's no wonder there's so much vandalism."

"Vincent sold his real estate investment to Misty to *save* this town. It was that or have cookie cutter developers buy it up and put in chain stores and generic, beachfront storefronts. As for the vandalism, is this what you mean?" Drew gestured around him. "This isn't because there are psychics in town. Why would I do this to myself?"

"To throw off suspicion, of course!" Ryan said. "And to trash Old Ben's place, obviously. You never did like Old Ben."

Old Ben had been the renter in Drew's current storefront fifteen years ago; the man had died at the happily retired and venerable old age of ninety-seven. Drew had never even met him. Ryan hadn't supported granting more fortune telling business licenses, but he'd never been a vociferous opponent, either. He'd made snide comments about newcomers whenever anyone who'd lived in Oracle Bay fewer than twenty years was mentioned, but Ryan's remarks had never seemed any more serious than "Old man shakes fist at cloud." Besides, Ryan's bookstore was a town landmark. People were willing to forgive a lot of crankiness for the sake of Title Wave. He'd announced he was vacating his space and selling his bookstore almost immediately after Misty'd bought all the Main Street store fronts from Vincent a couple months ago. But at the time, that had seemed like nothing more than a coincidence.

"Where is this coming from?" Drew asked, genuinely bewildered.

"Another store was targeted tonight," Ryan said. "Mine."

"I'm so sorry," Drew said. "But I had nothing to do with it. What possible motivation would I have?"

"You attract a bad element," Ryan said, wagging a finger in Drew's face. "I see those shady folks who've been hanging out at young Andy's den of iniquity lately, and your other friends have been sacrificing goats for your rituals. I have possible buyers coming in tomorrow, none of whom are of your ilk, so I'm sure that doesn't make you and your creepy friends happy, either."

Drew's jaw hung open, partially in shock after hearing Andy referred to as young, and partly at the idea that anyone was sacrificing goats for fun. "Listen, Ryan. We've been business neighbors for a long time. I'm sorry your shop was vandalized. I hope the damage wasn't too bad. If you'd like, I can help you clean up so you can have it in ship-shape to talk to your potential buyers tomorrow. I'm not interested in trouble. I'm not responsible for the influx of visitors we're having—just grateful for the additional revenue. But I am willing to help you out. Let me drop my cats off at home, and then I'll stop by and help out."

"I don't need your help. Just know that I have my eyes on you. There won't be any more unanimous votes on the city council, not as long as I'm on it anyway." Ryan's face had flushed a dull red while he was talking; now his cheeks were so ruddy, Drew wouldn't have been surprised to see steam coming out of Ryan's ears.

"That's not much longer, is it?" Drew shouted, his voice rising with frustration and exhaustion. "So your threat is pretty empty."

"What do you mean by that?" Ryan gasped, clutching his chest and staggering backwards melodramatically.

Drew fought to keep from rolling his eyes. Ryan never let go of his position as lead actor in most of the community theater's productions. "Aren't you retiring in a month and moving out of town? It'll be hard to maintain your council seat if you don't live here."

Ryan's mouth opened and closed over and over, like a fish gasping for water, before he turned and slammed the door. The confined kittens mewed pitifully in response.

Drew looked around the shop. "Good enough," he said. "It's been a day, and we are going home."

· · * ★ ★ ⭐ ★ ★ * · ·

It was close to ten when the combination of yoga, a hot shower, and some kitty snuggles calmed Drew down enough to think.

"Ugh. I was a jerk," he told Hercule. "Or at least, I was less polite than I could've been."

"Mew, mew." Hercule agreed.

Drew grabbed his phone and opened the text messages. He hesitated for a moment, thinking of Bill, then shook his head and started a group text to Sandy, Misty, Ceri, Paska, and Morgana; Jezebel was still out of town. "*Today has been weird. Desperately need friends, counsel, and beers. Meet at Andy's in 30?*"

The replies came in rapidly.

Paska: "*It is ten o'clock at night. I'm not as young as I once was. I'll see you there.*"

Morgana: "*Fine. But you're buying.*"

Sandy: "*I don't wanna be that person, but...I am. Can V come or is this super sekrit oracle bizness?*"

Misty: "*Same ?? from me.*"

Drew replied, "*Bring the menfolk. The more the merrier.*"

Misty sent a thumbs up and a goat emoji, while Sandy replied with a beer emoji. Drew grinned. Today might have sucked, but at least he had some of the best friends possible.

Feeling magnanimous and much friendlier, Drew decided to stop by Title Wave on his way to the bar to apologize and attempt to make amends. The lights were on and the door was ajar when he got there, so he poked his head in.

"Ryan? Ryan, it's Drew. I just wanted to stop by and apologize for our argument earlier. I was exhausted and rude, and I'm sorry." Drew walked into the store. It wasn't as neat as usual—Ryan kept things impeccably organized. Books from the window display were everywhere, and Drew recognized the telltale signs of fingerprint dust. An empty bottle of wine and two glasses were on the counter next to the register. Drew grimaced. Regardless of Ryan's feelings about him, no one deserved to go through this type of violation. "Ryan?"

He walked into the labyrinthine stacks. It was eerily quiet, and a growing uneasiness settled over him; he was intruding. Drew turned, intending to back out and come back tomorrow, when he saw a foot, toes pointing straight up. He sprinted across the small chaise-lounge filled clearing and headed into the romance section. Ryan lay on his back, eyes open and staring up at the ceiling.

Drew whipped his phone out of his pocket and dialed nine-one-one without taking his eyes off Ryan.

"Nine-one-one, what's your emergency?"

"This is Drew Hardy. I stopped by Title Wave to talk to Ryan—his door was open, and the lights were on—and found him lying on his back in the romance section."

"Is he breathing?" the woman's voice asked. "I'm sending paramedics, but I need you to tell me if he's alive."

Drew dropped to his knees next to Ryan and held his hand over his face, then felt for a pulse in his neck. "He doesn't seem to be breathing and I can't find a pulse. His lips are blue."

"The paramedics are almost there. Do you know CPR?"

"Yes."

"Put me on speaker and I'll talk you through it in case you forget."

Drew put the phone on speaker and started CPR. He made it

through three rounds before he was pushed aside gently by the EMTs. He picked the phone back up. "They're here now. Thank you."

"You're welcome. Take care, Drew." She hung up.

Drew watched the EMTs work on Ryan, but they didn't spend very long with him. "It's too late," one of them said. "He's been dead at least a half hour."

More sirens sounded outside, and Drew looked around for a chair. He was going to end his day the same way he'd started it—being questioned by the cops. He made his way back around Ryan, headed for the front of the shop, when movement caught his eye. A woman was tiptoeing out of the bathroom.

"Martha!"

The older woman with fading red hair and the wrinkles that came with a lifetime of sourness spun around. "Oh, Drew! How funny to see you here! I was just in the bathroom!"

The EMTs popped their heads up. "Martha—we didn't realize there was someone else here. Are you okay?"

She giggled. "Oh, yes. I'm okay. I stopped by to help Ryan clean up his shop and we had wine and then I went to the bathroom and everything's fine."

Drew exchanged a look with the EMTs. Martha was not fine.

"Shock," one of them mouthed. She stood up, walked outside, and returned with a blanket.

"Martha, why don't you come sit down," the EMT said. "I want to make sure you're okay."

"Okay." Her eyes drifted closed and she stumbled.

"Mike! Get up here!"

The second EMT raced to the front, took in the scene, and rushed out to grab the gurney. "How much wine did you drink with Ryan?"

"Jus' a little," she giggled. "Today is wine day, though. First there was wine at Drew's store. Then there was wine everywhere. And last, there was wine here!"

Mike came back in with the gurney, and they helped Martha up onto it. "I think she's just drunk, but better safe than sorry." They wheeled her out to the ambulance.

After a moment, Mike came back in. "She's getting some fluids and seems to be calming down. I'll stay until the cops come, and then we'll take her in. I called the coroner's office, and they're on their way, too. Are you okay?"

Drew ran his hand distractedly through his hair. "I'm fine, just... shocked. I was coming to apologize and found a body."

"Apologize for what?" Kyle asked, striding through the door, Chad hot on his heels.

Drew pinched the bridge of his nose between his thumb and forefinger. *This day just keeps on getting better.*

four

Drew sat on the curb with his face in his hands. It was midnight, and he still hadn't been released. He'd been fending off texts from the rest of the group; they'd been understandably concerned when he didn't show up to the night out he'd organized.

A light drizzle had started about thirty minutes ago, and he'd gone from distastefully damp to uncomfortably wet, bordering on disgustingly drenched. Even the small crowd that had gathered when the excitement started had mostly dispersed. Adriana was standing in the doorway of the vacant shop next door. Martha and Ryan were both on the town council with her, along with Misty and Gabrielle, the town's realtor. She was flanked by a couple other business owners with shops in the area, but everyone else had gone home.

Drew wasn't allowed back into the crime scene, but he wasn't supposed to leave, either. Technically, he could've left whenever he wanted, since he wasn't being charged. But every few minutes, Chad or Kyle stood in the doorway to glare him into submission, and he didn't want to deal with accusations of guilt and fleeing the scene later.

"Drew! Oh my god, what are you doing out here?" Ceri called, running down the street. "It is wet and cold and you're sitting in a puddle."

"I can't go until the cops let me go," Drew said. He'd been up for almost twenty-four hours—twenty-four very eventful hours—and couldn't even work up the energy to be annoyed at his circumstances.

"This is inhumane," Paska pronounced in a sepulcher tone. He was of medium height, well-built if a bit on the dad-bod side, and almost as pretty as Drew. Or at least he had been until he started growing an ill-advised beard. "Not bad for small town cops. I could do better, but this is an excellent way to get the chief suspect to confess."

"Confess to what?" Drew sputtered. "He was dead when I got there, his lips were blue—cyanosis, and he was a cranky, angry old man who'd had too much to drink and was under a lot of stress. He probably had a heart attack."

"That's what you want them to think," Paska said, nodding. "Wise."

There was no reasoning with Paska when he got into one of his weird moods, so Drew didn't try. He stood up, tucked his hands in his armpits, and wished he'd gotten a blanket from the EMTs, too.

Misty slipped an arm around his shoulder and the rest of the psychics moved in close to provide a buffer against the wind. "Are they charging you with anything or merely being jerks?" she asked.

"Jerks, I think. It's been almost two hours, though, and I'm cold and exhausted."

"Too bad none of us is a lawyer," Vincent said.

"We should pool our money and send Vincent to law school," Ceri said, tossing her red hair. "He's smart, logical, and between jobs; we definitely could use a lawyer. These last months have been agonizing."

"No thank you," Vincent said adamantly. "I'm not going back to school, and I'm not unemployed. I'm consulting."

Morgana, who almost always appeared to be channeling Morticia Addams, walked forward. "A lawyer is a good idea. I know someone. He may be reluctant to help us at first, but I can convince him. I'll leave as soon as the apocalypse is over."

Drew's eyes bounced back and forth among his friends. They were always enthusiastic, and he knew that banter was their way of diffusing tension—his way, too, when it wasn't his tension—but everything was moving too fast and he was having trouble keeping up.

"Are you okay?" Joseph asked.

Concern from Joseph McEwen, goat farmer and cheese maker extraordinaire as well as the best friend to his ex-everything, felt wrong. Drew dredged up a smile. "I don't even know. It's been a really long day."

"I can't even imagine," Ceri said. "I've been up almost as long as you and I'm exhausted. None of the day's trauma has been mine, and I'm still having trouble dealing. What do you need?"

"I need to go home, but I don't know when that's going to happen. Barring that, I need a blanket and something hot to drink."

"I didn't bring a blanket, but I brought cocoa spiked with schnapps," Bill said. "I heard what was happening—" he glanced at Joseph "—and wanted to do something. I'm sorry about earlier. I shouldn't have stormed off. Cocoa?"

Drew took the drink and let the heat of the cup permeate his fingers. "This is amazing. Thank you so much."

Bill shrugged out of his heavy Pendleton jacket. "Take this. Please. I'm warm enough for now."

Drew wanted to protest but didn't. He handed the cocoa off to Misty, put on Bill's jacket, and was overwhelmed with the scent of him. Bread and coffee beans and the faintest hint of the aftershave Drew had introduced him to when they were dating. His chest tightened, and he bit his cheeks to keep back the tears. He was so tired, and this was just like coming home. "Thank you," he whispered to Bill. He took the cocoa back and returned the hugs of all his friends who were wandering off into the night, leaving him alone with Bill. Then Drew looked at his former love—really looked at him—for the first time today.

Bill was a bear of a man. He was six feet tall with broad, well-muscled shoulders, a soft waist, and a sexy abundance of body hair. He was clean-shaven now, but when he wore a beard, it was all Drew could do to keep his distance. Now that his coat was off, Drew could just make out the sprinkling of dark chest hair curling around the collar of Bill's shirt. His dark brown hair and brown eyes nearly disappeared into the night.

"You came," Drew said. "For me?"

"Of course for you. I will always be here when you need me."

Drew opened his mouth to argue to the point, to throw out every time over the last three years that Bill hadn't been there, but it didn't matter anymore. "This won't be easy. There's a lot going on."

Bill grimaced. "I got a taste of it with Joseph. I'm sorry I ever doubted you. I'll make it up to you, and I'll be by your side."

Drew had never wanted anything as much as he wanted to kiss Bill in that moment. The streetlight in the background made a hazy glow around Bill's head and softened his demeanor. He took a half step forward into Bill's personal space, tilted his face up, and held his breath.

"You're free to go, Hardy," Kyle yelled. "Don't leave town."

The spell was broken; Bill took a step back.

"We need to talk," Bill said. He took a half step forward, not close enough for a kiss, but far closer than two Americans generally stood for casual conversation.

"I need to sleep," Drew replied. He yawned and blinked rapidly. His eyes felt gritty and one lower lid was starting to twitch. "It's been almost twenty-four hours and I'm exhausted. The kittens will need to be fed, too. Unless they magicked themselves out of the bathroom again and made sandwiches."

"What?" Bill asked, understandably confused.

Drew shook his head. He was babbling. "I have kittens now. I'll tell you all about it when we get together. But now, I have to sleep."

"Go, then." Bill pushed Drew gently in the direction of his house. "We have time to find our way back to each other. Sleep."

Drew started to take off the borrowed coat, but Bill shook his head. "Keep it. That way you'll have an excuse to call me tomorrow."

"Thank you. For everything."

"Always." Bill turned and walked up the street. Drew watched his ex until the mist swallowed him up, then turned the opposite direction and walked home.

DREW STUMBLED INTO HIS HOUSE, FIGHTING THE SLEEP THAT WAS threatening to overwhelm him. Tuppence and Hercule were passed out in a ball on his dark gray sofa, enthroned on a large pile of shredded toilet paper.

He shook his head, too tired to deal with the mess and mystery of how they kept opening the bathroom door. He trudged into the kitchen, closed the window that shouldn't have been open, and poured himself a glass of water. The doors were locked. The windows closed and locked. And the kittens had the run of the house.

Nothing for it now, but bed.

When Drew opened the door to his bedroom, all the lights were on, the windows were open, and there was a red rose laying across the pillow of the perfectly made bed. When he looked closer at the flower, he saw a piece of paper tucked underneath.

He knew he should call the cops again and not touch anything, but the thought of going through that again without any sleep was exhausting. He used a silk tie to pull the paper out and unfold it. The note read, "This is the beginning."

Drew set it back down, closed the windows with the tie, and left the room, pulling the door shut behind him. He headed into the guest room, stripped down to his boxer briefs, and crawled under the covers. He texted Bill, "*Were you here tonight? In my house?*"

The reply was immediate. "*No, of course not. I'd never be in your house without your permission.*"

"*I didn't think so. Just checking.*"

"*Is everything okay? Are you ok? Was there another break-in?*"

"*I'll tell you everything tomorrow. Promise. I'm fine. Just tired.*"

"*Come by for coffee in the morning. On the house.*"

"*It won't be early, but I'll be there,*" Drew promised.

"*Looking forward to it. Night.*"

"*Night.*" Drew set his phone on the night table, wished he'd brought the kittens upstairs with him, and fell asleep.

THE SUN STREAMING IN THROUGH THE EASTERN WINDOWS WOKE DREW MUCH earlier than he'd hoped the next morning. Disoriented, it took a moment before he determined that the reason the sun was at the wrong angle—and the room was a weird color—was because Drew was in his guest room and not his bedroom.

That thought was followed closely by the *why* of the whole situation. Drew bolted out of bed, disturbing the kittens who were dozing at his feet, grabbed his phone, opened the door, and marched across the hall to his room. He was ready to take pictures and maybe, if he was feeling patient, call the cops.

The room was just as he'd left it the morning before when he'd left with Ceri to go to the shop. Bed uncharacteristically unmade. No roses. No notes. The windows were still closed, and there was zero sign of disturbance.

"Mew!" Tuppence said, rubbing her head enthusiastically against his ankle. He reached down and picked her up.

"Wait a minute," he said to her. "I just opened the guest room door. It was closed. All night. How did you get in?"

"Mew!" she said again, trying to sink her claws into the webbing between his finger and thumb.

"Mew, mew!" Hercule agreed, head butting Drew in the shin.

"There is something off about you two. I would've figured it out already if it wasn't for you meddling kittens!"

Hercule ran to the doorway, looked back, and yowled.

"You're right. We need to get our priorities straight. First, breakfast, then sleuthing. Lead the way mysterious feline. I'd rather think about you than whether or not I'm hallucinating fixed beds and roses."

Drew sat in his shop and looked around. He hadn't ever turned the open sign around today. It felt like too much. Ryan was dead. Martha had been examined and released into the custody of Adriana, her only real friend in town. They were a quirky pair, but somehow suited each other.

The weeks after the Yule Ball were generally the quietest time of the year for Oracle Bay, but the absence of tourists this year was eerie. They'd started dropping off even before the Yule Ball. It'd been an odd Autumn. Between almost losing Main Street to a con man and his semi-ruthless developer, Sandy's shooting, magic goats, Etruscan goddesses, and the Christmas apocalypse, it'd been hard to keep the supernatural under wraps for both the innocent townsfolk and the tourists who drove the town's economy.

A knock on the door startled him out of his depressed reverie. It was gloomy in the shop. He hadn't turned on very many lights, and the late-afternoon winter sun wasn't helping at all. Drew trudged to the door after the knock came a second time. He pulled open the door so he could politely tell his unwanted customer to bugger off, but instead, his jaw dropped, and no words left his mouth. It was Bill.

"You didn't come for coffee and you didn't call," Bill said. "You're not answering your texts. You promised an explanation."

"I think I was just exhausted and hallucinating," Drew said. "Everything was fine this morning."

"Everything?" Bill asked. "Because you're sitting alone in the dark. How long have you been here?"

"Not long." He pulled out his cell phone to check the time. "Oh. Well. About seven hours."

"I thought we were getting somewhere yesterday, but if it was just your exhaustion talking, let me know now."

Drew dropped his face into his hands. "No. Definitely not. I don't know what's wrong with me. You'd think by now I'd be better at this —" he waved his hand vaguely between them "—whatever this is."

"By now? You're barely older than me. I don't think we're required to have our lives together until we're in our mid-forties."

Drew opened and closed his mouth, doing a credible imitation of a fish. He knew he had to say something. Their relationship had died spectacularly due to half-truths and not-quite-lies and skepticism. If they were going to reopen things, it had to be from a place of complete and transparent honesty. Over sharing rather than under. Nothing else would work. But what he needed to say was so far beyond the realm of regular human belief, he didn't know where to begin.

"You're not just a bit older than me, are you?" Bill asked. "That's why you were always so vague about your age. I thought it was because you hated being over thirty, but it's because you didn't want to tell me how old you really were."

"Would you have believed me?" Drew asked, as much gentleness as possible in his voice.

"Probably not," Bill admitted. "But I will now."

"I was born in the nineteenth century," Drew blurted out. "I'm certainly not as old as some of my compatriots, but I'm well over one hundred."

"That's…"

"A lot," Drew said. "I know. If this changes things, I understand."

"The only thing it changes is where I shop for gifts. I'm sure the AARP has an online store."

Drew scowled, but inwardly he was grinning like an idiot.

"Wanna go for a walk, old man?" Bill asked. "Or will that be too much for you?"

Now he let his grin break through. "I'd love to go for a walk. Let me grab a jacket."

Drew went into the back of the shop and came back with his coat and Bill's heavy Pendleton coat.

"I'm only taking this back because it looks better on me," Bill said, sliding his arms into the sleeves.

"It really does," Drew admitted. "I was swimming in it."

They walked out into the misty chill, and after Drew locked up, they headed to the waterfront.

"I'm sorry," Bill said. "I was an ass. The way I treated you... Even if you had been exaggerating or flat-out making the whole thing up, the way I reacted to your revelation that you were a real-life psychic was out of line and over the top. I didn't let you explain, I just shut you down and shut you out."

A weight that had been sitting on Drew's chest for almost three years lifted and he could breathe deeply again. "You were an ass, but so was I. I shouldn't have sprung everything on you, demanded you take my word for it with zero proof, and not given you any time to adjust before issuing ultimatums. Like I said earlier, I'm old enough to know better...to *do* better."

Silence, more comfortable than before, descended on them, and they walked along the oceanfront path without talking. Drew was awash in emotions. Relief, trepidation, and a hit of the hurt and anger he thought he'd beaten into submission. But above all the rest, he felt a swelling of hope.

They arrived at a break in the boardwalk. "Wanna walk to the end of the pier?" Bill asked.

The wind whipped up, carrying the smell of brine and ozone.

"It's going to storm," Drew said.

"That's the best time."

They walked to the end of the pier and leaned against the railing, not touching, but close enough that Drew could feel Bill's body heat. Drew stared out at the waves, barely visible in the light of the waxing moon behind them and the few boardwalk lights close enough to penetrate the growing fog. Something was happening, and Drew didn't want to jinx it by saying the wrong thing or looking at Bill at the wrong time.

"Do you ever think of trying again?" Bill asks.

"It's all I ever think about," Drew answered.

"Then why don't we?" Bill's voice broke, and Drew looked up and met his eyes. Drew lifted his hand, hesitated, then rested it on Bill's cheek, stroking Bill's face with his thumb.

"I'm too afraid," Drew confessed. "I don't think I can survive another broken heart."

"It'll be different. I know who you are now. I pro—"

"Don't make promises you can't keep," Drew said, smiling sadly. "There was more wrong between us than distrust." The anger that had bubbled up with the other emotions made its way to the forefront. "It took a magic goat and a divine kidnapping to get you to believe the man you professed to love might not be a pathological liar." He leaned forward and brushed his lips against Bill's. "There is nothing I want more than to pick up where we left off, but there are a lot of things to work through before we can."

"Then let's work through them," Bill said. "Let's start over. Let me take you out for dinner tomorrow night. We'll take it slow. Rebuild trust. Find our weak spots and build them up. I've been bereft without you."

Drew dropped his hand from Bill's cheek. "Starting over might be nice."

"You, me, a couple French 75s, and some real talk?" Bill asked. "How can you say no?"

"It does sound pretty irresistible," Drew admitted. "Make it night after tomorrow, throw in some raw oysters and steak tartare, and you might have me convinced."

"I'll never say no to oysters and tartare," Bill said. "And I'm free every night this week, so pushing it back a day works for me."

"Well, then. I guess we have ourselves a date."

five

Drew sat at his kitchen table sipping his fifth cup of coffee, avoiding the antics of the kittens as they played "pounce and chase" under the table, and ignored the steadily increasing number of text and voicemail notifications accumulating on his phone.

After he'd agreed to a date with Bill, they'd watched the storm until the wind became too rough, then walked back to Main Street and said their goodbyes.

There'd been nothing odd about his house. No open windows. No mysterious roses. No kitten destruction. Everything was perfectly normal.

Drew had lain in bed, but sleep had eluded him. He watched the clock read midnight, then one, then two. At half-past two, a crash from the kitchen had startled him out of a near-sleep. He'd rushed down the stairs, only to find two innocent looking fur balls sitting on the kitchen floor surrounded by cans of seltzer water. They'd tipped over the open boxes and spilled the contents everywhere. He'd picked up all the cans, put them in the fridge, and trudged back upstairs.

The last time Drew remembered seeing on the clock was 3:41.

And now it was half-past eight. He'd been up for an hour and a half—kitten breakfast is far more important than sleep—and was in no way ready to face the world.

A knock on the door pulled him out of his grumpy and tired reminiscing. He glared at the door, poured another cup of coffee, and ignored it.

The knock came again, followed by the bell. Drew slowly stirred some fresh cream into his coffee and pretended he couldn't hear.

There was the scraping sound of metal on metal followed by the door opening. "I know you're in here," Ceri said. "I'm coming to find you. Make yourself decent."

"I'm naked," he called out.

"That's okay," Ceri said. "I won't look." She walked into the kitchen, looked him up and down, and said, "Sitting in your underwear does not count as naked, you big liar."

"You weren't going to look," he pointed out. "I guess both of our pants are on fire now. What do you want?"

"Get dressed and come across the street. Things have been happening, and we have mysteries to solve."

"Should I wear my deerstalker?" he asked.

Ceri clasped her hands in front of her chest and widened her eyes. "Please tell me you can deliver on that."

Drew grinned. "What can I say? I like detective novels."

"How soon can you be there?"

"I need to eat something to protect my stomach against the six cups of coffee I've had, maybe put on pants and shirt... Thirty minutes?"

"Misty brought breakfast. There are plenty of pastries to go around, both sweet and savory. You're on your own for the clothing, though."

"I can be dressed and over in fifteen," Drew said. "Maybe twenty—gotta make sure the troublemakers have everything they need."

"See you then. And don't take longer, or I'll send Morgana over next time."

Drew shuddered. "Perish the thought."

· · · ★ ★ ★ ★ ★ · · ·

DREW WALKED INTO SANDY AND VINCENT'S HOME EXACTLY EIGHTEEN minutes later. He ambled through the kitchen, snagged a ham and cheese croissant, a cranberry scone, and another cup of coffee.

The rest of the psychics were gathered in the living room. Sandy and Misty were sharing the loveseat. Paska and Morgana bookended the couch, and Ceri was curled up in the overstuffed easy chair with a cup of tea. Jezebel was the only one missing from the regular group. Morgana hadn't had any luck talking Russell into joining yet. Everyone knew he was something, but no one could put a finger on what. Either Russell didn't know, or he wasn't talking.

"Should we invite Zeke?" Drew asked, apropos of nothing.

"I did," Paska said. "He's opening today, though, and didn't want to ask Andy—or more accurately, Brandy—for time off so soon after the apocalypse. The Pour House is like every business in town— unseasonably busy. The lingering gods, monsters, and general busy-bodies have kept everyone hopping."

Drew settled in between Paska and Morgana and took a second to adjust to being between two powerful and powerfully old beings. Their energy, unless they were trying to mask it, was intense.

Morgana picked up her cup of tea from the end table. "Settle down, Drew. You can't sit here if you're going to wiggle all over the place like an overeager puppy." Her dark eyes and hair contrasted with her pale skin and gave a distinctly Morticia Addams vibe.

Drew stilled and balanced his plate on his lap to take a drink. "Apologies Morgana. I'll try to restrain my exuberance to be so near your awe-inspiring presence."

She hid a grin behind her teacup. "See that you do."

Paska cleared his throat and the room fell silent. Drew didn't know how old he was, other than old, but he looked good for his age. He appeared to be in his early forties, toned without being musclebound, and had light brown skin, salt and pepper hair, and eyes so dark there was no definition between the pupil and iris. Paska quirked an eyebrow at Drew. Drew shrugged and grinned. Paska winked, then turned back to the rest of the room.

"This morning," Paska began, "when I went out to the workshop in the backyard where I keep my casting supplies and do most of my rune work, I discovered a break-in. The door was open, although it didn't look forced. It simply looked as if I'd forgotten to lock it."

Drew tried not to think about the things Paska—rune caster and bone reader—might have in his private workshop.

"Only one thing was stolen. A clay jar given to me by my mother. It held a set of rune stones made from the bones of...well, a man who was very important to me and to the people where we grew up."

Drew felt Morgana lean forward and look around him at Paska. "You lost his bones?"

"Whose bones?" Sandy asked.

"It doesn't matter who," Paska said. "All that matters is that they were important to me. What are the chances that you'd know any of my old chums, anyway, right?"

"Morgana knows him, though," Misty pointed out. Her dark, wavy hair, usually carefully confined in a bun, was wild today.

Ceri looked around the room. "Some of you are young, yet. But the older you get, the more secrets you have. Some of it is habit—you can't be giving away too many glimpses of the past without raising suspicion. Some is forgetfulness; there are a lot of hazy memories way back, and admitting you can't access them all makes an oracle feel old. And, of course, some of it is possessiveness. It's nice to be the only person to know something, and it's hard to trust others enough to share. You'll never learn everyone's secrets."

Misty pursed her lips, glanced over at Sandy, and said, "Those are fair points. I'm sorry I pushed. I am not going to forget, though. Any time you want to share the story, I am here for it."

"I'll keep that in mind," Paska said. "But for now, I want to know who stole my bones, how they got into my workshop, and how they knew what the most personally valuable items were."

Drew set his plate on the floor and twisted to face Paska. "Was anything else disturbed? Anything minor that looked more like a harmless practical joke than anything else?"

Paska shook his head. "I didn't notice anything else. Are you thinking of your sign and lightbulbs and skeleton?"

Drew nodded. "My focus stone was valuable because I had a strong connection to it and I'd spent years looking, but it has little value on the open market."

"I, too, have had an experience," Morgana announced.

"We all have," Sandy said. "At least Misty and I have. I don't know about Ceri, and of course, Jezebel isn't back yet."

Drew grabbed his phone and pulled up a notes app. After writing the details he could remember about Paska's story, he said, "Tell me. Morgana, if you wouldn't mind going next."

Ceri snorted. "Should've grabbed the hat, Sherlock."

"My shop, which is next to To A Tea, looked the same this morning as when I left it three days ago," Morgana began. "But when Paska called, he asked me to stop by on my way here. The door was unlocked, and the alarm system disabled. I've looked through the records, and the alarm was turned off with the override code at approximately midnight last night. It wasn't me, as I was asleep at the time, although I have no one to corroborate my story."

"I don't think you need an alibi for breaking into your own shop," Drew said. "But thank you for being so detailed."

Morgana nodded once, then continued. "Everything was in place. You have all been to Morgana's Mysteries and know that I keep a very tidy shop. Nothing was moved. I have several antique tea sets to set the mood, and every one was exactly where it belonged. I stepped into the back room where I keep my own tea set. It's not as old as Paska's lost items, but I've had that set for quite a while. I seldom use it for tasseography because the cups and saucers are all chipped, but that's what I drink from when I'm in the shop. It's the set that allows me to channel the beyond most accurately, and what I use for my own readings and other customers with more serious problems when I need a little more power. It had great sentimental value and now it's gone."

Drew finished his notes, dread pooling in the pit of his stomach. "Sandy?"

"My story is much like everyone's. My shop was unlocked. I don't have an alarm system, but I do have the squeakiest hinges on Main Street, no matter how well-oiled I keep them. Today, they didn't squeak. Not even a minor groan. Nothing was out of place, but the tarot deck that I use most often—the first deck I ever bought in college—was gone. In its place was a deck of playing cards, but every card was a Joker."

"Morgana, Paska...did either of you have replacement items like Sandy and I did?"

Paska shook his head. "Not that I noticed."

Morgana's lips tightened into a thin line. "Someone left four styrofoam cups stacked in the cupboard."

Drew noted it, then looked at Misty. "Your turn."

"I don't have tools to lose like the rest of you. I see through touch, although I know enough about palm reading to do a credible imitation of looking at love lines before I share whatever glimpse of the future I'm given through skin to skin contact. First Hand Knowledge was also unlocked. My aesthetic is the opposite of Morgana's, but none of my occult goodies were disturbed. The only thing missing was a pair of silk gloves I kept at the shop to wear as a costume. They weren't old or valuable or even particularly sentimental, but they were the gloves I wore to my Junior Prom, the one and only time I danced with Joseph before our recent...ahhh...rekindling. Or kindling, really. Nothing to rekindle."

"That sounds particularly sentimental," Sandy noted.

"Fine. It is," Misty admitted. "But no one could've known that. I've never told anyone."

"Everyone has secrets," Ceri said.

"And someone knows them all," Drew murmured. "Was anything left in its place?"

"Mittens connected by a long string. They were striped."

Drew shook his head slowly. "Okay, Ceri. Last but not least."

"Everyone knows the drill by now. Mirror Images was unlocked. Nothing disturbed. My scrying mirror and bowl right where I'd left them. However, the wall mirror in the business office in the back of the shop was gone. It was a terrible mirror and almost impossible to use for scrying. But it was my family's when I was a girl and was the first thing I ever saw the future in. I took it with me when they kicked me out, stole it really, and have kept it ever since to remind myself that I am more than they could've ever imagined. In its place was a weird Halloween mirror that glows purple and cracks every time I try to look at it."

"That sounds pretty awesome," Misty said. "As a Halloween decoration. But not a very good substitute for what's missing."

Drew leaned forward and put his elbows on his knees. "Has anyone besides us been targeted?"

"Adriana said she was missing some shop equipment, and when I talked to Antonia, she said she was missing one of her display tea sets," Morgana said. "I talked to her when I discovered my tea set missing."

"Ryan said his store had been vandalized, too," Drew said. "When he stopped by to yell at me for being a bad element or whatever." He shrugged. "It's not the first time I've heard that, and I'm sure it won't be the last."

"Do you know if anything went missing?" Paska asked.

"I don't. He was too busy blaming me to actually talk to me. I offered to help clean up, but he stormed out and slammed the door."

Silence blanketed the room. Something niggled at the back of his brain, but Drew couldn't put a finger on it. He shook his head and tried to concentrate on the matters at hand.

"It's possible someone is targeting only the psychics and the other thefts are a cover-up," Drew said. "I doubt Adriana was significantly attached to her equipment any more than anything else. Morgana, do you know if the missing tea set held any sentimental value to Antonia?"

Morgana shook her head. "Not as far as I know, but it might."

"And we don't know what, if anything, was taken from Ryan's before he passed away," Drew continued.

"Do we know how he died yet?" Paska asked.

Everyone shook their heads. "I assumed heart attack," Drew said. "His lips and fingertips were blue. I think that's a sign of cardiac arrest."

"Did anyone call Andy or Zeke or Russell to ask them if their businesses had been hit?" Sandy asked. "Andy might not be an oracle, but he is supernatural. And Zeke and Russell are both something."

"I talked to Zeke earlier," Paska said. "Told him why we were meeting. He didn't volunteer anything."

"He's not a business owner, either," Ceri said. "That might make a difference."

"Neither is Russell," Drew mused. "But he is the manager of the Sleeping Inn Restaurant and Bar. That might be enough."

"I'll call Russell," Misty said. She pulled out her cell phone and walked out in the kitchen to make her call.

"What about Andy?" Drew asked.

"Hearing nothing, I volunteer to check in with him," Ceri said.

"When's the last time you talked to him?" Drew asked.

"This morning before he went into work. If something happened overnight, he wouldn't have known by the time he left my place this morning."

Drew glanced around the room, but no one appeared surprised by the admission. Morgana looked a little more sour than usual, and Sandy was grinning, but this wasn't news to anyone. "Wanna check in with him?"

"Sure," Ceri said. She pulled out her phone and started texting.

She moved to put her phone down, when it vibrated with an incoming message. "The Pour House was broken into last night, but the only thing stolen was his display of tap handles representing the first beers he ever brewed. He is not impressed and apparently, almost set the bar on fire."

"Argh!" Drew groaned. "There's something there, but I can't put my finger on it."

Misty walked back into the room. "The Sleeping Inn wasn't hit, but Russell's house was broken into. According to him, he has a Ouija board collection, and the first one he ever bought—the one that's missing the original planchette and has been doodled all over by his college roommate—is missing."

"That is an interesting collection," Paska said. "Not that any of us can judge, but I think I know what we're dealing with now."

"You know who the thief is?" Drew asked.

"Oh, no. Not at all. But I know who Russell is." Paska refused to say anything further. "It's his story to tell and not mine. None of you want me spouting off about your talents when you're not around to defend yourself."

"One more thing," Misty said. "Drew, there's someone on your porch. Or at least there was a couple minutes ago."

"It's not the cops, is it?" Drew asked. "I cannot deal with any more police questioning today."

"It's not the cops. It's that guy you went to lunch with the other day."

"Oooh!" Sandy said. "Did you have a date?"

"No. Not until tomorrow," Drew said. "What do you mean the guy I went to lunch with?"

"To the Sleeping Inn," Misty said. "After he showed up at your shop?"

Drew exhaled with his eyes closed and tried to find a calm center to draw on. "Dio."

· · · · · ★ ★ ★ ★ · · · ·

Drew offered up his apologies. They all made plans to get together again in a couple days, then he marched across the street to confront the man sitting on his porch swing drinking chianti directly out of the bottle.

"Wine?" Dio asked.

"It's not even noon," Drew said.

"That wasn't a no." Dio grabbed a glass from the ground, filled it, and handed it too Drew.

Drew took a sip. "What are you doing here? I thought I made it clear that I wasn't interested in seeing you here. Or anywhere."

"I decided I wasn't a quitter. I'm not ready to give up on us yet, Drew Hardy."

"There is no us to hold on to," Drew said. "A three-month fling when I was on the rebound from a terrible breakup hardly constitutes an 'us.'"

"But you still talk about me," Dio said. "You have compared me to a god."

A dull red flush crept up Drew's cheeks. "Hyperbole."

"Wine dulls embarrassment," Dio said, refilling Drew's glass. "But it doesn't erase the words you've said."

"You're very charming and seductive," Drew admitted. "But you're not ever going to be anything more to me than a rebound guy. You were there when I needed someone, but I don't need that anymore."

"You might," Dio said. "I heard you're giving Bill the Barista another shot."

"How do you know? How do you know what I've said about you and what Bill and I are doing?" Drew took another sip of his wine.

"I get around," Dio smirked. "It's hard to keep secrets from me. You know that. After all, you bared your soul to me the day we met. I know all your hopes and fears."

"You caught me at a weak moment," Drew admitted. "I was heartbroken, more than a little intoxicated, and desperate for a sympathetic ear."

"And I kept you up all night drinking wine and talking," Dio grinned, taking another drink from the chianti. "But you, my dear psychic, kept one juicy tidbit back."

"I did?" Drew asked. He shook his head and looked down at his glass. It was full. Again. He took a sip, then paused. "How many times have you refilled my wine?"

"Only as many times as you emptied it," Dio replied.

"That's not an answer." Drew wasn't quite slurring, but he was definitely on his way to tipsy town.

Dio leaned forward and kissed Drew on the cheek. "I'll find out your last secret if I have to stay in town for a month to do it."

"Please don't," Drew said. He could feel his eyes starting to droop closed and he forced them open. "Just go."

Dio giggled. "And miss all this fun? Hardly! I had no idea little Oracle Bay could be so entertaining, but you sure know how to show a guy a good time." He skipped down the steps and out of sight.

Drew stood up, got his sway under control, and headed inside. Two very noisy kittens attempted to convince him they hadn't eaten in weeks, if not months. Dodging the furry, hungry obstacle course made his drunken walk to the kitchen even more hazardous. "If you guys murder me, that'll be the end of the kibble," he said. "Of course, I guess you could last awhile feasting on my corpse."

He made another pot of coffee and drank it black, alternating sips of coffee with gulps of water, in an attempt to sober up. Something about Dio always messed with Drew's self-control. He always ended up drinking more than he wanted to—more than he ever did in any other situation—when he drank with Dio.

He retired to the living room with his last cup of coffee, settled into the sofa with both sleepy kitties, and turned on the TV. Today called for some fictional murder. He vacillated between "Murder, She Wrote," "Hercule Poirot," and a new show he hadn't watched yet, "Miss Fisher's Murder Mysteries." In the end, he went with the familiar and queued up a little Jessica Fletcher.

After three episodes and one quick costume change—the deerstalker hat was sometimes necessary—he had an idea. He grabbed his phone and dialed.

"Hey Ceri. Remember that time about a century ago when we ran into each other in Los Angeles? You never did tell me what you were doing there."

He could almost see Ceri roll her eyes, but she answered anyway. "The same thing you were doing."

"Looking fabulous, hanging out with the stars, and ingratiating yourself with LA's finest?" Drew grinned.

"That's the ticket. You nearly screwed up my case." One hundred years had not yet dampened Ceri's irritation with Drew's arrogant bumbling and misogynistic assumptions about what she was doing and why.

"Sorry." Drew injected as much sincerity into that word as was possible over the phone. "I was in town following a lead and was a right sexist bastard who never even dreamed of running into a beautiful lady PI."

"It's fun to reminisce about all the ways you've been awful in the past, but that's not why you called. What are you thinking?" Ceri asked. "Of course, if that is why you called, that's okay, too. I have a notebook around here somewhere with a list I can read to you while you think of suitable ways to grovel."

"As much fun as that sounds, you're right. That's not why I called," Drew said. The idea that Ceri had a list of every time he'd screwed up was a little disturbing but not at all surprising. "Between the two of us, we have more investigative experience than the entire Oracle Bay PD, plus we have the benefit of being able to call on our other gifts."

"Have you tried calling on your other gifts to look at the situation?" She sounded genuinely curious.

"Of course. I assume everyone who can, has."

"Nothing but fog for you, too, then?"

Drew sighed. "Nothing but fog." Resignation tinged his voice.

"But you think we can do something about this?" Ceri asked.

"I think we can. How many cases did you solve for the LAPD?"

"Enough to deserve my own television show," she said. "I worked with them for almost ten years, off and on. What about you?"

"I worked in Chicago during that era, mostly. But that wasn't my first detecting rodeo. The Chicago PD owes me a huge debt of gratitude. They also owe me several thousand dollars—the cheap bastards shorted me on my last couple cases with them."

"What do you want to do?" she asked. "We can go after the entire Chicago Police Force, or we can look into our crime wave in Oracle Bay."

"Meet me at The Pour House tonight. We can talk it out and see where to go from there. I'm leaning towards staying local, but if you have any bigger ideas, I'm open to suggestion," Drew said.

"Sounds good. What time?"

"Eight?"

"See you then." Ceri hung up.

six

Drew was walking out the front door when his phone vibrated. He glanced at the screen. "Change of plan. Meet at Sleeping Inn."

Drew shrugged and headed towards the hotel. Ceri was already at a table in the back, sipping a glass of wine. Drew grimaced at the thought of more alcohol and ordered a club soda at the bar before joining her.

"Why the venue change?" Drew asked, sliding into his seat. She hadn't admitted to anything, but she hadn't gone out of her way to keep things a secret, either. Everyone had seen Ceri dancing with Andy at the Yule Ball, and Drew had watched them leave together long before the dance was over. Drew hoped Andy hadn't done anything egregious. He'd boycott Andy's bar if he had to, but The Pour House brewed the best beer on the peninsula.

"Seemed more appropriate," she said.

"Something up with you and Andy?"

"Tell me your ideas, Drew." A warning note permeated her voice, and Drew backed off. He and Ceri were close, but she was intensely private. She played her cards close to the vest and only showed them when she was good and ready.

"I think we should interview every business owner on Main Street to see if they've had similar experiences—maybe something that didn't seem significant except sentimentally—and see if we can draw any lines. Right now, the crimes are more nuisance than anything else. Sure, it's violating to have your business broken into, but no real damage is being done. Only pranks. But pranks where the perpetrator knows what's most valuable."

"That's a good idea. I haven't interrogated witnesses in a long time," Ceri grinned.

"Do you want to split up or team up?" he asked.

"Team up. We're both good, but we have different strengths. If we're together, we won't miss anything."

"Sounds like a plan." They clinked glasses. "Should we meet at one end of Main in the morning—say nine o'clock or so?"

"Nine sounds great. Which end?"

"The end with the coffee shop, obviously."

"Oh, you want to start with your boyfriend," Ceri teased.

"That's just an added bonus," he smirked. "And he's not my boyfriend."

"Yet," Ceri said.

"Yet."

DREW STOPPED OUTSIDE THE DOOR OF CAFFIEND DREAMS AND RAN HIS fingers through his hair. He was more nervous than was warranted, especially since all he was doing was going in for coffee, something he'd done countless times before.

"What are you doing out here?" Ceri asked. "It's raining and frigid. You look amazing. You always look amazing. Just open those big, beautiful gray eyes at him and he'll be in your thrall."

Drew took a deep breath. "I have a date tonight."

"I know. You've mentioned it once. Or twice, maybe."

"Don't be sour with me, wench. How many dates have you had with Andy?"

Ceri pursed her lips, gave him a look that would've quelled a lesser man, and said, "Approximately?"

Drew nodded.

"Zero. We aren't dating. It's strictly an FWB situation." Ceri shrugged, nonchalance echoing from every inch of her relaxed pose. The muscles around her jaw tightened though, and Drew eyed her thoughtfully.

"Whatever you need to tell yourself to get through the day." Drew knew better than to push, especially when Ceri was putting so much effort into pretending she didn't care.

"Anyway, it's old news. Those benefits have sailed." She started to shrug, realized she hadn't come completely out of her last dismissive shrug, and froze in a half-hunched manner before shaking off the awkwardness and letting her body flow back into his usual graceful posture.

Drew paused before yanking open the door to the coffee shop. "What do you mean? Are you okay? Why didn't you tell me?"

Ceri waved her hand dismissively. "Those kinds of arrangements are always temporary. Particularly when they're entered into with a fallen angel."

"He's only half fallen," Drew protested.

"That's not the point. The point is he was a demon, and they're not exactly long-term relationship material. The other point is that I am not looking for a long-term relationship. It was just refreshing to meet someone I could touch." She brushed past him, pulled open the door, and strode inside, leaving Drew with a whole host of questions he'd never even thought to ask before.

"Ceri!" he said, following her in. She gave him another *look*, and he backed off. She was right. This was neither the time nor the place. Drew took his place at the back of the line and kept his mouth closed.

When they got to the front of the line, Bill handed them coffees.

"What's this?" Ceri asked.

Bill smirked. "Caramel latte extra foam, and a quad shot espresso. I'm not the only one who can predict the future."

A slow smile crept across Drew's face. This was really happening. Bill was on board and he was being cool about it. Ceri was not as forgiving. "You're still a jerk, Bill," she said. "Even if you are a funny jerk who remembers my coffee order from three years ago."

"You haven't been here in three years?" Drew said, aghast. He pulled out his debit card to pay for the drinks.

"Why would I frequent the business of the man who broke your heart?" Ceri retorted.

"Because he makes the best coffee on the peninsula? Where did you get your espresso fix? Please tell me it wasn't..."

"Listen. The mermaid and I got to be close friends, and you don't need to judge us," Ceri said, taking a sip of her coffee.

Bill grinned. "I always remember my favorite people's drinks. And this is on the house."

"You don't need to—" Drew started.

"I do. Take the coffees," Bill pressed. "I'll see you tonight."

"If you insist."

"I do. Now go. You're holding up the line."

Drew walked out of the shop, followed by Ceri, and paused just outside the door again. "Where to next?"

Ceri looked around. "We've already talked to Sandy. Why don't we stop into Mind Your Manor and see if they've had any disturbances?"

"The realty company?" Drew asked. "Do you think..."

"We should be thorough, and Gabrielle and Bryan are observant."

"You're right," Drew conceded. "I shouldn't discount the mundane businesses. After all, Ryan said there'd been vandalism, and Adriana's wine shop was targeted."

"Get your head back in the game, Hardy... No lead is too small!"

"Should've grabbed the hat," Drew said. "Let's get to it."

They walked past the empty storefront next to the coffee shop and into the Oracle Bay realty office. Bryan wasn't there, but Gabrielle was sitting in her office, staring intently at her laptop.

"Hey Gabrielle," Ceri said.

Gabrielle looked up, grinned, and came out to the main room. She was short—not more than five feet tall—with dark brown skin, black, curly hair, and the most beautiful eyes Drew'd ever seen outside of a mirror. He was not at all interested in women, but her body, which rippled with darkly enticing curves, almost made him regret that. She was a good friend of Jezebel's, and as such, they'd spent time together socially, but Drew didn't know her well. Ceri, however, apparently knew Gabrielle a bit better.

"What's up?" Gabrielle asked. "You two finally shacking up together and need a new, romantic home to cement your unnatural love?"

Ceri laughed and Drew rolled his eyes. "You caught us out," Ceri said. "We need a cozy beachfront home where we can raise a family."

Drew shuddered. "Staaaahp. Even as a joke, it's too much. I'll leave the children to someone else. I've got my hands full managing my own life."

Gabrielle laughed, a deep, throaty laugh. "Y'all are breaking my heart. If you're not here to buy, what are you doing?"

"Can't people just stop in to chat?" Ceri asked.

"Not both of you," Gabrielle said. "This has something to do with the goings on in this town, doesn't it?"

"There's no way to pull one over on you," Drew said. "There's been a lot of mischievous vandalism in the last few days. We just wanted to know if you'd been hit, too."

Gabrielle rapped on the wooden table behind her. "So far, no. We've been lucky. Nothing odd here. Do you know who else has been messed with?"

"Besides us?" Ceri asked. "Morgana, Paska, Sandy, Misty. Also Andy, Adriana, Antonia, and maybe Ryan before he died. Russell's home was broken into."

"That's a whole lot of suspicious activity. Do you know if Jez's business was touched?"

Ceri shook her head. "She's still out of town, and we didn't want to compound things by breaking in to check on a break in. None of the items stolen have been of great monetary value, so we're gonna wait and see."

Gabrielle nodded. "Makes sense. I'll let you know if I hear anything else."

"I appreciate it," Ceri said. "Take care and stay safe."

"I will. And if you two change your minds and decide to give joint homeownership a chance, let me know."

"You'll be the first person we tell," Drew promised. "Cross my heart."

THE REST OF THE MORNING WAS VERY SIMILAR TO THE FIRST VISIT. THEY stopped at Deja 'Do—the most popular salon in town—but no one there had anything to add. The same was true at The Codfather—the best fish 'n' chips on the peninsula, and Aw, Shucks!—purveyor of fresh oysters, and other shellfish when in season.

Drew and Ceri looked down the rest of Main Street. A couple dozen storefronts, each painted a bright, cheerful color, decorated both sides of the wide street. But of those shops, half stood empty. Nearly every other one was shuttered and dark, and the diagonal parking spaces held only six cars.

"There are a lot of empty storefronts," Ceri said. "I don't remember it ever being this bad."

Drew shrugged. "A lot of people aging out of business ownership without anyone to take over—like Ryan. I know Misty is working pretty aggressively to fill up space. Vincent is helping behind the scenes."

"It'll be nice to have the street filled up. I hope Misty makes all new businesses pick punny names." She pushed open the door of Covington Wine Shoppe.

"You have questionable taste," Adriana said. The frost that accompanied her words raised goosebumps on Drew's arms. She was still mad about the Prosecco.

Ceri turned her sunniest smile on Adriana. "Aww, c'mon Adriana. Everyone loves a good pun. They make the tourists laugh and drum up business."

"I assure you, I get plenty of business without resorting to childish wordplay. Some of us like to be regarded as professionals."

"You do you," Drew said.

Her only response was an icy glare. Drew shivered.

"Did you need something?" she asked. "Because if not, you can go. I'm too busy to stand around and gossip."

The shop was conspicuously empty, something Adriana seemed to realize the moment the words came out of her mouth. Her lips thinned and tightened, and her eyes narrowed.

"I need a couple bottles of wine," Ceri said. "You know I'm hopeless at picking out anything that isn't Bordeaux. It's for an intimate dinner I'm planning. I'd like a bottle for the main course—we're having lamb—and a bottle for dessert and relaxing after. I'm planning something chocolate and decadent. Can you help?"

Adriana relaxed her shoulders and stood up straighter. "Of course I can help. Follow me. We'll find the perfect wines for you."

While Adriana was browsing, lips pursed and reading glasses perched on her nose, Ceri said, "I heard you had a break-in, too. My shop was one of the ones hit. Did you lose anything valuable?"

"Yes. It's so aggravating. I'd just purchased a new screw capper— the machine that puts the screw caps on wine bottles—and a bunch of caps, and the capper and the caps were all taken. I'd started making some of my own wine with grapes I'd purchased. I was planning on starting classes where people could come, make their wines and labels, and then come back when it was ready to drink."

"That's a brilliant idea!" Drew said. "It'll be so popular!"

"Unfortunately, I lost my big investment," Adriana sighed. "A couple thousand dollars is no small loss to any business."

"Ugh," Ceri said. "I'm so sorry. I didn't lose anything of great monetary value. Either way, though, it's so violating to think that someone was in your space touching your things."

Adriana reached out and placed a hand on Ceri's shoulder. "Thank you for understanding. You've always been such a nice young lady."

Ceri grinned at Adriana. "I do my best. Did you find some wine for me?"

Adriana grabbed two bottles off the shelf. "This Côtes du Rhône —it's a grenache heavy blend—will be wonderful with the lamb, and this Ruby Port will complement your chocolate dessert perfectly."

Ceri took the two bottles, paid, and said, "Thank you so much. I'll let you know how wonderful they are!"

They walked towards the exit just as Martha came rushing into the store. "Oh, it's so awful! Have you heard?" she gasped.

"Heard what?" Drew asked.

"It's Ryan! They're saying it was murder!" Martha's pale skin was even grayer than usual, and her faded red hair drooped around her shoulders.

"What do you mean, murder?" Adriana demanded. "I thought he had a heart attack!"

Martha lowered her voice and leaned in, whispering conspiratorially, "There've been a lot of overdoses lately—mostly people from Seattle or Portland, not good, local folk—so the medical examiner did an advanced drug test. They're doing them on everyone now, I guess. Trying to find the source of the problem."

"So how did they decide murder and not overdose?" Ceri asked.

"They said there was so much Fentanyl in his system that it was unlikely he would've taken that much accidentally," Martha explained.

"Suicide, then," Adriana said flatly. "It must've been suicide."

"That is a possibility," Martha admitted. "But the cops sounded pretty sure it was murder."

"How did you hear all this?" Drew asked.

Martha's eyes darted back and forth. "I listen."

"Okay," Ceri said. "Gotcha."

"You don't understand," Martha said. She tapped her ear three times. "I have ways to listen."

"Have you... Have you bugged the police station?" Drew asked through half-clenched teeth. The question was completely ludicrous, and he felt ridiculous asking it.

"You guessed my secret!" Martha crowed. "I've been listening for years."

"Just to the cops?" Ceri asked.

"Oh no. I listen to everyone." Martha looked around at her audience. "Well, not you three, of course. Only law enforcement and people I don't like very much."

"Well. Thanks for the news about Ryan," Drew said. "Ceri and I have to get going. Wine to drink and all that. Stay safe, ladies!"

Martha waved them out of the shop while Drew and Ceri beat a hasty retreat.

"Huh," Drew said. "That was certainly something."

"Yeah. It's weird that Adriana's theft wasn't sentimental, right?" Ceri asked as they walked away from the Wine Shoppe.

"That's where you're focusing? On the wine capper?" Drew glanced back over his shoulder at Adriana's shop, then came to a stop in front of one of the empty stores.

"Well, everyone else lost something that had more personal value than monetary. Why is hers different?"

"It's Adriana. It's possible that the most expensive thing in her shop does hold the most sentimental value." Drew leaned back against the wall of the shop after a cursory examination for spiders and nails and other things he didn't want on his coat.

Ceri laughed. "That's not nice."

"I know, but she doesn't like me, and it makes me cranky," Drew said. He felt like a bit of a jerk for implying Adriana cared about nothing but money, but he also thought it might be true. "What about Martha's revelations?"

"About Ryan or her penchant for eavesdropping?" The wind whipped up, bringing the smell of brine and a sudden chill to the nearly empty street. Ceri wrapped her coat more tightly around her body and tucked her hands under her arms.

"Both." Drew stepped back even further, trying to shelter his body from the damp, chilly wind.

"I'm definitely going to check my shop for bugs, as soon as I figure out how to do that," Ceri declared. "I have a date with YouTube coming up."

"Same," Drew agreed. "It's creepy." He pushed off the building, and they started down the street again.

"It does move her to the top of the suspect list," Ceri said. "If she was always listening, she might hear what we value most."

"What's the motivation, though?" Drew asked. "She doesn't seem the type for random mischief."

"I don't know," Ceri sighed. "We should talk to her again. Maybe without Adriana around."

"Definitely. But in the meantime, Ready for some tea?" Drew asked, opening the door to To A Tea.

"I am always ready for tea," Ceri said. "Especially if it comes with lunch."

CERI WAS SIPPING HER AFTER LUNCH TEA AND CHATTING WITH ANOTHER customer while Drew took a look around. Antonia's tea shop was probably the classiest thing on Main Street and hit every tea shop stereotype he could come up with. Pink and cream decor, lots of lace, and displays of the most mouth-watering confections. She'd been a pastry chef before moving to Oracle Bay, and her training shone through everything she did.

Drew paused to examine a small figurine of two kittens playing with a ball of yarn. Unlike the other knickknacks, this one wasn't white, pink, and gold. One of the kittens was a shiny black cat with mismatched eyes, and the second was an orange and black chimera with eyes identical to the first.

Antonia stopped by his elbow. "Isn't that precious?" she said. "I found it in the window yesterday morning. It doesn't quite fit with anything else, but they're so adorable."

"They really are," Drew said. "They look like troublemakers, though."

"All cats are troublemakers to some degree. Didn't you just find a couple kittens on your doorstep?" Antonia asked. "We have the same stories, except I'd guess yours are rather more work than mine."

Drew forced a laugh and widened his eyes a bit to inject fake sincerity into his face. "They're a handful, and that's no lie. I wouldn't trade them for anything, though."

"I always did like cats," Antonia said. "But my allergies prevent me from doing anything but admiring them from afar—mostly in YouTube video form. The internet sure is a blessing for cat enthusiasts, isn't it?"

This time, Drew's grin wasn't faked. "That's the best use in this day and age, that's for sure."

"You should start videotaping your cats and make them YouTube famous. They could get sponsorships for you!"

He laughed. "I'll look into it," he promised. "Can I ask you a question, Antonia?"

"Of course, young man."

"Have you had anything weird happen here? Has anything gone missing?"

"Not that I've noticed. None of my little figurines are gone, although I don't know where this one came from. Maybe a customer left it for me." Antonia lightly touched the kittens.

"Morgana mentioned something about a missing display set?" Drew prompted.

"Oh, yes. That. That was a bit odd. Come with me and I'll show you."

Drew followed her back into the kitchen with Ceri trailing behind. In the middle of a large table was an elaborate tea set with service for twelve.

"This is usually in the front window," Antonia said. "But yesterday morning when I arrived to open, the display case was empty, except for the kitten figurine. I must admit, it gave me quite a turn—this set was my great-grandmother's, and she in turn had it from the Queen's own palace. It was always family lore that Queen Victoria herself once took tea from this set. So, as you can imagine, it is precious. I was in a bit of a bother when Miss Morgana stopped by to inquire as to my health. However, after she left, I had a bit of gin to calm my nerves and did a thorough search. I found it put away in one of the cupboards. I don't know how it got there—none of my staff will admit to putting it away, and I'm inclined to believe them, but it didn't get up and walk away on its own, now, did it?

Drew and Ceri made small talk with Antonia for a while longer, then made their excuses, paid their bill, and walked out.

"That's a twist on things," Ceri said.

"This whole case is twisted," Drew grumbled. "It's so petty. Why take items of sentimental value and replace them with jokes? Why move a tea set around and place a kitten figurine—a figurine that almost perfectly mimics my brand-new surprise cats? It could be a coincidence, but at this point, I'm skeptical coincidence has any place in this town."

"We've all had sentimental items stolen," Ceri pointed out. "Adriana, who doesn't have an oracular bone in her body, lost some equipment. Ryan lost something unknown—maybe—and Antonia almost lost something of great value, but instead it was just hidden."

"Maybe all our stuff is hidden in the cupboards?" Drew suggested. "Did you look? I can't remember where I looked in my shop."

"Paska sounded like he'd been pretty thorough," Ceri pointed out. "But I don't know about everyone. It wouldn't hurt to suggest it."

"Let's do that then," Drew said. "Wanna head home for brainstorming and sitting down?"

"Not so fast," someone said.

Drew spun around. Chad and Kyle were standing in the street behind Ceri and him. Drew pasted a smile on his face. "What can I do for you officers today?"

"We need to question you about the night Mr. Cohen died," Chad said. "Preferably down at the station."

Drew looked around. "Why don't we head to the Sleeping Inn instead. I could use a break."

"It'd really be better if you came downtown," Kyle said.

"Do I have to?" Drew asked. He watched the cops' expressions change and knew that at this point, at least, he didn't have to.

"The Sleeping Inn, then," Kyle said.

"I'll catch you later," Drew said to Ceri. He walked to the end of the block and turned left towards the historic hotel and pub that stood between Main Street and the Pacific Ocean. He could hear the sounds of footsteps behind him, trying to keep up.

Drew didn't know exactly why they wanted to talk to him, but he'd spent enough time as a private investigator and watching every detective show he could find to know that they seldom wanted to question those who were blameless. He shook his head. If Ryan had been murdered—though it didn't seem possible for the cops to pin an overdose on murder and not suicide—Drew was not only the last person to see him alive, he was the first person to see him dead. That was suspicious, and he really couldn't blame the cops for giving him a second look. Well, he could blame them, but he'd probably do the same in their place.

Drew grimaced when he walked into the pub; Dio was sitting near a window with four bottles of wine, two men, and three women. Drew waved at Russell, then sat at the table farthest away from Dio. He ignored the cops, slung his arm over the chair next to him, and picked up a menu.

"This is serious," Kyle said, settling in across from Drew. "Not a dinner date."

"I wasn't thinking dinner," Drew said. "Just an appetizer and a French 75."

"Spinach and artichoke dip? Or the cheese plate?" Russell asked.

"Cheese plate and a side of olives," Drew said. "And you know my drink."

"Of course." Russell turned towards the cops. "And for you gentlemen?"

"I'll have a Coke and the spinach and artichoke dip," Chad said. Kyle glared at him but didn't say anything. There was a long pause while everyone looked at Kyle expectantly, and he steadfastly refused to look at anyone.

"Fine." Kyle barked. "Ginger ale and the steak tartare."

"Excellent choice, Officer," Russell said. "I'll be right back with your drinks."

No one said anything while waiting for Russell to return. When he did, in addition to the drinks they'd ordered, there was a carafe of wine and three full glasses.

"Compliments of the man in the corner," Russell said.

"We can't drink while we're on duty," Kyle said. "But our thanks."

"I'm just doing what I'm paid to do," Russell said, setting a glass of wine in front of each person next to their non-alcoholic beverages —and Drew's French 75. "Your food will be out in about fifteen minutes."

Chad picked up his wine and took a sip, appearing completely oblivious to what he was doing. Kyle followed suit, and before Drew could even begin to figure out how to comment on what was happening, he caught himself taking a sip of the Bordeaux instead of his gin and champagne cocktail.

"Here's the deal, Hardy," Kyle said, setting his glass down with more force than was necessary. "You're a suspect in the murder of Ryan Greenfield. You admitted to arguing with him the night he was murdered and were the last to see him alive. You also discovered the body. He has no family who stood to benefit from his death, so we're looking at contentious relationships."

"I wasn't the last to see him alive," Drew protested. "Martha was. She said she had a glass of wine with him before he died."

"She's since recanted," Chad said. "She was intoxicated."

"Whether or not she actually had drinks with Ryan, she was at the scene and had been drinking, even if it wasn't the wine Ryan had out," Drew pointed out. "She came out of the restroom after the EMTs arrived, which means she was there before me."

"It's your word against hers," Kyle said, taking a huge gulp of wine.

"Three people saw her come out of the bathroom. I hardly think that's just a 'he said, she said' situation," Drew protested.

Kyle waved away his protest and nearly spilled his wine in the process. "It doesn't matter. You're still the number one suspect. Tell us your abilie."

"Abilie? Do you mean alibi?" Drew asked.

"Thas what he said," Chad scoffed. "Abilie."

"Do you have a time of death?" Drew asked. "When do I need an alibi for?"

"Pfffftttt. Like we'd tell you all our cards," Chad said. "You tell us your stuff, and we'll tell you if it fits."

Drew pulled out his phone and recounted the events of the evening, complete with time stamped text messages.

"We'll need a copy of all that stuff," Kyle said.

"Of course. I didn't do it. I just wanted to apologize to the old man and help him clean up after his break-in."

Chad straightened up. "What break-in?" he asked. "There was no evidence of a break-in."

Drew sighed. "I said this the night it happened. When Ryan stopped by, we argued. He blamed me and the rest of the Oracle Bay psychics for making the town less classy, then said that he blamed his break-in on me, since I'd had one, too."

"Did he say what was missing?" Chad asked.

"No, but when I stopped by, I noticed the window display was messed up and there was fingerprint dust everywhere. That wasn't you guys?" Drew asked.

They looked at each other, then at Drew.

"I didn't dust for prints at the scene," Chad said. "I saw the dust and thought someone else had taken care of it."

"Same here," Kyle admitted.

Russell set food in front of everyone and surreptitiously filled the wine glasses.

The cops dug in, but Drew just stared at his cheese. The problem was on the tip of his tongue, but he just couldn't quite wrap his brain around it. He selected a piece of Oregon blue cheese and nibbled at it.

"We'll be in touch," Chad said, interrupting Drew's train of thought.

"Don't leave town," Kyle menaced. He downed his second glass of wine. "We've got fingerprints to take."

Drew watched them walk out, then turned to get the check.

"I'll send the bill to the police station," Russell said. "If they're going to conduct official business here, the station should pick it up."

"Thanks, Russell. See you later."

seven

Drew checked his reflection for at least the twentieth time. He was meeting Bill in thirty minutes so they could drive down to Long Beach for dinner. A first date. Kind of. He turned to pace the length of the living room and tripped over Hercule Purrot.

"Why are cats so homicidal?" Drew asked him, scooping the orange and black chimera kitten up to nuzzle his adorable little face. "The tripping instinct is a little out of control."

"Mew!" Tuppence complained, twining around his ankles. He picked her up in his other hand and sat down on the sofa. Stretched across his lap, side-by-side, the kittens rolled over onto their backs, exposing their tempting, pink bellies.

"You are both pure evil," Drew said. "I know what happens next, yet I'm helpless to resist you." He placed one hand on each belly and rubbed softly. They purred for approximately fifteen seconds before curling around his hands, claws fully extended, and attacking.

"Ahhhh!" Drew yelled, trying to extract his hands from the adorable furry death machines taking up real estate on his lap. "Evil!"

They let go, purred loudly while head butting the hands they'd just terrorized, and hopped down onto the sofa, one on each side of him. The tiny terrors curled up into fluffy balls and immediately fell asleep.

Drew checked out his hands. They weren't in too bad of shape. He washed them, checked his watch, took a breath, and headed out the door. He walked a mile through the mist, away from the ocean and towards the bay, to a large city block with no sidewalks and minimal streetlights. The block was completely taken up by a single home. It didn't look obscenely large from the outside, merely supremely haunted.

The property stretched up in gothic splendor, culminating in a tower on the south side and a second story wrap-around porch on the north side. The main floor's porch was intricately carved in the same pattern as the wrought-iron fence that surrounded the land. The house was painted a medium gray color that matched the ocean on a stormy winter day. In the misty evening, it looked as though it had succumbed to age and abandonment.

Drew shuddered a bit. He hadn't grown up in Oracle Bay, but even without knowing the truth, he knew this house was the target of a hundred dares by countless kids showing off for their friends. Bill had lived here his whole life—the kid from the haunted house— and had finally grown to embrace the weirdness of it when the rest of his family left town. Drew loved it. He loved every weird nook and cranny. He was especially fond of the secret staircase that led from the pantry to the third-floor cupola room—it had an amazing view of the Bay. But more than any of that, he loved the grounds. There was a labyrinth, a rose garden, an amazing herb garden, and the hot tub Bill had installed a couple of years after his family left Oracle Bay and left the house to him.

Drew hadn't been here since they'd ended things, and he found himself a lot more nervous than he'd thought he would be. He took a few long, calming breaths, opened the gate, and walked up to the front door to ring the bell.

No matter how many times he'd been there, Drew always expected a butler to open the door, a la Tim Curry in Clue. But, as always, it was just Bill.

He walked out, pulling a wool coat on, and shut the door behind him. "Hey," Bill said.

"Hey yourself. I walked over, since I assumed you'd be driving."

"I could've picked you up."

Drew grinned. "It didn't even occur to me to ask until I was halfway here." He shrugged. "I never mind a walk in the mist—it calms my nerves. I especially don't mind when I get to see the Walters Mansion."

"It's hardly a mansion," Bill grumbled. It was a long-standing joke between them. "And I'm glad I'm not the only one who needs their nerves calmed. I was five seconds away from pouring a small whiskey."

Drew grinned. "I guess anxiety shared is anxiety halved?"

"Something like that," Bill smiled back. "Are you ready?"

"Always. Is the driver pulling the car around?" Drew asked.

"You're going to give me a headache if you make me roll my eyes one more time."

"It's been so long," Drew sighed. "I have a lot of wealth-based mockery built up."

Bill sighed. "There hasn't been any regular staff since long before I was born. And I think if we're going to mock someone here for their old money, it isn't going to be me."

"Wait! This isn't fair," Drew argued. "You're not allowed to turn the tables like that. Besides, I don't come from money."

"But you're old enough to be your own old money, aren't you?" Bill countered.

Drew pouted. "I don't know how I feel about this. Maybe I liked it better when you didn't know who I really was."

"You mean when I refused to listen to who you really were?" Bill asked. "Did you really like it better? Because I think this is the far superior relationship model." He opened the passenger door of the silver Porsche 911 that Drew'd walked right by without noticing.

"What is this beautiful thing?" Drew exclaimed, sliding in. "When did you get this? I thought we'd take the van."

Bill closed the door behind Drew and got in on the other side. "About a year ago, I decided it'd be nice to have another car besides the bakery van, and I've always wanted a Porsche."

"I haven't seen this car anywhere. I wouldn't have missed it, not a gorgeous thing like this."

"Turns out, I don't go very many places." Bill turned on the car, carefully adjusted the mirror, and backed out of the driveway. "Most of the time, it's easier to take the van."

"You've left town, though, right? Gone to Seattle or Portland?"

"I've been up to see Joseph's folks a couple times, but he always drives," Bill shrugged. "You're the first person who's sat in that seat since I brought it home."

"I'm not the first person to, uh, sit in your passenger seat in the last three years, am I?" Drew asked. Heat suffused his neck and crawled up onto his face, making him grateful for the dark.

"That is, by far, the worst euphemism I've heard in a long time, Drew Hardy if that is even your real name…oh my god."

The heat of awkward embarrassment gave way to a thousand super-sized hummingbirds who'd taken up residence in his abdomen. "It's not the name I was born with, no," Drew said.

"I should've guessed," Bill said. "You do own a complete collection of first edition Nancy Drew and Hardy Boys books, which is fun, but a bit odd. Although why those names? I know you have every Agatha Christie ever written as well."

"Drew Hardy sounded more fitting. I did name my kittens Hercule Purrot and Tuppence Beresfurred, though. Dame Christie has representation in my house."

"I want to know," Bill said. "I know I don't deserve the knowledge, this special piece of you. I haven't earned it. But I want to know."

"There's almost no one alive today who knows my true name," Drew said. "I don't even remember the last time I said it out loud."

"You don't have to tell me," Bill said. "That might be more of a second date revelation."

Drew snorted. "I want to. Kind of. I'm a little afraid you'll laugh. There's a reason I changed it. Well, a reason besides needing a new identity once I discovered the oracular fountain of youth."

"I promise not to laugh," Bill said.

"Solomon Paine."

Bill made a choking noise.

"You promised," Drew said.

"I'm not laughing. I was…surprised. That is quite the name." Bill curled his lips around his teeth and bit down, trying to forcibly suppress his laughter.

"My parents had very high hopes for me, both in terms of wealth and wisdom. Alas, they died thoroughly disappointed in me. I failed them in so many ways."

"I'm sorry," Bill said. For a moment, he took a hand off the steering wheel and lightly touched Drew's thigh, before returning his hands to the classic ten and two position. "I know what it's like to be a disappointment."

"It's so far in the past it hardly matters anymore." Drew heard the lie in his words but hoped that Bill wouldn't.

"We've been apart for a while now, but not so long that I've forgotten how to listen for your truth. We don't have to talk about it. Not today, or not ever. But if you ever want to trust me with your story, no matter where we are in relationship to each other, I will listen."

Drew tipped his head back into the headrest and stared up at the dark ceiling, willing away the moisture that was gathering at the corners of his eyes. He might not have dated a lot in the last few years, but he was pretty sure, "don't cry on a first date," was still valid dating advice. "Where are we going tonight?" he asked, once he was confident his voice was under control.

"The Shelburne," Bill said. "I love their vibe. They have a great beer selection, and the food is amazing."

"I think Andy said they were starting to carry some of his brews," Drew said. "Between that and North Jetty, it'll be tough to decide."

"That's why the gods invented taster trays," Bill said.

"The gods, eh?" Drew asked. His humor was quickly coming back the further away the topic of parental disapproval was.

"Not sure which ones, but there are enough of them milling about, that one of them must be responsible."

The drive was almost too short. Drew caught glimpses of the ocean reflecting back the full moon in the cloud-scattered sky. "This drive would be amazing in the summer with the top down," Drew said. "Just driving south along the coast to the California border."

"Maybe we'll do that," Bill said, stealing a glance at Drew. "It's about time I put some miles on her."

"Oh, her? Your car's a lady? Have you named her?"

"Now it's your turn to promise not to laugh," Bill said.

"Cross my heart."

"I named her Dame Agatha."

Drew couldn't catch his breath. His face was hot, but chills raced over the rest of his body. A lump in his throat prevented him from speaking. Fortunately, it also prevented him from throwing up.

"Are you okay? Is it okay that I named her for you, or for your favorite author, rather?"

Drew nodded, realized that since it was dark and Bill was driving, he probably couldn't see him, then forced words past the lump in his throat. "It's okay. It's more than okay. I…" His words trailed off while he searched for the phrases that would express how he felt. "I am beyond honored. This is magnificent. You are magnificent. Thank you."

* * * * ★ ★ ★ ★ * * * *

DREW PRECEDED BILL INTO THE COZY PUB OF THE SHELBURNE HOTEL AND slid into a seat near the window. Bill sat across from him, smiled, then turned to look at the tap handles behind the bar.

"I don't believe it," Bill growled.

"What?" Drew asked. "Andy's stuff not on yet?"

Bill twisted back around to face Drew. "What is he doing here?" he growled under his breath.

"Who?" Drew asked, trying to crane around Bill without being too obvious.

"You know who."

Drew was about to protest that he had no idea who, when the bartender moved and opened up the view to the tables on the other side of the bar. Sitting at the bar with his ubiquitous bottle of wine was Dio. Drew whipped his body back into place and shrunk down in an attempt to hide behind Bill's larger body.

"I don't know why he's here," Drew whispered. "I didn't know we were coming here. I couldn't have possible told him."

Bill's expression softened from hardening anger to sheepish understanding. "That's true. The only one who could've told him is me, and I am confident I didn't share that information."

Drew's lips thinned and flattened as he attempted to hold back the wave of hurt threatening to wash over him. "Bill. Even if I had known where we were going, I wouldn't have told him. I might've told one of my friends, but Dio isn't my friend. I know I hurt you when I dated him immediately after we broke up, but it was a meaningless fling that didn't even last six weeks. I don't know why he's here now, but I do know it's annoying to keep running into him. Everywhere I go, he's there with his bottle of wine, getting everyone drunk...oh my god."

"Hello gentlemen!" Dio boomed. He'd managed to sneak up on them while they were intent on each other. "Fancy a glass of wine?"

Drew opened his mouth to decline and tell Dio to go away, but before he could say anything, Bill replied instead. "We'd love a glass."

"Two glasses, coming up! Only the best for the love birds. It's so nice to be present for a romantic reunion."

Drew took a sip of the wine that was in his hand then frowned at it. Something was wrong. He had a question. Or an epiphany. "We were going to have beer," Drew said.

"Nonsense," Dio replied, filling Drew's glass again. "Chilly winter evenings in cozy bars developing cozier feelings calls for a glass of tempranillo. Warms the heart and the body, if you know what I mean." He winked broadly, refilled Bill's glass, and set the bottle on the table. "Why don't you gentlemen keep this one. It's on me."

"The wine is always on you," Drew said.

"Oh, my dear boy. There is usually a price. I'm just not making you pay it. This time." Dio reached out and ran a thumb down Drew's jaw and sighed. "More's the pity, really."

"Hey!" Bill said. "That's not okay."

"You're right. My apologies to both of you. I'll be leaving now."

"For good?" Bill asked, either unable or unwilling to hide his hopeful eagerness.

"Not yet, I'm afraid. You'll have to put up with me for a bit longer yet. Something is wrong in Oracle Bay. Something weird that grates at my soul when I cross the border into your town. I need to find out what's going on. Otherwise, it'll bug me for ages." Dio waved a mock salute at them and walked out of the pub.

As soon as Dio had crossed the threshold of the building, a fog lifted from Drew's brain. He shook his head and stared suspiciously at his glass of wine. "I think something's wrong with the wine. It made me feel drunk after only a few sips."

"I couldn't stop drinking it, either," Bill said, shoving his glass as far away from him as possible on the small table.

Drew tilted his head and regarded the bottle Dio'd left behind. "When he came into my shop, everyone was drinking wine and he never ran out. It was the same at the Sleeping Inn."

"There was wine at Title Wave, wasn't there?" Bill asked.

"Yeah, there was. Martha said she and Ryan had been drinking it before he died," Drew confirmed. "Bill, I think Dio was left behind after our recent apocalypse."

"Left behind? Unraptured?"

Drew snorted with laughter. "Maybe. But that would mean we were, too. I meant he's a little more divine than most of the rest of the town's residents."

"I am trying not to be jealous, but when you call my romantic rival 'divine,' it's really pushing it," Bill teased. "Why don't you just spit it out. Who is he?"

"I don't want to say it out loud and be wrong, but..." Drew sucked in a deep breath and held it for a moment before exhaling nosily. "I think he's Dionysus, the Greek god of wine, merriment, and debauchery."

After dinner and a walk through Seaside to finish clearing their heads, Bill drove Drew back to Oracle Bay. The drive back was quieter. Drew didn't know what Bill was thinking, but whatever it was, the man wasn't ready to share. Drew was wondering about the wine Martha and Ryan had drunk. Martha had been uncharacteristically giggly when he'd never known her to be anything but quiet and grumpy before.

"Should I tell Chad and Kyle about the wine?" he asked Bill.

"Tell them what?" Bill asked. "That we drank wine some stranger gave us and it made us feel tipsy and foggy and maybe he gave the wine to Ryan, too?"

"It sounds ridiculous when you put it like that," Drew admitted. "But there is something there, I just know it."

"You're right," Bill agreed. "There is. But let's find a way to convey the information without getting you in more trouble. They're already way too interested in you. I don't think you want them looking any deeper into your actions."

"My actions are blameless," Drew protested.

"Of course they are. But let's be honest. Innocence is always a shield, and sometimes, people become convenient targets because of who they are or what they look like and not what they've done. Don't make yourself a target."

Drew ground his teeth. What Bill was saying made sense, but it was the twenty-first century. He'd hoped things would be better by now. "I haven't lived this long to go back into hiding," he said. "You don't know what it's like. It's bad enough when your family disowns you, but having your love be a crime..."

Bill started to say something, but Drew held up his hand. "I will find a way to alert the police to the possibility of something being wrong with the wine if they haven't already looked in that direction. There was some left in the bottle at the crime scene."

"Thank you," Bill said softly. "I don't know what it's like to have lived in any other era than now and I forgot that you do. I'm sorry."

Drew twisted his mouth into a smile, grateful Bill couldn't see his misshapen expression. "You don't need to apologize. It's not every day you're in a car with someone who predates the Civil War. It's one thing to intellectually know I'm a super-geezer. It's another completely to internalize it. Let's call it good, shall we?"

"Absolutely. Do you want to take me home, or would you like to grab a beer?" Drew asked, tone hopeful. "I'm not sure I'm ready for this night to... Oh my god."

They'd rounded the last curve and hit Oracle Bay's Main Street. An ambulance, what looked like every firetruck in the area, and four police cars were blocking Main a little further down. The flashing lights revealed a growing crowd on the other side of the emergency vehicle blockade and a white-sheeted figure on the ground.

"Is that your shop?" Bill asked.

"Yes," Drew said. "The shop with the dead body is my shop."

"At least you have a solid alibi this time," Bill said.

"I shouldn't need one," Drew said.

"Do you think someone is trying to frame you?" Bill asked. "Maybe because you spurned them for another?"

Drew felt a genuine smile creep across his face. "I adore that you read romance novels the way I read mysteries. I don't think anyone's trying to frame me. I don't know much about Dio—beyond the stories he told me when he came to town the first time. Is he a particularly murderous deity?"

"I think they're all a little murderous if they don't get their way," Bill said. "That's why they're gods and we're not."

"We should find out," Drew said. "I want to know what we're working with here. I don't know how Dio could've framed me. No one knew Ryan and I were going to argue and that I'd stop by his place later to apologize and discover his body. And whoever that is in front of my shop now...I've not been in town all evening. I'd think a god would be better at pointing the finger at me—especially since he already knew I had an alibi."

Bill huffed out his disappointment. "I really, really want him to be guilty," he admitted.

"I know." Drew reached over and patted his hand. "But I don't want to overlook a murderer because we find someone else irritating."

"You're right. Wanna round up your freaks and get a beer at The Pour House?" Bill asked.

"We're not freaks," Drew said. "We're weirdos."

"You're my favorite weirdo," Bill said. "Thanks for going out with me tonight."

Drew flashed a smile at Bill. "I'll text everyone, but even if it's just you and me, it'll be good."

"Fair warning, I need to be to work by four-thirty tomorrow morning, so I'm not sure how late I'm good for," Bill reminded him. "I've gotten used to going to bed early most nights. It's easy when there's no one to talk to."

"I don't want to keep you up. Wait. That's a lie. I definitely want to keep you up, but I understand that you'll have to leave earlier than I will."

"I'm very much looking forward to the night you keep me up past my bedtime," Bill grinned, punctuating his statement with a rakish wink.

Drew felt heat suffuse his body and settle low in his abdomen. "Ummm... Yes. Uh." He shook his head, feeling as foggy as he had earlier with Dio's wine. "I mean, that does sound delightful when it's the right time for both of us."

"I hope that time is sooner, rather than later. It's been a long three years, and I've missed you a lot," Bill said, the heated look in his eyes belying his casual tone.

"Tonight, we have a divine mystery to solve, but we should plan a second date," Drew suggested. "Maybe stay in and watch a movie."

"Netflix and chill?" Bill suggested.

"That sounds perfect. And now, unless you want to get arrested for making out in front of emergency vehicles and a crime scene, we should head to the bar. I need a cold beer." *And a colder shower.*

Drew and Bill slid into chairs in the back room that had been effectively reserved for the psychics since Sandy moved to town. Drew was a little surprised to see Ceri sitting at the bar already. She'd been spending a lot of time at The Pour House lately, but after casually tossing out that things were over between her and Andy while they were investigating, he hadn't expected to see her here on her own.

"Are you going to tell Ceri we're here?" Bill asked.

"She saw us come in. She's probably waiting for Andy to have a minute so she can tell him what's up and let him know the freeloaders are back."

"Freeloaders?" Bill asked.

"Psychics drink free in The Pour House," Drew explained. "And since you're here with me tonight, you'll get to take advantage of Andy's generosity, too."

"Hey guys," Brandy said, setting down coasters, glasses, and three pitchers. "Andy wanted y'all to enjoy his latest experiment tonight. After you give it a shot, you're welcome to have anything else you'd like, of course. On the house." Her lips pursed in disapproval.

"How's the new management gig going?" Drew asked.

"Other than disagreeing with a few pre-existing policies—"

"Like free drinks for charlatans?" Drew teased.

She flashed him a grin. "—like free drinks for local small business owners who spend a lot of time in the bar, it's great. Zeke is backing me up behind the bar and I've had four new servers start in the last week. Hiring people is more expensive, of course, especially since Andy insists on paying everyone a living wage and providing insurance and benefits," her smile belied the disapproval her words indicated, "but our customer service complaints have already all but disappeared. Plus, we've been busier than ever since the weird fog and cold snap we had a couple weeks ago. The weirdest customers— the ones that didn't leave after the cosplay weekend Andy hosted when he shut the place down and handed out beer and food like he didn't have bills to pay —are starting to disappear, but more people are driving up from Long Beach and even Astoria to drink here. And the new people are much, much better tippers than those other folks."

Andy strode up behind her. "She's not telling enough of the story," he said. "In the two weeks since she's been in charge of managing the bar, I've created two new beers, and she's tightened the books just enough to be turning the kind of profit I would never be able to manage. She's the best thing that ever happened to my bar."

Brandy's cognac-colored eyes lit up, transforming her light brown face from attractive to radiant. A smug grin flitted across her face. "I just love it when people recognize my business acumen," she said. "It's so much better than any pleasure of the flesh one could devise." She closed her eyes for a moment, and when she opened them again, the brilliance had been replaced by mild pleasure. Brandy was all business again. "I'm headed back to the bar. I'll come back and check on you in a bit, but if you need something in the meantime, you can wave down Kat or Lilah. I've let them know not to bother you unless you flag them down."

"Thanks, Brandy," Drew said. "You're amazing."

"I really am," she agreed. "Andy's lucky to have me. He has no head for business."

"I am sitting right here," Andy protested. "You're not supposed to trash talk the boss where he can hear you."

"I always forget that rule," Brandy said as she walked away.

"You are lucky to have her," Bill said. "I wonder if she'd be interested in being the business manager for—"

"Don't even finish that sentence," Andy said. "I will smite you and send you in the deepest bowels of hell if you steal my bar manager from me."

Bill laughed. "You'll smite me? What kinda talk is that?"

Drew squirmed a little in his seat. "I don't think I ever got around to explaining who Andy is," he said.

"What do you mean, who he is?" Bill asked. "Is he another psychic?"

"Not exactly," Andy murmured. "And to be fair to Drew, there haven't been many opportunities to explain, he only found out a few weeks ago. I've been keeping my background pretty close to my chest since I moved to town."

"Just tell me," Bill said. "It can't be any weirder than finding out my ex's rebound guy is the god of wine, right?"

"He's a fallen angel," Drew said.

"Your ex is the what?" Ceri asked. She was standing in the doorway of the private room, one hand covering her mouth. "Oh, no. You insisted he was a demigod, and no one believed you."

"Wait a minute," Bill said. "Andy is a…fallen angel? Like a kicked out of heaven, sent to hell with Lucifer fallen angel?"

"Yes," Andy said. "It didn't stick, though, and now I'm here. I am not on the side of either heaven or hell."

"Okay then," Bill said. "It'll take some processing, but once you've been kidnapped by an Etruscan goddess and rescued by a psychic and another goddess disguised as a goat, nothing is far-fetched anymore."

Andy reached over and clapped him on the back. "You're a good man, Bill Walters. And now that we've gotten me out of the way, let's talk about the wine god. Which one is he?"

"Dionysus," Drew said. "I'm almost positive. I don't know a lot about him—as a god, I mean. Or as a person, either. We didn't really get to know each other that well."

"You're not supposed to start talking about new business before everyone shows up," Misty chided. She walked around the table and sat down next to Bill. "Joseph sends his regrets. One of the kids is sick. Nothing serious, but he didn't want to leave her."

Andy poured the beer and handed the glass around the table while everyone else trickled in.

Paska was the last to arrive. He glared at Drew while downing the glass in front of him. He'd nearly drained his drink when he stopped abruptly, slammed the glass down on the table, and wrinkled his nose. "What is this?" he sputtered. "I was expecting the Pearly Gates Pale. This is...not a pale."

"It's new! Apricot Angel sour. Do you like it?" Andy asked. He could do angelic innocence better than almost anyone, but there was no mistaking the devilish twinkle in his eye now.

Paska picked up his glass and took a cautious sip. "It's much better when I know what to expect. It's a crap pale."

"I like it," Misty declared.

"Not my style," Sandy said. "Too puckery."

"Why are we here?" Morgana asked. "I am an old woman and you interrupted my bedtime routine."

Drew rolled his eyes. "Whatever, Morgana. I probably just interrupted your midnight broomstick flight."

"If I had a rolled-up newspaper right now, I'd use it," she grumbled. "Get on with it."

"Is it about Martha?" Sandy asked.

"Martha?" Drew looked at Sandy quizzically. "What about Martha?"

Sandy exchanged uncomfortable looks with Misty and Vincent. "There's been another death," she said. "Martha was found about an hour ago."

"In front of my shop," Drew said. "I didn't know who it was, but I saw." He filled everyone in on his and Bill's date, up to and including their theory about Dio.

"Do you think your party god is killing people?" Morgana asked.

"I don't know. I was hoping you all could help me figure it out. I don't know much about the Greek gods—not even the ones I've met in real life, apparently. Some of you have a lot more experience with gods and monsters than I do."

"I don't have experience," Sandy said. "But I do have education. My mother was a Classics professor who also taught a lot of courses on Greek mythology and literature. Anything I don't know, she will. Unless someone here has more direct experience, she might be our best bet."

"Where is your mom?" Misty asked. "Still in the Aegean?"

"On her way here, actually," Sandy said. "I managed to stall her for a while, but she's beginning to think I'm deliberately keeping her from meeting Vincent because I'm ashamed of her, and I can't stand in the face of that. She's back in the States as of yesterday morning. She and my step-dad Jonah landed in Seattle and are planning on driving down tomorrow."

"It'll be great," Vincent said. "No one is nervous about this at all."

"Do you think she'd mind being pulled into this?" Drew asked. "How much does she know about—" he waved his hand around to encompass everyone at the table "—all this?"

"A bit. None of the scary or dangerous stuff. But, she's my mom," Sandy said. "I tell her everything."

"What are we going to do if we decide Dio is killing people?" Ceri asked. "Hand him over to the authorities? Find proof somehow that will stand up in court?"

"It'd make more sense to get in touch with Zeus," Andy said. "He has his flaws. A lot of them, actually. But he is committed to keeping everyone in line. It's hard enough surviving out there without a solid worship base. He wouldn't want rumors to spread that one of his people was on a murder spree. Well, maybe Ares. That'd be in character and would probably increase belief."

"Did you meet Dio when the rest of his pantheon was in town?" Drew asked.

"This is so weird," Bill muttered. "Just talking about meeting gods."

Drew reached under the table, found Bill's hand, and squeezed it. When Drew started to pull his hand back, Bill's grip tightened.

"I don't remember meeting him," Andy said. "Anyone else?"

Everyone shook their heads.

"If Dio is the god of wine, and it sounds plausible based on the events since he's been spotted in town, is it possible he's responsible for the other crimes as well?" Morgana asked. "I'd appreciate recovering my tea set."

"Can I ask a potentially stupid question?" Bill asked. "I know I'm not a member of your usual crowd, but Drew assured me it'd be okay for me to be here tonight."

"I am delighted that you're here," Ceri said. "And there's no such thing as a stupid question."

"Only stupid people," Paska muttered. "Ask away."

"If all of you are powerful psychics, how come you're not using your powers to see what's going on?"

"That is not a stupid question," Andy said. "Just a little impolite."

"We've all tried," Morgana admitted. "Something is going on that is dampening our powers."

"And we've all had our most powerful diving tools taken from us," Paska said.

"Not all of you," Bill said. "I know how Misty works."

"You wish you knew," Misty scoffed. "And you're right. I am the divining tool in my case and only my gloves were taken. But I can't see anything, either, beyond the most mundane things. I've been making Joseph be my guinea pig, and other than seeing that one of the kids was going to fall mildly sick and recover in a couple days, there's nothing. I haven't tried with anyone else, so I can't guarantee I'm completely powerless, but between what I've gotten from Joseph and what's happening with everyone else, I don't think there's much point."

"It's like there's a heavy fog over everything," Ceri said. "I can see shapes and movement, but not enough to be useful.

Bill reached his free hand over and grabbed Misty's arm above the leather of her driving gloves.

She ripped her arm out of his hands. "That was not okay," Misty snapped. "Do not force me into reading you."

"I'm sorry. I didn't think..." Bill trailed off.

Misty's expression softened. "It's okay this once. But never do that again. Ever. Or I will reverse the link and force you to see everything I've ever known."

Bill blanched a bit and apologized again. Misty smiled. "Luckily for you, you're my boyfriend's best friend and you're not currently breaking my good friend's heart. I will let it go. Now, do you want to know what I saw?"

Bill nodded. Misty leaned over and whispered something in his ear. Bill's ruddy skin turned redder and the blush spread down his neck and across the tips of his ears. Misty laughed and leaned away.

"What was it?" Drew asked.

"Tell you later," Bill replied. "I've got to go. Early morning tomorrow." He stood, grabbed his jacket, and dropped a kiss on Drew's cheek. "I had a great time." He fled.

"What did you say to him?" Drew asked.

Misty grinned wickedly. "He's got a lot on his mind right now, and a vivid imagination. I merely repeated his fantasies back to him."

"You're evil," Drew said.

"Absolutely." Misty turned back to the rest of the group. "Anything else we need to do tonight?"

"If anyone has discreet contacts in the Greek pantheon, it might not hurt to make some inquiries," Paska said. "A few character references would not go amiss."

Drew sat at the bar with his fourth Lucifer Imperial Stout. The rest of his friends had left shortly after Bill. Even Ceri was nowhere to be seen—although neither was Andy, even though the bar was still packed. Drew didn't know why he was still sitting there. He should've gone home at the same time as everyone else. It wasn't like him to sit and drink alone. He grimaced at the beer, then tilted his head back and chugged it.

"You know, that beer is packing an eleven percent punch," Brandy said, grabbing his glass before he could slam it onto the bar. "You should slow down."

"Are you cutting me off?" he asked.

"Should I?"

Drew took a breath and stood up. "I'm going to the restroom and then grabbing a water. I'll let you know when I get back."

Drew walked across the crowded floor to the restrooms with nary a weave, then stopped to grab a glass of water from the cooler at the far end of the bar before heading back to his seat. Zeke stopped in front of him. "Brandy says I can get you another beer, but she would like to recommend something in the lower ABV range."

"What's the ABV of that sour Andy poured us earlier?" Drew asked.

"Right around five percent," Zeke said.

"Let's give that a try, then. I don't know if I gave it a fair shot earlier."

Zeke returned with a pint of honey-colored beer. "Angel Apricot for you. I understand you're having a bit of a god problem?"

"Do you know him?" Drew asked, taking a sip of the tart beer.

"Unfortunately, I don't know much outside my own pantheon,"

Zeke admitted. "I always rather hoped that if I ignored them hard enough, they'd go away. All the other gods really mess with a guy's commitment to monotheism sometimes, you know?"

"My parents were religious folk, but the church and I really didn't take to each other," Drew said. "I stopped attending long before I started questioning anything but my place."

"We're useless, then," Zeke shrugged. "Won't be the last time."

"I'll drink to that," Drew said, raising his glass. He knew he was drunker than he appeared. He might not know a lot about religions or mythology, but he did have over a hundred years of drinking behind him, and a good handle on how to mask his intoxication—at least up to a point. He should leave. He took another sip of his beer, then resolutely set it down and slid off the bar stool. He waved to Brandy and Zeke and headed out. Just before he reached the door, someone rushed by him, yanked the door open, and ran out into the night, long, red hair streaming behind her. Drew shook his head, grabbed the door as it started to swing closed, and followed Ceri outside.

By the time he got to the sidewalk to begin his walk home, Ceri had already peeled out of the parking lot. Drew watched her tail-lights until they disappeared into the distance. Right after they winked out of sight, Andy appeared beside him.

"Andy!" Drew gasped as his pulse sped up. "Don't be creepy."

"Is she gone?" Andy asked.

"It looked like she was headed towards home and that she didn't want to be bothered," Drew said. "I don't think you'll be welcome there right now."

"I won't bother her," Andy said. "I just want to make sure she got home safely."

"Let me," Drew said. He pulled out his phone.

"*Hey speed racer. That was some exit. Text me and tell me you made it home safe and that you're sorry you didn't offer me a ride.*"

"It'll be a couple minutes," Drew said. "Don't go anywhere." He took one step and then another away from Andy.

"I'm not going anywhere," Andy said. "Why are you looking at me like that?"

"This is the first time I've seen your wings all up close and personal," Drew said. "They're intimidating. They're also not as black as I thought. They're silver."

"Sorry you had to see that. I lost control of my emotions, and they have a bad habit of popping out when that happens," Andy sighed. "At least I didn't set anything on fire this time."

"You'll need to check those bad boys out," Drew said. "It's night and I have been drinking, but they are definitely more gray than black."

Drew's phone beeped, and he pulled it out of his pocket.

"So sorry I didn't offer you a ride. I didn't see you. Fortunately, you're a ten-minute walk home. Tell that idiot I made it safe."

Drew turned his phone towards Andy. "She's fine."

"Idiot?" Andy exclaimed. "I'm the idiot? If anyone is acting irrationally here, it isn't me."

"I'm gonna head home," Drew said. "You should probably do the same. Or go back to work. Or whatever. Let me know if you need anything." He turned and walked back towards town. He'd only gone a few steps when he stopped and turned back. Andy was still staring in the direction Ceri'd drove off into. "She really does care for you," Drew said. "Give her time."

"Time," Andy said, almost too quietly for Drew to hear. "Not sure there's a lot of that left."

"What?" Drew asked.

"Nothing that affects you," Andy said before he turned and walked away.

nine

Drew woke up too early the next morning. His mouth was dank and fuzzy and the pounding in his head…wasn't in his head. Someone was at the door.

He slid out of bed and drew the curtains. The too-bright-to-be-winter light streamed in and fanned the flames of his headache, making him wince. He squinted down towards his front porch. Though Drew couldn't see who was at the door, the police cruisers out front offered a valuable clue.

He swore as he made his way to the bathroom. Once he'd brushed his teeth and downed a couple aspirin, he felt a little better. At least his headache wasn't keeping time with the cops' knocking anymore. With a robe over his bare chest and pajama pants, Drew made his way downstairs. He yanked open the door, surprising Chad in mid-knock, and stepped out onto the porch.

"Officers. What do you want?" He'd meant to be cheerful and disarming and pleasant, but a hangover and a seven AM waking time made him surly.

"Wouldn't you rather talk inside?" Kyle asked. "It'd be more comfortable for you, especially since you're not dressed yet."

"The fresh air will do me a world of good," Drew said. "What do you want?"

"Martha Webster was found dead last night."

"I heard," Drew said. "And saw, as well. My return home was blocked by all the emergency vehicles on Main Street."

"Return home from where?" Chad asked. He leaned forward intently and pulled a small notebook and a stubby pencil out of his pocket.

"Long Beach. Well, Seaview, really. I had dinner with Bill Walters at the Shelburne."

"Can anyone besides your boyfriend corroborate your story?" Kyle asked.

"He's not...you know, never mind. Yes. Although I didn't know anyone else dining at the Shelburne last night, there were servers who would probably be able to verify our presence there, and Bill paid with a credit card, so you'll have that if you need it as well. I'm not positive, but I wouldn't be surprised if his car keeps track of where it's been and when, and there might be cameras at the Shelburne. I've never looked for them, but it's a possibility."

"Why didn't you come see what was going on at your shop?" Chad asked. "Didn't you want to know?"

"Of course I did," Drew said. "But it looked like there was a body, and I didn't want to get in the way. I figured if you needed to talk to me, you'd find me. And here you are. Early in the morning. Lucky me."

"Are you okay?" Kyle asked. "You look a little pale."

"Just hungover," Drew said. "Hungover, sleep deprived, and thrilled to be talking to you fellas."

"Why are you hungover?" Kyle demanded.

Drew rolled his eyes then winced. "Too many imperial stouts at The Pour House last night. Brandy warned me too late."

"And how long were you there?" Kyle barked.

"Bill and I headed there when we couldn't get through town. A few friends joined us. That was probably about ten-thirty. I can grab my phone and see what time I texted everyone if it helps. They all left by about eleven-thirty and I sat at the bar until one-ish. Again, I could verify the times on my phone. I texted Ceri as I was leaving."

Chad wrote everything down in cramped, stilted writing; the half pencil, like the kind you use at Pub Trivia, all but invisible in his massive hand.

"Am I a suspect?" Drew asked. "Was Martha's death a homicide as well?"

"How'd you know it was Martha?" Chad asked.

Drew blew out a long breath. "We live in Oracle Bay, Chad. Someone found her and called it in. Whoever that was probably told their friends and neighbors. There were a ton of people out there last night watching, and although she was covered by the time I arrived, someone must have seen her. This is not the kind of town in which you can keep secrets. I think Sandy Franklin told me, but it could've just as easily been her fiancé, or Misty, or someone else I saw at The Pour House last night. Where did you work before coming here?"

"Portland," Chad said. "Kyle was in Eugene."

"Both of those towns are significantly bigger than Oracle Bay. It's not weird that everyone knows who died. It's not weird that I've talked to both of them in the last week. The only thing that's weird is that Martha was at the scene of Ryan's murder, acting strangely, and now she's dead."

"Dead in the exact same way," Kyle said under his breath.

"You were there, too," Chad pointed out. "Maybe Martha walked in on you while you were murdering Ryan and you tried to bump her off that night before she talked, but failed, so had to finish the job."

"That does make a certain amount of sense," Drew agreed. "But you questioned Martha after she was released from the hospital. Wouldn't she have mentioned me then?"

"Not necessarily," Kyle said. "Not if she was scared or confused. She was not in her right mind that night. If she was intimidated, but you weren't confident she'd stay that way, you could've murdered her to prevent her from talking."

"Do you know time of death?" Drew asked. "Because I was at the Shelburne shortly after seven."

"Still being determined," Kyle said, elbowing Chad when he opened his mouth. "I think we have everything we need for now. Don't leave town."

"Don't leave Oracle Bay, or don't leave the peninsula?" Drew asked.

Neither man had an answer for that, and Drew snickered a bit. "I'll let you know if I'm going farther than Ilwaco."

"You do that," Kyle said. "Thank you for your time."

Drew offered a tight grin then stepped back into the house, slamming the door behind him and almost tripping over Tuppence and Hercule. "You two will be the death of me," Drew said. He leaned down and scratched them under their chins. "Time for breakfast?"

Their contented purrs turned into enthusiastic mews as he filled their bowls with kitten kibble.

"I think I'll go out for coffee today," Drew said. "It feels like an espresso drink kind of morning."

DREW WAS SITTING BY THE WINDOW IN CAFFIEND DREAMS ENJOYING A LARGE mocha and a ham and cheese croissant. The line was out the door—unusual for a weekday in winter — the tourist influx usually died off after Christmas and didn't pick up again until mid-March when the whales started appearing off the coast. This year, however, that didn't happen. At first, those in the know had chalked it up to the gods and supernatural creatures lingering after the apocalypse, but now, most of the customers appeared human, and every business was feeling the uncomfortably satisfying sensation of having more business than they'd planned to handle.

"I'm going to have to follow Andy's lead and hire some more

help," Bill said, sliding into the seat across from Drew and wiping his face on a white rag. "Jules is fantastic as a backup for me, but she is not interested in picking up any more hours, and is, in fact, threatening to leave me altogether to go to college."

"The nerve of her!" Drew exclaimed. "Doesn't she know that bettering herself with a university education pales in comparison with filling in as a barista on the odd weekends and holidays you don't want to work?"

Bill threw his rag at Drew, and the sweaty end caught him in the face.

"Ewww..." Drew plucked it off his face and held it up, pinched gingerly between his index finger and thumb. "Like I want your sweat all over your face." Bill opened his mouth, but before he could say anything, Drew leaned forward and placed his hand over Bill's mouth. "Don't say it. I know where you were going—I saw that look in your eyes—and I would submit that your business when your line is just about out the door again is the wrong time to make dirty jokes."

"Fine," Bill conceded. "But at some point, you're going to have to put up with my filthy mind again."

"I'm ready, but this is neither the time nor the place."

"You're right, as always," Bill said pushing himself to his feet. He groaned. "I'm going to have to invest in a pair of clogs if business keeps up like this."

"Just hire someone," Drew said. "Clogs are never the answer. Least sexy shoe ever."

"Are you sure they're the least sexy?" Bill asked.

"Positive."

Bill walked around the counter and greeted the first person in line—a line that hadn't been there five minutes ago when he'd sat down. After taking her order, he walked to the espresso machine and grinned at Drew. "Challenge accepted."

"That was not a challenge!" Drew called out.

"Sounded like one to me." Bill shrugged. "I'll talk to you later. Do you have plans tonight?"

"I don't know. I guess it depends on what happens with Sandy's mother. I'll let you know, though," Drew promised.

"See you later." Bill handed the woman her espresso drink and made small talk with her while her payment processed.

Drew watched as long as he could without being creepy, then walked outside and further down Main Street. The front of his shop was still cordoned off, and although he could go through the back, there was no way he was getting walk-in customers today—not when a police barricade prevented access to his front door.

He walked the rest of the way home and was less than a block away when his phone buzzed.

"Mom is down for the QA session. Come over and let's talk."

Drew shifted course slightly and went to Vincent's and Sandy's place across the street. He knocked on the door. Vincent opened it before Drew could drop his hand. Vincent had a slightly wild look around his eyes.

"How goes it with Sandy's folks?" Drew asked.

"They're great. Really nice. Very interested in our lives. Lots of questions! I am having a great time," Vincent insisted.

Drew chuckled. "Where's your family? I don't think I ever asked."

"My father died when I was in high school—massive heart attack at age thirty-eight, and my mother died ten years later to the day of pancreatic cancer."

"I'm so sorry," Drew said.

"It's been a few years since mom passed, and it doesn't hurt as much as it used to," Vincent said. "I was an only child, as were both of my parents, so I didn't have any siblings or extended family."

"Well, you have family now!" Drew said. "Sounds like Sandy's parents are ready to add you to theirs."

"Not sure I'm ready," Vincent muttered. "It's weird to go from zero to full family in less than three months. It didn't seem real when they were off in Greece, but now that they're here for a stay of indefinite length, I am really feeling the family pinch."

Drew clapped Vincent on the shoulder. "You'll get used to it."

"Easy for you to say," Vincent pointed out. "You have as much family as me, and from what I've heard, Bill's family isn't much a part of his life, either."

"This is all my family, though," Drew said. "The psychics, their partners and friends, you. I have the best family because I chose them, and they chose me. Being part of a family that you weren't born to is pretty amazing. You know they love you for who you are and not because they feel a sense of obligation. Now let's go. I'm eager to meet Sandy's mom and see what she has to say about Dio."

"Come on in, then," Vincent said, moving out of the way and ushering Drew in. "You're gonna love Dione and Jonah."

Drew was braced for a barrage of questions as Vincent introduced him. He was not, however, braced for a barrage of hugs.

"Sandy's told us how wonderful you were for her when she first moved here. We're so grateful she made friends who could help protect her from that repulsive cabbage of an ex-husband." Dione said, hugging him warmly.

"Everyone was glad to help. Even if she hadn't fit in with our group of friends, we wouldn't have left her to fend for herself. She is a good fit, though, and was able to help save the town," Drew replied. Dione might have been at least a century and a half younger than him, but she was his friend's mom, and automatically got parent-deference. Plus, Dione gave the best mom hugs Drew had experienced in decades.

"With a lot of help from everyone, especially Vincent," Sandy said.

"We are all the best," Drew agreed. "Every single one of us is amazing."

"I can't wait to meet the rest of your friends," Dione said. "Didn't you say more of them are on their way?"

"Yes," Sandy said. "Drew lives across the street, so he had the shortest commute, but everyone else should be here soon. We've all been forced to temporarily close our businesses."

"Why, though?" Jonah asked. "You could still open and just use your knowledge instead of your skill to do readings, couldn't you?"

"I could," Sandy admitted. "I read tarot cards all through college without any supernatural aid. I'm not sure that'd work for anyone else."

"I could make stuff up," Drew said. "But it'd be pretty obvious. There's no skill that'll help me read futures in a crystal ball, unless I employ old times charlatan tricks and get an assistant to pick their pockets and eavesdrop on them ahead of time."

"Oh, well," Johan shrugged. "It was just an idea. I feel bad for all of you losing your livelihoods like this."

"Thanks, Papa Jo," Sandy said, smiling at him.

Twenty minutes of semi-stilted small talk later, the doorbell rang.

"I'll get it," Vincent volunteered. He fled from the room rather faster than was necessary.

A murmur of voices floated down the hall from the foyer.

"Sounds like everyone else is here," Sandy said.

"I don't hear Paska," Drew said.

"That's because I know how to keep my mouth shut when there's nothing else to say," Paska retorted, walking into the room. "Unlike you young people, I know the value of silence."

"You young people?" Jonah asked, quirking up an eyebrow.

"A lot of the people here are a lot older than they look," Sandy said. "I can't really tell you more than that, but it's no good making age assumptions with these folks."

"I've lived with your mother for a couple of decades, and she's barely aged," Jonah said. "In fact, I think retirement and travel have done her a world of good. If I didn't know better, I'd swear she was younger now than when we met."

Dione instantly became the focus of all the psychic's stares.

"How old are you?" Morgana asked. "To my eyes, you look as though you're in your mid-thirties, but knowing that Sandy is less than a decade younger than that, it is clearly impossible."

"I'm a year shy of fifty," Dione said. "Although I'm not sure why I'm telling you. It's rude to ask a lady's age."

"If you are forty-nine and your daughter is nearly twenty-nine, you were quite young when she was born," Morgana said. "But not ridiculously so. Who was her father?"

"Morgana!" Sandy exclaimed. "That is a super personal question!"

"Wasn't he your mom's college boyfriend or something?" Ceri asked.

"That's a bit of an exaggeration of his stature," Dione admitted. "I met him on my semester abroad and discovered I was pregnant as that semester was coming to a close. He flew back to the States with me but didn't stick around long. I hadn't expected him to, honestly. He didn't seem the settling down type, which is why I'd been so careful to not get pregnant." She shrugged. "Sometimes things don't turn out at all the way you want them to, but I'm glad I have my baby girl."

"I want so badly to ask you if you regret anything, but it seems rude to do so in front of Sandy," Morgana said.

"You just asked her in front of me, so I don't think you're that concerned about being rude," Sandy said. "Does it matter right now? Don't we have bigger problems on our plate?"

Morgana sat in one of the many chairs scattered around Sandy's and Vincent's living room and leaned back, crossing her arms. "You're right. Let's talk about Dio. Who has a picture?"

"I do," Drew admitted. "I'll find it." He pulled out his phone and scrolled through the pictures. While he searched, he gave the overview to Dione and Jonah. "This man who goes by Dio has been seen in Oracle Bay a lot over the last couple of weeks. He always has wine with him, and he pushes it on everyone around him. The wine bottles seem bottomless—they never run out. People who would never normally partake in multiple glasses of wine, especially in the morning or at their places of business, are drinking to excess. Things are going missing, and two people are dead. We know for sure that they were both having wine the night the first person—Ryan, owner of Title Wave bookstore—died. At this point, I don't know if Martha was having wine before she passed."

"We are beginning to suspect he is Dionysus," Morgana said. "It sounds a bit ridiculous, but he has such a hedonistic aura, and combined with the ever-flowing wine... We've had quite the influx of gods lately, and it's not out of the realm of possibility.

Drew found the picture he wanted, zoomed in on Dio's face, and handed it over to Dione. "This is Dio."

Dione took the phone, glanced at the picture, and blanched. Her light olive skin took on an almost sickly cast and her hand started to shake. "How long has he been here?" she asked. Her voice was still steady, but she kept her eyes on the screen.

"A couple weeks is all, as far as we know," Drew replied. "He's kind of a showboat, so I don't know if he could've stayed under the radar at all."

"And he is your ex-boyfriend?" she asked.

"More of a fling that I had a few years ago when I split from Bill —the guy who runs the coffee shop and bakery in town."

Dione rolled her lips in and bit them together before handing the phone back to Drew. "He is the spitting image of the man of whom we spoke earlier. Sandy's father."

Sandy's jaw dropped. "What? How is this possible?"

"Well, if he is a god, he wouldn't age unless he wanted to," Morgana said. "What name was he using when you knew him Dione?"

"Denis," she said. "Why is he here now, so soon after my Sandy moved to this town? Do you think he's here for her?"

"I'm an adult woman," Sandy said. "He can't come for me at this point. The only thing he could do is introduce himself to me and give me twenty-eight birthday and holiday gifts. Maybe throw a little retroactive child support your way. He can't take me away."

"She's mostly right," Morgana said. "The gods, particularly the ones that aren't part of the Christian pantheon, must work on behalf of the good of all those who live on earth now. They are bound by a treaty. There will be loopholes, of course. And some will break the rules because they can, but overall, they are bound. It's too early to start testing their leaders. He could, of course, offer her something she wouldn't want to refuse to convince her to break ties with earth and go with him to Olympus, but based on what I've read and heard from everyone here who's known him intimately, that is out of character. Dio doesn't want to be responsible for another person. He wants to have fun and convince everyone else to have fun, too."

"This is so weird," Dione muttered.

"Look at is this way, sweetheart," Jonah said. "Your conquests include not only a god among men—clearly me—but also an actual god. How many other people can claim that?"

"Drew can," Dione pointed out. "Well, just the actual god part. Not the 'Jonah is a god among men' part. I don't think."

"The only man we have in common is Dio. Or Denis," Drew said. "But yeah, this is really weird."

"My bio-dad is a god?" Sandy said. "And a god who's kind of a jerk? Eurgh."

"If you've been holding back and can actually keep our wine bottles filled with wine-goddess magic, I am very disappointed in you," Misty said. "You should practice. See if you can do other liquors. I want a Long Island Ice Tea fountain at my wedding."

"Have we learned anything useful about Dio yet?" Ceri asked. "We've learned a lot that's interesting, but we haven't gotten to useful. We were hoping you'd have some insight into Dio's habits and character based on your studies, but it does sound like you'll have even more knowledge than we hoped for."

"I'll do my best," Dione said. "It's been quite a shock and I'm still adjusting."

"Let's take a break," Paska said. "Sandy could use some time alone with her family, and we all need to regroup and figure out what questions we should ask."

"Fine," Misty said. "Let's meet back here in thirty minutes. We need to figure out if Dio is a danger to our town or only our livers."

ten

Drew grabbed folding chairs from where they were stored in the back hallway for group meetings and set them out. He had a dozen small tv trays that he interspersed among the chairs. Misty set up coffee, the rest of the pastries Bill had left after his morning rush, and small plates and napkins. They'd decided to move to a larger, more neutral spot than Sandy's living room, and Drew's shop afforded them the most privacy. The front door was still cordoned off and the back wasn't numbered, so you had to know which was the right one in order to access the shop.

Sandy and her parents were the first after Drew and Misty to arrive. They were followed closely by Paska and Morgana. Ceri came in last, ten minutes past the agreed upon meeting time, and with Andy in tow. "Zeke said he knows nothing about the Greeks and wants to keep it that way," Ceri announced. "Russell pretended he didn't know why I'd ask him to show up. I wanted to bring wine but was afraid we'd get carried away and end up intoxicated."

"Dione, can you tell us what you know of Dio—first what you know of the god in general, then what you know of him as a man."

She shrugged. "You know much of what I'm going to tell you.

Dionysus, known as Bacchus in the Roman pantheon, is the god of wine, debauchery, theater, madness, and fertility. Oh, damn him straight to hell." Dione huffed. "He ought to disclose that. It's not fair. Drew, you should consider yourself lucky you skipped that part."

"No one has ever congratulated me on not getting pregnant before," Drew admitted. "Thank you. I think."

"So, he's the god of wine and sex and drama?" Ceri asked.

"That's a very basic interpretation," Dione confirmed. "There are a lot of nuances to his story depending on the source. He's known as the twice-born and has drawn parallels to Jesus."

"Jesus was a big wine fan, too," Ceri pointed out. "And he was able to make magical wineskins that never went empty."

Dione laughed. "What I'm not sure about is how a god manifests. Will he manifest as the central figure in one of the Bacchic cults? As a leader of a murderous Bacchanalia? Or as the more modern depiction of a jolly lad with ivy vines, wine, and magical cats?"

"Oh my god," Drew muttered. He rubbed his head. This headache was really messing with his cognitive function. "When he showed up at my shop, he was wearing a leopard-print shirt and a necklace with leaves on it. I thought maybe it was marijuana leaves at first—you see a lot more pot jewelry than you'd expect—but I bet it was ivy."

"So if he was inciting Bacchanalia, he could also be responsible for the murders, right?" Andy asked. "Those were violent events."

"Yes," Dione said. "He wouldn't necessarily be committing them himself, though. The bacchanalia was a religious rite where wine was consumed to inspire divine madness. It is that madness that could lead to violence. Have you noticed any young women about, possibly carrying pinecone-topped sticks or wearing snakes?"

"Can't say that I have," Andy admitted. "And my bar usually draws the more interesting elements."

"He's likely here alone, then," Dione said. "There's not enough mayhem for his maenads to be involved."

"This isn't enough mayhem?" Sandy demanded. It was the first time she'd spoken since arriving at Drew's shop. "Stuff has been stolen. People are murdered. Secret fathers are being outed. And there is a lot of drunkenness."

"You haven't been drunk, though," Vincent said. "The couple times Dio's offered us wine, you've always refused. I haven't, and I don't like wine nearly as much as you do."

Drew held up his hand. "We need to talk to Dio, I think. But first, we need to decide if we think he's responsible for the murders, either directly or indirectly."

"I don't think so," Dione said. "Admittedly, it's been almost thirty years since I've known him and how well can you ever know anyone, but it doesn't fit with the mythology or the man."

"I agree," Drew admitted. "It's suspicious, that he's here now and there are deaths happening, but I don't think it's him."

"What about the mischief?" Andy asked. "The break-ins and weird, sentimental thefts?"

"That's more in the realm of possibility," Dione said.

"He's the god of drama, right?" Jonah asked. "This is very dramatic."

"I'd be more inclined to blame one of the more well-known trickster gods, if we knew of one in town," Andy said. "This is first-rate mischief that goes beyond laughs and straight into annoying. But I haven't seen any divines besides Dio in over a week."

"Who's the Greek trickster?" Misty asked. "I'm only familiar with Native American and Norse tricksters."

"There are a number of tricksters associated with the Greek pantheon. Hermes as the god of thieves and liars is always prominent. Eris, goddess of discord usually comes in at the top of the list, as well. But it's hard to ignore Dionysus. He can shift shape, take on different characteristics, and is unpredictable." Dione sighed. "Some sources claim he's truly androgynous, able to take on any aspect he pleases. But regardless, playing tricks like this—tricks that would really tug at the heart of someone—is right up his alley."

Drew signed heavily. "I don't want to confront him. I just want my ball back and for him to go away."

Sandy scooted her chair over next to Drew's. "At least he's not your dad," she said. "But, on the bright side, you could've been my step-dad! Wouldn't that have been fun?"

Drew leaned away from her, pursed his lips, and gave her some serious side-eye. "A young man such as myself? Be your step-daddy? I think not, darlin'."

"Are you Southern?" Sandy asked. "Your accent just now…"

"I'm sure I don't remember," he drawled, poorly.

"Does anyone here have a way to contact Dio?" Morgana asked. "I'd like to solve the mystery of my tea set and move on to find the murderer, if we're certain it isn't the god."

"I do," Drew said. "Unless he's changed his number."

"Should we call Adriana? She lost something, too." Ceri said.

"Oh, definitely not," Drew said. "If we find her bottle screwer or whatever is missing, we can return it to her as a surprise gift. No need to bring her in at this stage. I'm not sure she's ready for a deep dive into Oracle Bay's secrets."

"I wish we had access to Martha's place," Ceri said. "I'm sure everything is off limits, but I'd really like to go see who she was listening to besides the cops."

"I thought she was a good suspect for the murders," Drew said. "But I wonder now if she overheard the wrong thing."

"Or told the wrong person about her illegal hobby," Ceri said.

"Let's see if we can get Dio to come down now," Paska said. "There might be a way or two to check out Martha's bug collection this evening."

Drew pulled his phone out of his pocket and headed outside to make the call. He didn't need to—the signal in his shop was always fantastic—but this call was hard enough to make without anyone else listening in. He scrolled through his contacts and hovered his finger over Dio's name. He'd introduced himself as 'Dio Neesus, like Liam Neeson but with an s.' Dio Neesus. Dioneesus. "I can't believe it took me this long to catch on," Drew muttered. "It's been right here in front of me all along."

He didn't call Dio. Instead, he found Bill's number and called him. It rang through to voice mail. "Hey Bill. It's Drew. I needed to let you know that there's a bunch of us at my shop, hoping to get it ready to reopen soon. I'm gonna invite Dio to stop by to meet the rest of the group and wanted you to know. You're welcome to come over any time. I can't wait to see you again. In a non coffee shop setting. I mean for our date. God. I'm babbling, aren't I? Anyway. Hope you're well. See you soon. Love—the croissant I had today. Bye."

Drew pounded the end call button and shook his head. *That went well*, he chastised himself. *You really couldn't have been more awkward if you'd tried.*

He took a deep breath and called Dio.

"Drew! Baby! I'm so glad to hear from you! Does this mean you've changed your mind and you'll run away to Corfu with me?"

"Can we talk?" Drew asked. "Can you come to my shop? Enter through the back, the front is still a crime scene."

"Of course. Now?"

"Yeah. That'd be good."

"I can be there in thirty minutes. See you soon."

Drew hung up. "Can't wait," he growled at the phone. "Ugh."

"Who are you ughing?"

Drew whipped around. A tall, black woman with dark, tightly curled hair stepped out of the shadows. She was wearing a long trench coat and an oversized red, floppy hat that made her look like a globe-trotting thief. "Jezebel?" Drew asked, stopping just short of hitting teenage excited squeal territory. "Where in the world have you been, Carmen Sandiego? I can't believe you're back! When did you get here?"

"About an hour ago," she said. "I dropped my stuff at home, checked my messages—it took forty minutes to get through all the group texts—and then stopped by my shop to see if I'd been hit the way the rest of you had. And the hat is fabulous, right?"

"One hundred percent. But more importantly, have you been targeted, too?"

"Why don't we go inside," she suggested. "I'd rather tell my story once, and some of us aren't used to the cold and damp."

"Some of us?" Drew asked. Two cloaked figures stepped forward out of the gray, misty shadows that pocketed the alley's corners in darkness.

"I made some friends."

DREW PULLED OPEN THE DOOR TO HIS SHOP AND LED JEZEBEL AND HER TWO cloaked companions through the back rooms. While they walked, Drew filled Jezebel in on the day's events, including the fact that Dio was on his way over right now, he was possibly responsible for all the thefts, and he was Sandy's biological dad.

"I know I left in the middle of the apocalypse, but I'd kinda hoped things had started to slow down by now. We've had too much excitement lately. I was looking forward to a few weeks without magic goats or the end of the world, and now there's a flirtatious god with sticky fingers making his way around town?" Jezebel said, shaking her head.

"That's the gist of it," Drew said. He grabbed three more folding chairs and opened the door to the main shop area. "Look who I found lurking in the alley," he said, stepping aside and letting Jezebel precede him into the shop. Her dark skin had an amber glow under the shop lights, and when she took off her hat, he could see that her black hair was longer than it'd been before—her natural curls created a perfect halo-like dome around her head.

"Jezebel!" Misty squealed, running forward to envelop her in a firm hug. "I've missed you so much. Did you learn everything you'd hoped? Who are your friends? Are you hungry? Thirsty?"

"One question at a time," Jezebel laughed. "I'm not hungry or thirsty at the moment but have no doubt I will be soon. I cannot wait to have some fried food and a beer. Or nachos, maybe. I don't even care if they're good. My...companions...prefer to be called Pythia and Trophonius in this time and place."

"Greek oracles," Dione said. "I was named for one, as was my mother, and hers before her. I probably made a mistake not carrying on the family tradition."

"What is your name?" One of the cloaked figures asked. All that was visible was her black hands interlaced on the dark gray of her hooded cloak. Her face was hidden in shadows.

"I am Dione," she said. "This is my husband Jonah and my daughter Cassandra, although she is usually called Sandy."

"Dione," Pythia said. "We've been looking for you for a very long time. We must talk when the business here is done."

Sandy's mom smiled a tight smile that didn't reach her eyes and grabbed Jonah's hand. "Sure thing," she said. "Any time."

"Mom, you don't have to talk to the creepy cloaked figures just because they said so," Sandy said. She leaned into her mother's side and grabbed her free hand.

"Do you trust them?" Dione asked, the tension in her jaw relaxing.

"Yes," Sandy said. "Jezebel is vouching for them by bringing them here, and that's good enough for me. But it doesn't have to be good enough for you. Don't do anything that makes you uncomfortable."

Dione squeezed Sandy's hand and sat up a little straighter. "Thanks, baby girl." She turned towards Pythia and Trophonius. "I will consider your request and let you know if I have any time available for you."

They nodded at Dionne in concert, further cementing their status at the top of the creepy column.

"Jez—what went missing for you?" Drew asked. "You said you'd had a theft, too."

"In my shop, I have a lot of star charts," Jezebel explained. "My ceiling and most of my walls are plastered with them. But there was one map of the constellations I'd gotten in a book at the Scholastic

Book Fair when I was eight, and that was when my fascination with both astronomy and astrology began. I displayed it under glass on the table where I'd sit with my clients. That table was always covered with a cloth, but I liked it there for good luck. It was missing, and the tablecloth was neatly folded. There was something left in its place I'd never seen before. On the table were ten wine glasses, each showing a different part of the night sky. And each glass had different initials on it. There was a JJ—Jezebel Jones. You all were there. Drew Hardy, Misty Greene, Cassandra Franklin, Paska Cooper, Morgana Bellflower, Ceridwen Kenny, Russell Black, and then a few I didn't know. EM?"

"Ezekiel Matthews," Andy said. "He's a prophet of the Christian god."

"Okay...I guess I did miss some stuff. The last one was SR."

"What's Sybil's last name? Sandy asked."

"Greene, same as me." Misty said. "Or at least I think so."

"Maybe someone new will be joining us," Paska said. "I like that we all have our own glasses now. No more mix-ups!"

"It's weird, though," Sandy said. "No one calls me Cassandra. Everyone who knows me calls me Sandy, and those who don't call me Alexandra. And how many people know Zeke's full name?"

"Probably Brandy and me," Andy said. "Slightly fewer people than who know that he's a prophet."

"Or that Russell is gifted," Morgana said. "None of us even know his gift yet. Well, none of us except Paska."

"Every step forward creates more questions rather than answering them," Ceri complained. She was sitting as far away from Andy as possible, Drew observed.

The back door swung open. "Guess he's here," Drew sighed. "I'd better go show him in."

Bill walked in almost as soon as Drew finished speaking. "The idiot's right behind me," he said. "I think he's pouring wine."

"It's probably best none of us have any," Drew said. "Feel free to dump everything in the garbage." He pulled the garbage out to the middle of the room.

"Sandy, if you see any of us drinking what we ought not be drinking, can you take our glasses and toss them?" Paska asked. "You're the only one who seems immune at this point."

Dio walked into the room balancing an enormous tray covered in larger-than-average wine glasses filled to the brim with red wine. "Who wants happy hour?" he called.

"It's not even noon," Drew pointed out.

"It's five o'clock somewhere. Isn't that what you Americans say?" He walked around the rough circle of chairs and handed out the wine. Sandy stood a few paces behind him, holding the garbage can.

When he got to Dione, he stopped and stared. "Didi? What are you doing here? When? I didn't feel you come into town!"

"Can you do that?" Dione asked. "Feel the presence of past lovers?"

"Only the ones I care about the most," Dio said expansively. "Love has an energy...

"Anyone else in the town besides me and Drew?" she asked.

Dio did a slow turn and looked at each face. He peered closely at Pythia and Trophonius. "I don't think so, although the hooded people are a little difficult to get a bead on."

"What about your kids?" Dione asked. "Do you feel them, too?"

"Of course!" he said expansively. "Hard to miss the energy that comes from your own offspring."

"Hi dad," Sandy said. "So nice to officially meet you at last."

Dio dropped his tray of drinks. It fell perfectly—none of the glasses tipped even a bit, and no wine spilled. "That's impossible! Who?" He looked around.

"Who do you think, idiot?" Dione said. "I know being a god can make possible the impossible, but even you have to admit it's a bit far-fetched that your fling with Drew three years ago would've resulted in a twenty-eight-year-old woman."

"You make a good point," Dio said, straightening up. There was a glass of wine in his hand that hadn't been there moments before. He took a long drink. "Why didn't you tell me?"

"I did! I thought that's why you flew back with me."

Dio stared at her. "Weren't you the college girl doing a semester in Greece? You were so hungry."

"That's enough of that," Dione said. "It doesn't matter that you don't remember I was pregnant. I didn't need you in my life to begin with."

Dio shook his head. "Your name is Dione. What is your daughter's name?"

"Sandy. Cassandra."

He slapped himself in the forehead. "You named your daughter Cassandra? When did you pick out that name?"

"I'd planned to name my first daughter Cassandra since I was ten years old," Dione said. "How is that relevant?"

"I didn't believe you," Dio said. "Of course I didn't, not with a true-born oracle named Cassandra in your womb. Her presence, before she was fully formed, would've channeled the power of the original Cassandra and rendered your words unbelievable."

"Rather convenient," Sandy muttered.

"It is one of the better excuses I've heard for abandoning your pregnant girlfriend," Morgana said. "Very inventive."

"This isn't why we're here," Drew said. "I am very excited for you all to have an extended family reunion. Later. Now, we have some questions."

"Ask away," Dio said expansively. "Have some more wine while you're at it."

"We know who you are," Sandy said. She walked around with the trashcan and collected the full glasses that had appeared in everyone's hands. "You've already admitted most of it."

"I admit nothing!"

"You admitted you could feel the energy of mortals, didn't protest being called a god, and have weird superstitions about oracles named Cassandra. You're wearing an ivy-leaf pendant on a chain that looks like vines, you're obsessed with wine, and even though we all just dumped our glasses for a second time, everyone in this room is holding a full one again, and most of us didn't even notice," Drew said.

"Pfffttt...what a bunch of superstitious nonsense," Dio said. He drained his glass and looked around the room. "Maybe if the lot of you—this whole town!—didn't drink so much, you wouldn't be hallucinating gods everywhere you look."

"Do you know what just happened here?" Ceri asked. "Or do you believe you wandered into town for no reason?"

"What do you mean, no reason? I came to check up on the one that got away!" Dio explained. "The whole time we were together, Drew wouldn't shut up about that awful barista. I was hoping he'd be over him by now."

"Really?" Bill asked, scooting his chair a little closer to Drew's and dropping the glass of wine in his hand into the garbage.

"I was a mess," Drew said. "You're all I talked about to anyone who would listen for months."

"There are several of us here who will attest to that," Paska said. "Dio, or Dionysus, actually, three weeks ago, this place was crawling with divine beings. There were several from your pantheon here. I'm surprised they didn't call you in."

Dio disappeared.

Several moments of silence had elapsed before anyone one else spoke.

"Did he just...disappear?" Jonah asked. Drew noted that Dione was holding his hand tightly, although the narrowing of her eyes indicated she was angry rather than scared.

"I have never wanted a class of medicinal wine more than I do right now," Misty said. "And that's saying something."

"What do we do with this?" Sandy demanded. "We don't have

answers about the break-ins, the thefts, the murders, or anything. All we know is that my bio-dad is a Greek god who abandoned my mother because my presence made him doubt her story. Anything else he's said or admitted to could be false. How do you polygraph a god?"

"If any of us could access our powers with accuracy, we could find out," Paska muttered.

"He took objects of power from each of us," Ceri said, tossing her hair behind her. "Not necessarily the objects we use on a daily basis, except Drew and Sandy. But objects that we keep and draw on either consciously or unconsciously. Is it possible those thefts were thefts of power as well as sentimentality?"

"Mine wasn't an object of power," Misty protested.

"But yours was a symbol of your power," Sandy said. "Your gloves are as much a part of your power as my cards are of mine. They represent the dampening of power, and they had great sentimental ties to said power."

"It could fit," Morgana mused. "Between that and the miasma of bacchanalia that follows him around, it might be enough to render our oracular skills useless."

"If he isn't your murderer, the atmosphere he brings with him would be enough to incite strong feelings into violence where there'd been none before," Dione said. "If someone was angry at your two victims and the aura of excess caught up with them, they would be almost powerless to resist."

"I think anyone here could resist," Paska said. "We are all very strong-minded. Even the regular humans like Bill and Jonah are probably relatively immune."

"You didn't mention me," Dione said.

"You were included," Paska said. "We've all succumbed to the wine, but it was easier to resist once I knew what was happening. Did everyone else find it to be so?"

Everyone, including Bill and Jonah nodded.

"Is anyone here still of the opinion Dio is the murderer?" Paska asked.

A subdued chorus of nos echoed in the room.

"He is too wrapped up in himself," Drew said. "Dio might pretend to be interested in the pleasure of others, but it's only another way he finds gratification. His entire MO is based on what will give him pleasure. He finds pleasure in inciting the passions of others, in tricking them into things they might not want, or think they want, but he doesn't do anything but lead the horses to water. Or wine, in this case."

"I agree," Dione said. "He takes pleasure in generosity—being a generous host or a consummate lover—but it's his own pleasure he's interested in. He wouldn't hesitate to kill if it was necessary and brought him pleasure. But these murders sound very impersonal. It's impossible to say whether or not he knew them well enough to want them out of the picture, but if he's only been back a couple weeks, how would've he gotten to know them well enough to want them gone?"

"He was here for a few months three years ago," Bill said. "Maybe he's been harboring a grudge?"

"I don't think he's the type to harbor a grudge," Jezebel said. "He is a ball of energy. Long game is not his style."

"Agreed," Drew said. "He's not the murderer. Just the thief. Probably. We need to track him down and get our stuff back."

"And get him gone," Misty said. "I'd like my powers back. In addition to all of this being very annoying, and the murders being horrible, I've come to rely on my foresight to pick good renters for my vacant properties. The last thing I want is someone moving in and naming their property Covington Wine Shoppe." She pronounced shoppe with two syllables, shop-pee, and wrinkled her nose in disdain. "Give me puns or give me death."

"I think I know where Dio is," Drew said. "He'll be drowning his sorrows—and possibly attempting to drown himself—on the deck of The Sleeping Inn's bar."

"Should we all go and confront him?" Sandy asked. "Or will that make him run?"

"Let me go," Drew said. "I'd like Paska, Ceri, and Dione to come, too, though." He looked at Dione. "You can wait inside. I want backup in case things go a bit pear-shaped, is all."

"You got it," Paska said. "See you there."

eleven

Drew opened the sliding glass door separating the Sleeping Inn's bar from the expansive deck overlooking the Pacific Ocean. In the summer, the deck was always packed, but starting in mid-September to late April, few people were interested in outdoor seating on the Washington coast.

Rain was ubiquitous in the Pacific northwest, so much so that by spring, most people only noticed its absence. Today, however, the rain was pairing up with the wind and clouds so dark they were nearly black, causing even the most hardened of denizens to scurry inside.

Dio stood at the railing, a bottle of wine dangling from one hand and a full glass in his other. There was a circle of perfect dryness around him, and although he looked miserable, he didn't look soaked. Drew, on the other hand, was drenched before he'd even made his way across the deck. "Why don't you come inside?" he yelled at Dio, hoping his voice was carrying above the roar of wind and surf.

"So you and your sneaky friends can peek into my brain and be mean to me?" Dio whined.

"Be mean to you?" Drew asked. "This isn't middle school. We need our things back."

"I was only trying to help," Dio sulked.

"You'll have to excuse me, but I'm not sure I understand how."

"Everyone was so uptight when I showed up. Many of you had worked yourselves to exhaustion. That redheaded friend of yours was on the verge of collapse," Dio pointed out. "You needed fun. Relaxation. A vacation from your jobs."

"So you broke into our businesses and stole from us?" Drew snapped.

"Everyone has a seat of power. Some people hide it, but it's power, nonetheless. I took the batteries, if you will," Dio explained.

"And in place of our batteries, you left jokes?"

"Everyone loves a laugh." Dio shrugged and took a sip of his wine. Drew did the same.

"I don't like being cut off," Drew said. "My ability to see into the future is very much a part of who I am. How would you like it if you no longer had the ability to make mischief and keep everyone drunk?"

"It happens from time to time." Dio shrugged. "But I don't need divine power to have fun. Last time I was in town, I was as close to being an ordinary mortal as it's possible for me to be. We had a good time, didn't we?"

Drew took another sip of his wine before answering. He ignored the implication that he'd chosen to spend time with Dio rather than been supernaturally seduced. "We did. You were just what I needed at that point in my life. But a lot has changed in the last three years. Hell, a lot has changed in the last three months. Things are different, somehow. And what I need is my ball back."

Dio snickered. Drew rolled his eyes, but gave in and laughed, too.

"You know what I mean. We all need our things back and for the drunkenness and violence to stop. You may not have committed those murders, but a bunch of drunks high on emotion are a recipe for unexplained brutality."

"Of course I didn't murder anyone. And I didn't cause any murders, either. I am here solely to bring the fun back."

"You bring passion and wine. Not everyone is a happy drunk. I've seen a lot of people end the night in the drunk tank because booze triggers aggression."

"You don't understand," Dio said. "I have perfect control over what emotions I incite. You're right. I am a god of passions, but the only passions I'm raising are lust and intemperance. If an orgy had broken out on Main Street, that'd be me. But, the violence isn't related to me at all."

"But the victims had been drinking wine," Drew protested.

"You can't convince me no one in this town drank wine before I showed up. Don't you and your friends have an expense account at the wine shop?"

"Fine," Drew said. "Will you come inside and tell us where our things are? I'll vouch for you for the murders."

"I guess this prank has run its course," Dio sighed. "Another glass of wine?"

Drew looked down at the empty glass in his hand and swore softly under his breath. The wind howled by to drown out his curses, but Dio smirked anyway. "Not so immune to me after all, are you?"

"You're too charming for your own good," Drew said.

Dio linked his arm through Drew's. "We had fun, though, didn't we?" he asked wistfully.

"We did. Will you leave town? Find a new place to play tricks?" Drew asked.

"It's time. I might check in with a few of my brethren. Find out why I didn't get an invite to the apocalypse. Again. Or I might head to Vegas. That is a delightful town to be me in."

Drew stood with his hands on his hips in front of the decrepit looking garage on an abandoned plot of land on the bay side of town.

The rest of the psychics stood in a loose semi-circle around him. The rain was giving them a temporary stay, but the dark clouds piling up behind them on the western horizon announced the reprieve wouldn't last long.

"This garage looks sketch," Jezebel said. "No way is it weather-proof. If our stuff hasn't been ruined, I'll be surprised."

"The padlock is shiny and new," Sandy said. "But the rest looks like it could be on the historic register."

"I don't think the historic register is interested in aspiring garages," Drew said. "But it's not inspiring confidence." He strode forward and slid the key into the lock. He pulled the double doors out and open, then stepped into the dim space and turned on his cellphone flashlight. "He said there was a light switch over here," Drew said.

"Are you sure?" Misty asked. "I don't see any electrical wires coming in."

"Here it is." Drew flipped the switch, and the place lit up like a warehouse superstore.

"Holy macaroni," Jezebel said. "Are we in the TARDIS?"

The space was large, open, and industrial. Round, bright lights ensured that every corner was illuminated. Small tables formed a circle in the middle of the space, each one displaying a single item or group of items.

"It's bigger on the inside, right?" Sandy asked. "I'm not imagining things."

"It is," Morgana confirmed.

"You know, after everything that's happened since I moved here, I didn't think a Mary Poppins shed would be the thing that sent me over the edge," Sandy said.

"Mary Poppins?" Ceri asked.

"Her bag is bigger on the inside," Sandy replied.

"She's a timelord. Obviously," Jezebel said.

"Let's find our stuff and get out of here," Drew said. "This place makes me uncomfortable."

Paska nodded. "My guts are twisted up tighter than—"

"Watch yourself, old man," Morgana interrupted.

Paska glared at her. "Tighter than two coats of paint, as I was about to say. Crone."

"Do you always bicker like this," Russell said, strain evident in his voice. "Can't we find our stuff and leave? Or I could leave, and someone could bring me my things later."

"My cards are over here," Sandy called from the back of the room. "It's much further away than I thought. I see a tea set and an old mirror, too."

Morgana and Ceri headed back towards Sandy. Drew, Paska, Jezebel, Misty, and Andy followed Russell in his near sprint the other way. Twenty minutes later, everyone had their items in hand except Drew.

"I can't find my ball," he said. "Has anyone seen it? It's blue."

"Is that it?" Jezebel asked, pointing into the center of the circle.

The light was so bright it was difficult to see anything, but when he squinted, he could almost make out a table with a light blue round object on it.

"Maybe? How do I get there?"

"If I were you, I'd just push one of the empty tables out of the way and walk," Paska said.

"That sounds simultaneously too easy and rather dangerous," Drew warned.

"You're letting this place get to you. It might be a weird storage container, but it's a storage container nonetheless," Paska pointed out. "You have the key. Walk in."

Drew took a deep breath and did as Paska suggested. The table slid out of the way, and he speed-walked to the table. It was his crystal ball on a stand decorated with stylized wine bottles and bejeweled vines. He tried to take just the ball, but the stand came with it. He shrugged and walked back out even more quickly than he'd walked in. "Let's get out of here."

"With pleasure," Russell said, leading the way out of the shed.

Drew handed his crystal ball to Sandy and closed the doors, replacing the lock. When he put the key in to activate the latch, it blazed with brilliant white light then disappeared.

Paska sighed. "I guess I won't get a second shot to snoop in there. Pity."

"I just want to get out of here and never come back," Drew said.

"Wait! Are we back online?" Ceri asked.

"If one of you wants to shake hands, I can tell you," Misty said. "Unless someone else wants to try."

Drew held his hand out to Misty. She pulled off her gloves and grabbed his arm. For a second, her expression was unchanged. Then her eyes widened, and her jaw dropped. She grinned at Drew, winked, and said, "Oh yeah, we're back online. And Drew is going to have a *very* interesting time soon. I don't want to spoil the fun, so I'm not going to say anymore. Just that he might want to buy stock in Chapstick."

Drew and Sandy followed Jezebel and her companions back to Jez's shop. Dione and Jonah were waiting for them outside, and the seven of them walked into *Your Lucky Stars*.

Papers were strewn everywhere. Star charts were hanging off the ceiling and walls like curling flypaper.

"You said you could use a bit of help straightening up," Sandy said. "You didn't say your place had been ransacked."

"It hadn't," Jezebel said. "When we arrived earlier, there was a couple weeks' worth of sandy dust on everything and the central table where the star chart had been was askew, but there wasn't..." she gestured around her. "This."

This was certainly more than dust and a mussed table.

"It could've been Dio," Drew said. "He could've done this while we were retrieving our stuff. But why?"

"Perhaps it was meant as a show of power?" Dione suggested.

"What's this?" Jezebel asked, pulling a large basket out from under her table. It contained four bottles of wine—one each of red, white, rosé, and sparkling—a large container of soft chèvre from Joseph's farm, three bars of goat's milk soap, some hard sausages bearing the logo of Natalie Dale, the local hog farmer and artisan charcuterie producer, and a handful of gift cards to a handful of local restaurants. The brown woven basket was decorated in red and green ribbons and adorned with holly berries and mistletoe.

"That looks a lot like the basket I saw in Ryan's shop the night he was murdered," Drew said.

"I've seen them in various businesses for the last couple weeks," Sandy offered. "Is there a card or a tag? I got the impression they were from the City Council."

"Did you get one?" Jezebel asked, digging through the basket looking for the tag.

"No. And I don't think any of *us* did. Drew?"

"I didn't get one and hadn't noticed I was left out. Are the wines from Adriana?" Drew asked.

"They're not her new shop label, but if they are gifts from the City, then I can't imagine they'd get the wine anywhere else. These are Oracle Bay baskets, and she is Oracle Bay wine," Jezebel said.

"If no other oracles received this gift and it was waiting for Ms. Webster in her ransacked shop, I wonder if this gift is as innocent a nod to local commerce as it seems," Trophonius said. His low intonations somehow made his mostly modern speech patterns heavy with portent.

A quick knock on the door interrupted further conversation. Jonah glanced at Jezebel, who nodded, then walked over and opened the door.

Bill walked in with a large tray of coffees. "I thought you all might need a pick-me-up after this—holy crap! What happened in here?"

"That's what I'd like to know," Jezebel said.

Bill handed her a coffee. "Mexican mocha?" she asked.

"Of course." He finished handing round the coffees, apologizing to Dione, Jonah, Pythia, and Trophonius for not knowing their preferences and only having the choice between lattes and Americanos for them. Jonah and Pythia took lattes, while Trophonius and Dione took the Americanos.

"Bill, did you get a basket like this?" Drew asked, holding up the gift in question.

"Yeah. Last week. I also made croissants for the baskets, but since Jezebel's went out so late, it's not surprising those didn't make it in. They'd be terrible by now, anyway."

"Did you know that none of the psychics received baskets?" Sandy asked.

"What do you mean?" Bill asked. "All the business owners were supposed to get one. Your names were on the planning list when accounting for how many of everything to provide."

"I didn't get one," Drew said. "And unless Misty knows more about this, since she's on the City Council, none of us knew about it. We weren't asked to provide gift certificates."

"That's bizarre," Bill said.

"Who's on the council?" Dione asked.

Bill and Drew exchanged looks with Sandy and Jezebel.

"Misty, Adriana, Ryan," Drew said. "Who are the other two?"

"Gabrielle—she owns the Realty business in town," Jezebel ticked the names off on her fingers. "Antonia was on the council until last year; I voted, but I can't remember who took her place.

"It wasn't...Martha, was it?" Drew asked. "I always forget about her. Unless she's complaining about something, she fades into the background."

"It was," Bill confirmed. "I voted for Frank—he owns Deja 'Do, but somehow he lost to Martha."

"That is weird," Drew said. "But not sure if it means anything."

"It means that three-fifths of the council members wanted fewer psychic businesses," Sandy said.

Drew flexed his fingers. "Maybe it's time to see if I have my oracular mojo back, too."

Dione twisted around to the low bookshelf behind her where Drew had set down his ball. "I can grab this for you. I'm excited to see someone else work their magic." She grabbed the ball and her entire body straightened and stiffened. Ball firmly in hand, Dione slowly turned back to face the center of the room. Her eyes were wide and vacant. A bell rang somewhere, and she jolted back to herself, handing the ball to Drew.

"Mom? Are you okay?" Sandy asked.

"Did you hear the bell?" Dione asked, eyes darting around wildly.

"Yeah. It sounded like the one that was in my shop when I first moved here. I didn't ever find it, and it only rang the first time I...oh. What did you see?" Sandy asked, leaning towards her mother.

Dione looked around the room and seemed to shrink a bit under the weight of six pairs of eyes all trained on her. "Nothing that I understood. Except for the babies. I saw a lot of babies. Grandbabies."

"Mother," Sandy said. "That is not relevant, and since you only have the one kid, I'm not sure it's even possible."

"I haven't seen an oracle utilize her full powers for the first time in a very, very long time," Pythia said. Her voice sounded distant and a faint echo bounced around the room before she spoke again. "Your oracular blood does run true."

"Question," Jezebel said. "If Dio, Dionysus, is Sandy's father, and his other local excitement was Drew, do you think he seeks out psychics? Or is he even conscious of it at all?"

"Your question has merit, and it is one that is particularly fascinating to me as I hadn't thought of it myself. Let us revisit it at a more opportune time," Trophonius said.

Dione was still staring at the ball, hands behind her back, looking wide-eyed and vaguely horrified.

"I'm gonna take her home," Sandy said, grabbing her mother's elbow. "I'll catch up with you later." She and Jonah led Dione out of the shop.

"We will speak more to the new Oracle," Pythia said.

"If Dione wants to, I'll make sure she knows where to find you," Drew replied. "But regardless of your roles in all this, she still gets to choose. If she leaves here soon, she'll be able to tuck those powers away, for the most part."

"It is as you say," Pythia replied, her voice more distant and the echoes louder now. "She must be made aware of all options and responsibilities."

Drew sat down at Jezebel's table. "Sorry to contaminate your star space with my crystal," he said.

"I have so many jokes I want to make. None of them appropriate," she replied. "Get on with it, ball boy."

Drew pulled his crystal ball in close, placed one hand lightly on either side, and closed his eyes for a moment. The stress lines on his face faded, and his jaw visibly unclenched. He shook his shoulders to loosen them up, then opened his eyes, took three deep breaths, and gazed into the crystal ball. His eyes unfocused, and his gaze softened. After a few moments, Drew closed his eyes again, let go of his ball, and pushed his chair back. He scrubbed his hands over his face, then looked at the waiting crowd.

"I can See, with a capital S," he said. "But trying to focus on Dio yields almost nothing. It's like a translucent mist follows him, everywhere obscuring my vision."

"What about the gift baskets?" Jezebel asked. "Anything there?"

"Nothing we don't already know. They were a City Council gift, all the items were donated by local businesses, and the local psychics were originally left out."

The front door opened, and Misty strode in. "How's it going? I ran into Sandy and she said things were a lot more chaotic than you'd expected."

"It'll be a bit of work to clean it up," Jezebel admitted. "But it's not terrible. Thanks for the basket, by the way." She nodded towards the chair it was sitting on.

"Ohhh, no," Misty said. "Those were delivered a couple weeks ago. I wouldn't eat the cheese, and you might want to check with Natalie to see how shelf stable the sausages are."

"It showed up today," Jezebel said. "It wasn't here this morning.

"Weird," Misty said. "Adriana told me everything that was going to be delivered had been when I asked for a couple extras to woo potential business owners."

"Did you get one?" Drew asked.

"Of course not. It'd be silly to send myself a gift," Misty said. "But every business owner not on the council and currently in town was supposed to receive one."

"I didn't get one," Drew said. "Neither did Sandy. And she believes that none of the oracles did."

"Bill, did you get one?" Misty asked.

"I did, and I made enough croissants for everyone to have their share."

"I'll take this up at the next council meeting," Misty muttered. "Not sure it's important now."

"Ryan had a basket," Drew said. "Even though he was on the council."

"Small town government corruption is weird," Misty said. "But that's the least of our worries now. Let's get Jez's shop cleaned up."

"Hopefully there will be some kind of clue," Drew muttered. "That's going to be the only way these mysteries get solved."

twelve

Bill and Drew stopped outside of Have a Ball. Drew couldn't bring himself to meet Bill's eyes, so he kept his own gaze on the ground.

"Your sign is fixed," Bill said. "I was looking forward to spending some quality time with the Amazing Ramiro, but I guess I'll have to settle for having a ball with Drew."

"I don't want you to settle," Drew said to Bill's shoes.

Bill reached forward, tipped Drew's chin up with his index finger, and looked down at him. "It's never settling when it's with you," he said, then stepped forward to close the gap between them. He lowered his mouth to Drew's, whose lips parted with anticipation. When their lips met, Drew let out a soft sigh of satisfaction and twined his arms around Bill's neck.

"Is this okay?" Bill whispered against Drew's face, his warm breath stirring fires that'd been dormant a long time.

"More than okay," Drew replied, moving even closer to Bill and closing the minuscule gap that had remained. He moved one hand up and twined his fingers in Bill's hair. The other hand found purchase on Bill's face. "I've missed this so much."

"Then why are you still talking?" Bill asked.

Their lips met again, and they stumbled backwards in the afternoon mist until Drew's back hit the door of his shop. His breath came in short, hot gasps. "This is probably not..."

Bill backed off and put a couple feet of space between them before Drew could even finish his sentence. "Probably not what?" He crossed his arms in front of his body and shifted enough to place his torso perpendicular to Drew's.

"Probably not the best place," Drew said. "It's late afternoon. It's Main Street. And there are at least three dozen people in a two-block radius. I'm about five seconds away from trying to get your clothes off, and the last thing I need is an arrest for indecent exposure at the spot where a body was found a couple days ago."

"Oh," Bill said. "Yes. All very good points."

"Are you blushing?" Drew asked.

"Of course not. Why would I be? Nothing embarrassing about losing control so badly you forget about a murder. I feel like a monster." Bill tilted his head away from Drew in a tempt to hide the blush that stained his cheeks.

Drew cleared the hanging remnants of crime scene tape from the door. "Come in. I just need to put my ball back where she belongs, and then we can get some dinner before seeing what Netflix has to offer?"

Bill walked forward. "That sounds like a pretty good plan."

"You're not a monster," Drew said behind him. "Sometimes it's easier to forget. And sometimes we genuinely forget for a moment. The brain has a remarkable capacity to protect us from stress. I've seen people forget the most extraordinary things over the years. So much has happened in the last two months. If your brain blocks a murder in favor of pleasure for a few moments, that doesn't make you a monster. If you remembered and did nothing, maybe... But you're not that kind of guy."

"Are you sure?" Bill asked. "I've been rather horrible to you."

"I'm positive. If you really were a monster instead of deeply hurt by what, to any rational human, appeared to be egregious and poorly constructed lies, I wouldn't have spent the last three years dreaming about you. I would've moved on, literally and figuratively. And I wouldn't be here with you now desperately wishing you'd kiss me again."

Bill moved forward and closed the gap between them. Drew tugged at Bill's shirt and released it from the waistband of his pants.

"I'm not sure this is the right place, either," Bill said. "The floor is bare, the table is definitely not big nor sturdy enough, and I really was looking forward to getting you into my bed again, not against the wall in full view of anyone who looks through your picture window."

Drew let go of Bill's shirt. "You're killing me," he complained. He clenched his fists in an effort to keep his hands from straying back to Bill's body.

"I'm killing us both," Bill said. He shifted back and forth from foot to foot. "Drop off your crystal and let's get going. Your evening plans sounded delightful."

"Fine," Drew said. He picked up the satchel from where he'd placed it when they'd first walked in, flipped on the light switch to illuminate the room, and stared. On the middle of his table was a holiday basket nearly identical to the one Jezebel received. "That's weird," he said. "Why are they being delivered now?" He moved it onto the chair and placed the ball back in its place of honor.

"One basket arriving at the business of someone who'd been gone a while was unusual, since whoever delivered it had either broken in after the place was ransacked or at the same time and didn't report it. Two delivered baskets in two locked business two weeks late? That's fishy," Bill said.

"I'm sorry, Babe," Drew said. "I think I need to make some calls."

"We have plenty of time ahead of us," Bill said. "I'm not even thirty yet. You can have me for the next fifty years if you want me."

"That won't be nearly long enough," Drew said. "But I'd rather have only fifty years than nothing." He pulled out his phone and started texting. "Everyone loves a group text," he said.

"*I got a basket, too. Anyone else been by their shops today?*" he asked.

"*You have impeccable timing, as usual,*" Morgana replied. "*I'm about to walk into mine.*"

"And now we wait," Drew said. "Want to grab dinner? It might be our best chance."

"Let's head to the Sleeping Inn," Bill suggested. "I'm feeling like oysters and champagne would be an excellent appetizer."

Drew smirked at Bill. "Still hoping for the movie?"

"I haven't seen the new Marvel flick, and I know how much you like some good action." Bill waggled his eyebrows and threw in a slow wink.

"Your innuendo is a little thick," Drew said, laughing.

"I'm out of practice!" Bill exclaimed. "You gotta cut me a break."

Drew locked up and followed Bill out to the street and down the block to the Sleeping Inn.

They had just begun their main courses when Drew's phone alerts started.

"Everyone got a basket," Drew said, scrolling through the messages.

"Basket?" Russell asked, bringing over two beers—no one particularly wanted wine yet. "I got a basket today."

"You?" Drew asked. "You're not even the owner here. Nor do you have a shop."

"I'm not sure I'd be the most popular psychic on the block, even if I had the talent," Russell said. "Who wants to talk to the dead?" He paled and clapped one hand over his mouth. "Damnit!" he whispered. "This is all Paska's fault."

"You're a nec—"

"Don't say it," Russell hissed, looking around frantically. "Do not *ever* say that word."

"No promises, but I'll keep it to myself for the moment," Drew said. "How is this Paska's fault?"

"He kept insinuating that he knew what my so-called gift was," Russell said. "I forgot that not everyone knows. Are you going to tell them?"

"I don't know," Drew replied. "It'd be easier if everyone did know. That way you would know we were all safe to talk to, and anyone who does know wouldn't have to constantly watch their tongue, so they didn't give away a secret."

"Fine. Tell whoever." Russell sounded a bit sulky.

"It's an amazing gift," Drew said. "And you would be very popular. There's a reason seances were all the rage in the early twentieth century. What I wouldn't have given for your talent then. I could've made a fortune."

Russell stared, jaw moving up and down in soundless surprise.

Bill saw his overwhelm and leaned in. "What's important right now is that Russell received a holiday basket today. He has that in common with every single psychic in town. And since no one but that subset of people knew Russell had any extra special talents, either there is a leak among the oracles and various others in the know, or someone heard something they shouldn't have. What's the plan?"

"There is no plan," Drew said. "Yet. I'm still working on what to do with the information, practically speaking. Good investigations take time and planning, not running off half-cocked on a hunch. That's for television time limits."

"Did Andy and Zeke get baskets? Did anyone ask them?" Bill inquired.

"Hm. I don't know. They aren't in my Oracles Assemble! text group, since Andy's not a seer and Zeke, like Russell, refuses to play along. I'll ask Ceri." Drew said.

Ceri, can you text Andy and see if either he or Zeke got a basket? Russell got one, which is...interesting.

She sent back a middle finger emoji, but he knew she'd reach out anyway. Ten minutes later, also known as the beginning of the dessert course, Drew had a reply.

Zeke didn't, as far as he knows. There was nothing for him at the bar. He'll let us know if there's one at his house when his shift is over. Andy is a yes.

Drew reopened the group text, added Andy and Russell, and said, *Andy and Russell got baskets, too. Zeke didn't. (Can someone add him? I don't have his number.) With the timing and the audience, it makes me think someone knows who the not-quite-normal residents are. I just don't know how. Ideas? Next steps?*

He put the phone down and went back to the dessert. It was a beautiful bread pudding with a whiskey hard sauce and fresh whipped cream. Drew took a bite and moaned. "This is beautiful," he said.

"Not as beautiful as you," Bill said. "Thank you for being here with me when things are still so weird."

"I'm beginning to fear that weird is the new normal," Drew confessed. "It started off as fairly mundane weird with Sandy's ex and Vincent's past. But things are progressively getting stranger. Goats and gods and...I can't think of another 'g' word that would fit."

"Gazing comma crystal?" Bill suggested.

"That'll have to do. I can't come up with anything better."

Drew's phone beeped. "It's Ceri," he said.

"We need to do another sweep of the town. I have an idea. Meet me in the morning."

"Free until morning," Drew said. "I have some thinking and planning to do, but I can do that almost anywhere.

"When are you going to reopen your shop?" Bill asked, looking intently at the bread pudding.

"Monday, I think. I need a few days. Do you have any time off coming up?"

"I can see if I can get someone to come in Sunday morning. Then I'd have Saturday afternoon until Monday early morning. Why?" Bill asked, not bothering to disguise the hopeful gleam in his eyes.

"I'd really like to hole up in your house."

"What about the kittens?"

"Argh. You're right. And speaking of, I should go feed them. They're probably destroying my house by now. Dinner was supposed to be thirty minutes ago." Drew's voice took on an air of panic as he remembered the destruction the two tiny creatures could wreak.

"You can bring them to my place on Saturday," Bill said. "Provided they like me, of course. Where did they come from? Did you ever figure it out?"

Drew grimaced. "I didn't. It was weird, but they were tiny and cute, so I made allowances. And then things started getting a bit haywire, and it got pushed to the back burner."

"Do you think they're tiny divinities?" Bill asked, helping Drew with his jacket. They walked out of the restaurant and into the light mist that'd been ubiquitous all day.

"If they are, I don't understand the point."

"Joseph had an Etruscan goddess disguised as a goat for as long as his family has been goat farming. I don't know if anyone saw the point until it was time for her to make one," Bill pointed out.

"Ugh. You're right. I've been spending too much time with my head in the sand. They are awfully wily, even for kittens. They escape from places they shouldn't be able to escape from. Maybe it's time to look into them further." Drew wrinkled his face. "I'm not sure how to See animals."

"Maybe Misty can, if she holds them?" Bill suggested.

"We could invite her and Joseph over for a double date this weekend. It wouldn't hurt to ask," Drew agreed.

"You should give her a heads up ahead of time. I think she'd appreciate that rather than having kittens thrust at her while she's eating."

"While she's eating?" Drew asked. "Why would I do that?"

"That's the only time she doesn't wear gloves. Maybe she takes them off when she's alone with Joseph, but I wouldn't bet money on it," Bill said.

"You're very observant." Drew aimed some side eyes at Bill and pursed his lips suspiciously.

"That's why I'm such an amazing barista. I remember everyone's favorites. And their habits," Bill aimed an over-exaggerated wink at Drew, drawing a grin to Drew's face.

"That's almost creepy, but not quite. Unless you're using your powers for evil."

"I don't usually choose evil." Bill smirked. "However, I do remember some of your favorite things, and I am considering using those for a little bit of evil."

Bill and Drew walked into Drew's house. Frantic mewing greeted them.

"Oh no, little fuzzies! Are you so hungry?" Drew crooned. They wound around his ankles, somehow managing to achieve a forward momentum, and led him to the kitchen. After Drew fed them and righted the houseplant that had mysteriously fallen into the sink, he joined Bill in the living room.

"One more thing about the weirdness, and then it's movie time," Drew said.

"We can talk about anything you want," Bill replied. "We don't have to do a movie tonight."

"I need something to take my mind off things," Drew said. Butterflies were taking flight in his stomach, although he couldn't find a reason for their sudden appearance. He took a deep breath. Talking about psychic stuff was always a little nervy. That must be it. "It's weird Russell and Andy got baskets and Zeke didn't. If someone can tell who we are, how did they miss him?"

"I don't know. He's pretty new to town and very quiet. It'd be easy to overlook him," Bill offered, sliding a little closer to Drew, stopping just short of physical contact.

"You're probably right. Something bugs me about the whole

thing, though. It feels like this has something to do with the murders. I just can't put the pieces together." He was trying to be logical, to work through this puzzle, but all Drew could think of was the infinitesimal distance between his left thigh and Bill's right one. The hairs on his arm stood up as if in response to a dose of static electricity, and he felt his breath quicken.

"You will," Bill said, slinging his arm around Drew's shoulders and pulling him close, finally bridging that distance that had existed for too long—for moments and years. "But for now, let's watch a movie. Maybe make out a little. And get some sleep."

"Will you stay?" Drew asked. He almost bit his tongue clamping his jaw shut again. They'd agreed to go slow, but the heat generated by sitting on the couch, touching only outer thighs and one arm around one back was overwhelming. The thought of more. More heat. More touching. Skin against skin. Lips... Drew was drowning in anticipatory sensation.

"I shouldn't," Bill said, but the way he trailed his hand from Drew's shoulder to run down his jawline belied his intentions. "I'll have to be up by three-thirty to walk home, shower, and dress before heading in for the morning."

"You have clothes here," Drew said, as nonchalantly as he could, tilting his head to give Bill more access to his neck. "You left a few things, and I've been holding on to them. Just in case. And I'll get up and drive you home in the morning if you want to go home first. Or I can drive you to work." Drew turned his body towards Bill's, and Bill's hand slid back around Drew's shoulders then flatted on his chest, sending a pulse of desire from his touch throughout Drew's body.

"You'll get up at four o'clock in the morning?" Bill said, licking his lips. "That doesn't sound like you."

Drew shrugged. He was no longer tentative about his desire. They'd said they'd go slow, but no one said they couldn't change their minds. "There's not a lot I wouldn't do to get you to stay tonight. How about it?"

"Well, as long as you don't mind me using your shower and getting ready, I won't say no. You can drop me off at work, and I'll walk home after." Bill leaned in and brushed Drew's lips with his. Sparks jumped between them, and both men gasped.

"Deal," Drew said, exhaling in short, quick bursts. "Oh, but part of the deal is you have to make me coffee in the morning."

"Still have the espresso machine I bought you?" Bill had brought his other hand into play and both were slowly sliding down Drew's chest towards his abdomen.

It was getting difficult to think. Drew shook his head. "Of course."

"Then you can have a coffee before you take me to work. And if you come to Caffiend Dreams with Ceri, I'll hook you up with a caramel latte, extra foam." Bill paused at Drew's hips and grasped them firmly.

"You are too good to be true." Drew planted a hard kiss on Bill's lips. He'd meant it to be short and teasing, but it turned into something intense and long.

"If you keep kissing me like that, we're gonna miss the Netflix part of Netflix and chill," Bill gasped, breaking off the kiss.

"I won't tell if you don't," Drew replied before silencing Bill with his lips.

DREW WAS WAITING INSIDE CAFFIEND DREAMS, CARAMEL LATTE IN HAND, when Ceri walked in, catching him mid-yawn.

"Late night?" she smirked.

"I was in bed much earlier than usual, actually," Drew countered. "But was out of bed much earlier this morning. I do not like anything that could be referred to as 'the crack of dawn.' It's unnatural and becoming much too common for my preference lately."

"Poor baby," she said, getting in line. "Why were you up so early today? Another break-in?"

"I'm positive you already know, Ceri," Drew said.

"I do, but I want to hear you say it out loud." Ceri smirked at Drew until he dropped eye contact.

"Me, too," said the person behind them. Drew spun around until he was face to beard with Joseph McEwen.

"Joseph. You're growing a beard," Drew said, then shook his head. "Apologies. You probably already knew that. I need more sleep."

For the first time in three years, Joseph smiled at Drew. "I had a feeling that's what was going on, but it's nice to have my suspicions confirmed."

"How does Misty feel about your new facial adornment?" Ceri asked, nose wrinkled into disapproval.

"I'm almost ashamed to admit this, but it was her idea," Joseph said, shrugging. "If it makes her happy, I'm willing to give it a shot. If I get tired of it, it won't take but a minute to get rid of it, and it does cut down on my grooming routine."

"Hey guys," Bill said as they reached the front of the line. He locked eyes with Drew and the air between felt warmer.

"I'm gonna need a cold shower if you two don't stop that," Ceri said, fanning herself.

"What?" Bill asked, then took a deep breath and tore his gaze from Drew's. "Sorry about that. What can I get you all? The usual?"

"Quad shot espresso," Ceri confirmed. "But, if you have fresh cream, I want some room."

"Same for me," Drew said.

"You want a quad shot espresso?" Bill asked. "After two espressos at home this morning and a latte?"

"Give it to me," Drew said.

Ceri snorted.

"So mature, Ceri," Joseph said. She stuck her tongue out at him. "I'll have a cup for drip and a twenty-ounce iced mocha."

Bill rang everyone up and started on the drinks.

"Where's Misty?" Ceri asked.

"She was still sleeping when I came into town for coffee," Joseph said. "She is not a morning person."

"Me, neither," Drew yawned. Their coffees were ready in short order, and the line was nearly out the door when they walked out into the overcast but dry morning.

"Bill needs to hire someone to help him out in the mornings," Joseph observed. "Business has been through the roof lately."

"He needs to stop opening at seven and have an evening coffee shop and bakery," Drew said. "I'd forgotten how early four is. I much prefer four in the morning to be late."

"It's not that bad," Joseph said. "I don't get up until about five, but you get used to it."

"I don't know that I want to," Drew yawned.

"Not even for your schmoopy bear?" Ceri teased.

"My what now?" Drew said. "I have never used that term of endearment before. It's terrible."

She laughed. "Ready to go canvass the neighborhood again?"

"As ready as I'll ever be," Drew sighed. "I wish I had more confidence the cops were going to figure it out. Correctly. I don't like being a suspect."

"Confidence in the cops? When have you ever had that?" she laughed.

Drew shrugged. "It could happen."

"I don't imagine it'll happen for many of us here, at least not for a while," Joseph said. "Getting hypnotized by a rogue goddess might be a great excuse for being an awful cop—certainly better than anything else I've ever heard—but it's still tough to believe that the force is competent. And with Daniel and Roger out on administrative leave, we have two replacements that don't even know Oracle Bay. Good luck with your investigation. Let me know if there's anything I can do to help."

"There is one thing," Ceri said. "Can I ask you a question?"

"Of course. I'll even let you have more than one," Joseph teased.

"So funny. Did you receive one of the City Council holiday baskets?"

"I did. It arrived a couple of weeks ago. Like Bill, I donated enough soap and cheese to cover every business owner in town. Misty and I really didn't talk about it, so I didn't know she hadn't gotten a basket and she didn't know she was on the list. She assumed the council members wouldn't get baskets and didn't check in with anyone to make sure her fellow council members had done their jobs. I have a copy of the email I got from Martha requesting the donations and letting me know how many I needed and to whom the baskets would be delivered. Let me know if you want me to forward it on."

"Martha sent the request?" Drew asked. "Interesting. I don't know why yet, but it feels like it's all related."

"I'll send it along when I get home," Joseph said. "Now I've got to get home, wake up Misty, and assuage her anger with this iced mocha."

"Thanks a lot, Joseph," Ceri said. "See you later."

"We need to head back over to the Pour House," Joseph said. "I missed the last get together. I've developed a terrible fear of missing out, now, because I was the last to know about Dionysus. Say...do you think he had something to do with your kittens? I'm suspicious of all animals when gods are around."

"Oh," Drew said. "I hadn't even thought of that. The kittens just kinda...are now. It's like they've always been here."

"Maybe something to look into. Ask your ex if he's still around. Divine animals are a lot of trouble, especially when they don't even produce anything useful," Joseph said. He was grinning, but his tone was serious.

Drew sighed. "One more thing on the list. See you later, Joseph."

thirteen

"Do you want to visit Gabrielle and Bryan first or Antonia?" Drew asked.

"Let's check in with the realtors first," Ceri said. "Hopefully it's early enough that they won't be out showing homes yet."

"See? This is why I keep you around. You're the smart one."

Ceri smacked his arm playfully. "And I keep you around because it's nice being appreciated by a pretty, dumb man."

Drew widened his eyes and looked at her. "You think I'm pretty?"

She scrunched her eyes closed. "Stop that. You aren't allowed to use your magic eyes on me. We're supposed to be friends."

Drew laughed and pulled open the door to Mind Your Manor. "As you wish, my lady."

"Oooh! You're back!" Gabrielle clapped her hands. "I have the perfect listing."

"Gabrielle, you've been to my house," Ceri said. "Can you imagine for an instant that I would ever want to leave? Besides, Drew's thrown me over for another."

Gabrielle sighed heavily in mock disappointment. "I heard he was seen dropping off a certain William Walters this morning at an ungodly hour. Word on the street is the two most eligible bachelors in town may have rekindled their romance."

Drew rolled his eyes. "It was four-thirty in the morning. Who on earth was up that early?"

"It sounds like something Martha would've done," Ceri said. "Who else is that much of a busy-body?"

Gabrielle shrugged. "You'll have to ask Bryan where he heard it from. He was bursting with the juicy gossip when I got in this morning. Truth be told, I think he's heartbroken. He was hitting up Caffiend Dreams several times a day for the last few months, and I don't think it was the pastries luring him in."

Drew squashed down a weird and unwelcome pang of jealousy and plastered a grin on his face. "I guess it's lucky for me he didn't make a move sooner."

"She's teasing you," a voice boomed from one of the offices off the main room. Bryan walked out and immediately overwhelmed everyone else with his presence. He was six and a half feet tall with the shoulders of a linebacker and skin the color of ebony. "Gabrielle knows I'm seeing someone, and she knows that someone isn't Bill."

Gabrielle shook her head. "I have been trying to figure out who, so I like to throw out random guesses and hope that something sticks. You'd think my brother of all people would be a little more sensitive to my pathological curiosity. He loves gossip as much as I do."

"Not when it's about me," Bryan teased.

"But when it's about me, it's fair game?" Drew asked. This time his smile was sincere.

"The whole town has been rooting for you guys from the moment you broke up," Bryan protested. "Of course I'm passing on the happy news as soon as I hear it."

"Who told you?" Ceri asked.

"Antonia," he replied. "I stopped in for some tea this morning before work."

"It doesn't matter," Drew muttered. "It's just harmless gossip."

Ceri shrugged. "Just curious. I've lived here for a few years now, but the way small town news spreads still baffles me."

"Speaking of small-town things," Drew segued, "Did you guys get a holiday basket or two?"

"We didn't get ours until yesterday," Ceri said. "We're out on a jealousy tour to see if your baskets were better than ours."

Gabrielle laughed. "Yeah, we each got one. I'm on the City Council, so it wasn't a surprise. They were identical as far as I know. We didn't compare baskets, and I didn't put them together. Some gift certificates to local businesses. Cheese and soap from Joseph, baked goods from Bill, wine from Adriana."

"Who delivered them?" Drew asked.

"I don't know," Gabrielle said. "It could've been any of the council members, I suppose. Adriana and Martha were heading up the basket giveaway, though. They were delivered while I was out with a client and Bryan was in the conference room with new potential clients. We've been ridiculously busy lately. I've never been this booked after Christmas. I'm running out of houses to sell. Unless Drew sells his and moves in with Bill. That'd be convenient. For everyone."

"We just started dating again," Drew said. "Slow down! I promise that if I sell my house, you'll be the first person I talk to."

"Of course I will. Now, I hate to kick you guys out, but I have a client coming in ten minutes."

"See you around," Drew said. "Bryan, are you gonna be at the next BGMN?"

"Like you could keep me away," he answered. "See you then."

Drew and Ceri walked out of the Realty office and towards To A Tea. "Still doing big gay movie nights?" Ceri asked.

"Yeah. It'll be nice not to have to coordinate with Bill while not actually speaking to each other, so we don't both show up. There's not really a secondary gay scene in Oracle Bay."

Ceri laughed. "I'm surprised there's a primary one, honestly. In a town this size?"

"Location, babe," Drew drawled. "We really like this laid-back coastal vibe. Great place for us older folks to retire."

Ceri shook her head and pushed open the door to To a Tea. A bell tinkled softly over their heads.

"I'll be right with you!" Antonia's voice floated towards them.

"She has more cats," Ceri said, pointing at the scene created around an antique tea set in the display window. Drew walked over. Instead of the two playful kittens that looked exactly like his mystery cats, there were a dozen. Half were perfect miniatures of Hercule Purrot and the other six were exact copies of Tuppence Beresfurred.

"They keep appearing!" Antonia said. "I don't know who's leaving them for me, but I do like to find them. They give an old lady little bursts of joy. It's almost like they're magical."

"We just wanted to ask about your holiday basket," Ceri said. "Did it arrive okay?"

"Oh, it did. The wine was wonderful—not that I'd expect anything else from Adriana. Although that young man of yours, Drew, what was his name?"

"Dio," Drew said through a tight smile.

"That's right. He certainly knew how to find a good vintage, didn't he? I found myself more mellow than I'd expected more than once when he was around."

"Do you remember who delivered the basket?" Drew asked.

"I don't. It appeared on the counter one morning. I was working in the back and didn't hear the bell. Does it matter? Is there something wrong with them?"

"Oh no," Ceri said. "We were just curious. It might've been Martha, and with everything that happened…"

"Yes, terrible shame, isn't it," Antonia said. "And two murders in as many weeks? Makes you wonder what's going on in the big world that it's slipping into our sleepy town. Although, if you were going to ask me which two folks would get themselves bumped off, those two would have been at the top of the list. Ryan ran a good store, but he wasn't brimming over with charm, now, was he? And Martha..." Antonia clicked her tongue against the roof of her mouth. "She was a kind soul deep down. Possibly. But she sure did enjoy putting her nose in everyone's business. If you were in your own room in the dark of night with the curtains drawn and you sneezed, she would be telling folks about your pneumonia the next morning. It was almost surprising that the nice bit of gossip about you and your young man didn't come from beyond the grave."

"Who did you hear that from?" Drew asked.

"Adriana, of all people," Antonia said. "And a proper surprise that was. She's never been much of a gossip, mostly because I didn't think she was interested in anyone but herself. But perhaps the mantle of town gossip needs a person to rest on. She and Martha were quite good friends. It makes sense she'd take up her companion's life work."

Drew was struggling not to laugh. Antonia looked like a prim and proper old woman, but she was brimming with snark. "Thank you so much for your time," he said, grinning at her. "A conversation with you is always a delight."

"Go on with you then. You don't need to butter up this old woman. Save your charms for your boyfriend."

Ceri hugged Antonia gently. "Take care. I'll be back for tea later this week."

· · * * ★ ★ ★ ★ ★ * * · ·

Ceri and Drew stood in front of Covington Wine Shoppe.

"I don't want to go in," Ceri said.

"At least she likes you," Drew said. "She's still mad at me for liking prosecco she didn't have in the shop."

"That doesn't make sense," Ceri protested.

"Ask Sandy how it went down sometime," Drew said.

"I believe you. It just doesn't make sense." Ceri opened the door and walked into the shop.

"How'd your dinner go?" Adriana asked. "Were the wines good?"

"Alas! The dinner was postponed, but I'll let you know as soon as I get feedback."

"Hmmph," Adriana said. "Do you need more wine?" She still hadn't spoken to Drew.

"Not today. I just had a question about the holiday baskets."

"What about them?" Adriana asked. "That was weeks ago."

"Well, a few of us only received ours yesterday. And we were curious, since you and Martha headed up the basket committee, if there was something going on with that. For the most part, the people who got their baskets late were those of us who work in the fortune telling shops in town, and for some reason a couple bartenders."

Adriana ducked her head down and sniffled dryly. "When I went over to Martha's to help get things in order, I found those baskets undelivered. She'd volunteered to deliver everyone's. I didn't want anyone to be left out, so I delivered them to everyone who hadn't received one. My most sincere apologies. It's too bad Ms. Greene didn't feel it was necessary to announce she hadn't received hers. We could've found and corrected this problem sooner had she spoken up." Her head came back up and she dashed her hands against her eyes as if to wipe away tears. "But now you have your baskets, so all's well that ends well, yes? Have you had a chance to enjoy your treats? The wine is special. I made it myself."

"Say, did your capper ever reappear?" Ceri asked. "My stuff did, and so did Drew's and a few other people's. In fact, everyone I know that had something go missing had it returned. I was hoping you did as well."

Adriana looked back and forth between the two of them long enough to make the silence awkward. She tilted her head back and forth as if weighing different options. "It did," she finally said. "I will be able to resume making wines again."

Ceri clapped her hands. "That's wonderful news! And I can't wait to try the ones in the basket. Maybe the murders will be solved soon, and we can all toast to justice!"

"To justice," Adriana said. She swallowed noisily and cleared her throat. "I don't want to keep you from your walk. Stop back in when you need some wine for one of your meetings! And let me know how you like the wine I made."

"We will," Drew said, leading the way out of the shop. They walked to the middle of the boardwalk and looked around to make sure no one was near.

"Something's up with her," Drew said.

"Definitely. She makes my spidey sense tingle," Ceri agreed. "She's sketchy, but I don't know how or why."

"We need to keep an eye on her. She knows a lot more than she's saying, and I think she had something to do with Martha's death."

"Ugh. Agreed. But hunches are not enough," Ceri said.

"Wanna try a couple readings?" Drew suggested. "Maybe we can call Misty, too."

"We could steal her corpse from the morgue and see if Paska can do something with her bones," Ceri suggested.

"I don't think that should be our first go-to," Drew said. "Becoming body thieves is more of a last resort activity."

"Spoil sport," Ceri said. "But if you insist. Let's go scry."

· · · · ★ ★ ★ ★ · · ·

"That was a colossal waste of time," Drew grumbled. "Maybe we *will* have to snatch Martha."

"But why didn't it work?" Ceri asked, sipping a porter in her booth at the Pour House. "I thought Dio's veil was lifted when we got our stuff back."

"Unless..." Drew said, jaw clenching. "He's back in town?"

"He promised he'd leave," Ceri protested. "Didn't he?"

Drew thought back to his last conversation with Dio. "He did.

But he didn't say when he was going to leave, and I left it open-ended."

"That'll teach you," Ceri muttered. "He left just long enough for us to regain our confidence and then came rolling back into town."

"No one's drinking wine, though," Drew said. "I haven't seen anyone having wine today. Even Adriana's was completely empty."

"We need to find him and ask him to be a little firmer about his exit strategy. His immediate exit strategy. It's weird not being able to scry."

"Hey y'all," Misty said from the end of the table.

Drew and Ceri both jumped.

"I wanted to introduce you to Leslie Grace. They're in town looking at Title Wave and the adjacent empty space."

Drew and Ceri reached out their hands and shook Leslie's in turn. Leslie was white, in their mid-forties, and tall—maybe a smidge over six feet. Their hair was neon green with a fantastic undercut, horn-rimmed glasses framed hazel eyes, and a wide smile that radiated joy and authenticity pulled the whole look together.

"What happens to Ryan's inventory and business?" Ceri asked. "It only now occurred to me that since he died before selling his business, the lease of the space wouldn't necessarily include those things."

Drew held out his hand. "It's nice to meet you Leslie. You can ignore Ceri's questions." Ceri stuck out her tongue at him and Drew grinned. "What are your thoughts on Oracle Bay so far?"

"It's a pleasure to meet you both," Leslie said. "Oracle Bay is a charming town. Very diverse for such a small, out-of-the-way place, isn't it?"

"It's not bad at all," Drew said. "Where have you been living?"

"Portland for the last few years," Leslie said.

"Do you mind if we join you?" Misty asked. "I'm trying very hard to lure Leslie into our town so they feel like they can never leave. Figuratively of course. We hardly ever tie people up and keep them here by force."

"It's been what, four years or so since we've had to resort to that?" Ceri asked, picking her beer up again.

Leslie grinned. "If the rest of the town is anything like the folks I've met so far, I think I'm going to like it here. Great views, lots of puns, and a wide range of characters."

"Oh, there are a lot of characters here, all right," Andy said, putting two beers down in front of Leslie and Misty. "You're in the company of some of the most...characteristic."

"I'm not sure that makes sense," Misty said.

"Mmm... The beer is wonderful as well!" Leslie said.

"Thank you," Andy said. "This is my place."

Leslie turned the glass around and looked at the logo. "Devilishly good brews?"

Andy winked. "It's all true." He looked at Ceri, but she looked down at her drink and avoided his gaze.

"What kind of plans do you have for Title Wave and the empty storefront?" Drew asked as Andy walked away, shoulders slumped.

"I am hoping to make a deal with Ryan's estate to keep the inventory and business name," Leslie said, leaning forward and leaning their arms on the table. "As for the other side, I'm still debating. I have two ideas that are vastly different but oddly not present in Oracle Bay. The first is an upscale cocktail lounge. Oracle Bay has a brewery and a restaurant and bar in the hotel, but not a place to dress up, drink fancy shmancy drinks, and avoid small children."

Misty clapped her hands. "I want this so badly. I even have a name for it. Olive or Twist. It'd be perfect next to the bookstore. And there could be literature-themed cocktails."

"Like what?" Drew asked.

Misty huffed. "I'm not a mixologist. I'm an ideas person."

Leslie laughed. "I like it. There are definitely some punny drink names out there. The other idea is a tattoo shop. I can't believe a place like this doesn't have one."

"I just rented out one of my Main Street properties to a tattoo artist. She's been working on the interior and staying well out of sight for the last couple months, but she's planning on opening in March." Misty sighed. "Imagine Joseph all inked up."

"Is there a punny name already picked out for that one?" Leslie asked.

"It's a secret," Misty said. "I don't even know yet."

"Well, there goes that idea," Leslie laughed. "I guess it's punny literary cocktails for everyone."

"Will you run the bar and the bookstore?" Ceri asked.

"No. A close friend of mine is an amazing business person and bartender, though, and if I can convince her to move here, it would be perfect. I'll obviously need to hire a couple more people to help out with both businesses. Right now, it's all dependent on whether the former proprietor's family is interested in cooperating." Leslie tented their fingers, a move that exuded a combination of gleeful anticipation and mischief. "I'm waiting to hear back from their lawyer. I don't want to push too hard on this, they just suffered an unthinkable tragedy, but I was on my way to meet with him before everything happened."

Ceri kicked Drew under the table. When he glanced at her, she had widened her eyes and was winking—poorly—at him. Drew shrugged. He had no idea what she was getting at and wasn't sure he wanted to know. He wanted to ask Misty if her gift was muffled again but didn't know how to in front of Leslie. Drew thought about ways to subtly suggest to Leslie that they needed to go to the bathroom or check out the view or grab a Connect Four game board from the shelf in the back of the room, but before he came up with something remotely reasonable, the front doors swung open with such force that they made an audible thunk against the walls.

A large, white man, closer to seven feet than six, stood in the doorway in jeans, Doc Martens, and an open denim vest holding a large cardboard box.

"That is a lot of look," Leslie said.

"I am looking for Zeke," he said. "I have a delivery for him.

Zeke came out from behind the counter, wiping his hands on a bar towel. "I'm Zeke."

The man set down the box, pulled open the top, and pulled out a basket. "Here's your holiday basket. Sorry it's late." He thrust the basket towards Zeke then reached into his back pocket and pulled out a phone. He shoved that in Zeke's face. "Sign here."

Zeke finger-signed, and the man backed out of the bar, pulled the doors shut behind him. The box was still on the floor. Zeke looked around, dropped the basket back in the box, and carried it behind the counter and out of sight.

"Well, isn't that interesting," Drew said.

"What was that?" Leslie asked.

Misty pasted a smile on her face. "This year, the city council gave gift baskets to all the local business owners as a thank you for their service to the town. Most of them went out a couple weeks ago, but the deliveries were...disrupted, and a few people got theirs this week. I'm not sure why Zeke was on the list; he doesn't own the place. But the baskets are full of items from other business owners. It was meant to be the beginning of a fun holiday tradition."

"I like it," Leslie said. "The only way you could sell me harder on this town is to tell me that there's karaoke at the brewery every weekend."

"Unfortunately, no," Misty laughed. "Although my boyfriend would be over the moon if that happened. He's a karaoke fiend."

Leslie drained the rest of their beer. "I have a lot to think about. And a little bit of waiting. If you don't mind, I'll see myself back to the hotel and give you a call tomorrow."

"That sounds great." Misty stood up, proffered her hand, and watched Leslie leave the bar. "I like them," she said.

fourteen

Drew sat on the living room floor and waved the long feathery wand back and forth while Hercule and Tuppence growled at it and attempted to make it pay for its crimes. After a while, they got bored and started a game of hop and pounce with each other and occasionally Drew's feet.

Tuppence mewed loudly and ran to the bathroom door. "Your stuff isn't in there anymore, silly. What do you want?"

The black cat jumped up and hit the door handle. The door swung open while Drew stared, jaw unhinged.

"How? That's not possible." He got out his phone, closed the door, and hit record. "Do it again."

Tuppence ran over to Drew and twined around his ankles, purring madly. Hercule stalked into the kitchen, followed by a small entourage of one kitten and one man. The chimera cat jumped onto the window sill, and before Drew could shoo him down, the kitten put his head under the window handle and stood up. The window opened smoothly, and Drew had it all on tape.

He stopped recording and sent the video to Misty with a terse message. *"They can open doors, too. Are your skills still online? I need help, and you know the most about weird animals."*

Her reply came moments later. *"Not sure dating a guy with a goddess-possessed goat qualifies me as an expert. I haven't tried to read anyone since the test. Why do you ask?"*

"Ceri and I couldn't see anything today. Meant to ask earlier and got sidetracked."

"I'll give it a shot. Is Dio back?"

"I don't know. No wine is appearing, but also psychic fog. Shrug." Drew shrugged his actual shoulders as he hit send.

"I'm gonna ignore that you typed 'shrug.' Now about those creepy cats... Do you want J and me to come over, or can you bring the cats here?" Misty sent two cat emojis, several goat emojis, and, for some reason, a clown face.

"Why there?"

"My number one idea is tossing them in with the latest kids to see if the divine parentage in them recognizes anything in your little monsters."

"Do you think that will work?" Drew eyed the phone with skepticism, hoping his expression penetrated cellular space and smacked Misty in the face.

"I'm flying blind here. I have no idea. I'll try to read them. But I don't know if that's possible. Or if anything's possible."

"I'll scoop them up and drive over." It was better than his ideas, that was for sure.

"Heads up. Bill's here."

Drew leaned back and regarded the last message with mixed feelings. On one hand, they'd only gotten back together over the last few days. Bill didn't owe him anything. On the other hand, he'd been hoping—no, expecting—Bill to show up or call or something any minute. That he'd skipped getting in touch and gone straight to his best friend's house caused a pang that Drew didn't want to identify; one that he was a little ashamed of. Maybe they had a standing weekly hangout. This didn't mean Bill was there to complain about or mock Drew in any way.

"Cool." He typed back, even though that was the furthest from what he felt. "C'mon kittens, we're going for a ride!"

He found the cat carrier he'd bought at Live Long and Pawspurr, opened the door, and watched as both cats barreled in, nearly tripping over each other. Drew latched the door behind them, filled a bag with supplies, and headed out to Joseph's.

* * * ★ ★ ★ ★ ★ ★ ★ * * *

Misty was waiting in the driveway when he pulled up. "Let's head into the barn first," she said. "Joseph is separating the kids from the does, so there are fewer goats to keep an eye on when you let your kittens loose."

Drew didn't know what to say. Every time he got used to the new normal of Oracle Bay, things found a way to get a little bit weirder.

He followed her into the barn, not even considering who might be there with Joseph. Once he saw Bill helping Joseph herd the kids into the central area of the barn and away from their mamas, he froze, cat carrier in hand, and stared, caught in Bill's eyes. Bill looked good. He had that quintessential sexy dad bod, ruddy, tanned skin, and dark, tousled hair that Drew had dreamed about in the years they were apart. Seeing him here, in blue jeans and a button-down flannel shirt that Bill only wore when he knew no one would see him —"I don't want people to think hipster when they think of me, regardless of how comfortable and how true the label is," ignited fires that had been banked for three years, except only the night Bill had spent at his place. Flames had been fanned, but nothing more. It'd been the most chaste bed-sharing situation Drew'd spent with another man since...a while. It hadn't felt weird at the time. It was late. They'd both been tired. Bill had to get up insanely early the next morning. And there'd been smooches. But now Drew was second guessing everything.

Bill strode forward, still holding Drew's gaze. He placed his hands on Drew's shoulders. "I'm so glad you're here," he said. "I've missed you." He bent down and captured Drew's lips in a searing kiss. Drew felt his knees start to buckle and wrapped his arms around Bill's torso to hold himself up.

"You missed me?" Drew asked, hating how much hesitation he could hear in his voice but not being able to stop himself.

"Of course, you ridiculous man," Bill said. "I've missed you for years. But everything's intensified now. I thought it'd be easier to be apart once we were together, but it's harder now, because I know that instead of a pipe dream, being in your arms is a real possibility."

"Oh," Drew managed. "Um. Well. I've always been so confident, but you make me feel vulnerable."

"I think that's what love is," Bill said. "Finding the person with whom you feel safe being vulnerable with."

"Can confirm," Misty said.

Drew felt his cheeks start to heat up and took a step back. He'd forgotten about their audience and the reason for his visit.

"We have years," Bill reminded him in a whisper. "And hopefully, if I play my cards right, we'll have tonight."

"Ahhhh," Drew said, looking at Misty and blushing furiously.

"We weren't that bad when we first got together, were we?" she asked Joseph, who was standing behind her holding one of the kids.

"Of course not," Joseph scoffed, as Bill and Drew said in unison, "You definitely were."

"I like it," Misty said. "You two making eyes and lips at each other is so much better than where you were the last few years. I have no complaints. As long as you don't get carried away and start stripping down in the barn, that is. It's cold and dirty in here."

"I promise," Drew said. He checked behind him to make sure the barn door was closed, then opened the cat carrier. "What do you think might happen?"

"I honestly have no idea," Misty said. "But a lot of these kids are either children or grandchildren of a goddess, so I thought they might recognize your kittens if they have anything divine going on.

"How?" Bill asked. "I mean, how will you know if the divine in the goats recognizes the divine in the kittens?"

Misty bit her lip and looked over her shoulder at Joseph. "Ummm...I was hoping it would just be...obvious. Contrary to popular belief, I am not an expert in occult animals. I merely fell in love with someone who had a magical goat."

Drew shrugged and opened the door to the carrier. It's not like the goats were going to harm Hercule and Tuppence. The worst that could happen is everyone got scared and ran to separate corners.

The kittens strolled out of the carrier, sniffed each other, the floor, Drew's ankles, Bill's shoes, and then sat down between the two men and began cleaning themselves in earnest.

"This is ridiculous," Drew groaned. "An entirely new space, full of new, very different smells, and the first priority is to bathe?"

"Cats are weird," Joseph observed.

The four humans and eight kids watched the two kittens groom themselves, then each other. Finally, satisfied with the smoothness of their fur and cleanliness of their backsides, Tuppence and Hercule set out to explore. They started from near the door—and away from everyone else—and made their way to the center of the room. Tuppence was particularly enamored with Joseph's boots; she draped herself over one foot and began purring enthusiastically.

"I hate to say it," Misty said, "but these seem like run-of-the-mill ordinary cats to me."

No sooner were the words out of her mouth when Tuppence unentangled herself from Joseph's boot and joined Hercule in inspecting the first kid.

The tiny noses of the cats gently booped the much larger nose of the baby goat, and all three animals took large leaps back.

"Mew?" Tuppence looked at Drew.

"Do they smell familiar?" Drew asked. "Like fellow goddesses or whatever?"

"Mew," Tuppence replied, charging forward, twining herself

under the goat's body, then climbing the kid and perching between its shoulder blades. "Mew!" she cried.

"I think my kitten just conquered your kid," Drew said.

"I can't argue with that," Joseph said. "I have barn cats, of course. So the goats are used to feline presence, but I've never seen anything like this."

"What do you think, Misty?" Drew asked.

"I can't tell the difference between magic cats and regular, impertinent cats," she admitted. "I thought there'd be more. I can't tell you what more, but more… Your video was damning."

"Damning or divine?" The woman's voice echoed through the barn. A shape took form in the center of the barn between the kid who was being tamed by Tuppence and the humans present. The shape slowly solidified into a translucent woman with olive skin, long dark hair, thick eyebrows peering out over dark brown eyes, and a thick and shapely body. The mother goddess of the Etruscans, even in a non-solid state, exuded calm and comfort and quiet wisdom.

"Uni," Joseph said, reverence coloring his tone. "I didn't think to see you again, especially so soon."

"My base of worshippers is here," she said. "I find it difficult to stay away."

"You have a worship base here?" Misty asked. "That was fast."

"Your partner, and many of your compatriots, worship me as a goddess. They don't yet make offerings, but they believe, and that is more than I've had in millennia."

"Huh," Misty said. "I never thought of it like that. I wonder why gods don't manifest more frequently to drum up belief."

"Likely because it's difficult to manifest, and most people don't believe without proof—also difficult. Our situation was unique. And whether they worship me in the old ways or not, there are a lot of believers now," Uni explained.

"So what about the kittens?" Drew interrupted. He'd been spiritually unyoked since he'd left his parents' home in his late teens and wasn't interested in talking about belief. "Are they normal?"

"Oh no, decidedly not," Uni declared. "But then again, what cats are?"

Drew huffed. "That isn't very helpful."

The goddess grinned. "They are not typical of the cats most people get in cat shops. These have a spark of something divine. They aren't what I was, but they have…gifts."

She smiled, stroked Joseph's arm, and disappeared.

"Well, that was almost enlightening," Misty said. "Your cats aren't goddesses in disguise, but they aren't normal either. Don't you feel like you've learned a lot?"

"Sure. A lot of nothing," Drew said. Hercule rubbed against his ankle, so Drew picked the cat up. "I'm glad they're not gods, but I wish I knew what gifts they had, beyond opening doors and windows they shouldn't."

"I wonder where they came from," Misty said. "Who would've given you kittens? Especially vaguely magical kittens."

"Dio," Bill said. "It was right when he was making his presence known. He'd have access to magic cats. And he probably knew how much Drew liked the idea of cats if not the actuality of pet ownership."

"What do you mean?" Drew asked.

"You talk about cats a lot," Bill said. "You show people cat videos. Your Twitter timeline is ninety percent cats, as is your Facebook. You think they're adorable. I know that you think you're not home enough to take care of them, and that you don't believe you'd be a good pet owner, but anyone who you were in a superficial relationship with would one hundred percent think you were sending out a constant plea to the universe for kittens. And maybe Dio was right. You do seem into this. Maybe I should've gotten you a cat instead of believing you when you said you didn't have the time or the energy."

Drew took Bill's hand. "Thanks for listening to me. I didn't want pets. I can't deny I adore these tiny miscreants, but this is not what I wanted. But you're right, I do have a cat video problem. It's not my fault that's why the internet was invented…"

"I thought the internet was for porn," Joseph said.

"That's use number two," Misty said. "Right after cats."

"Thank you guys," Drew said. "I guess I'll take them home. Unless..."

"I'll touch one of your cats," Misty said. She pulled off a glove and handed it to Joseph. "Give me a kitten."

Drew handed Hercule over, and Misty stroked him with her bare hand. "Either there's nothing, or the mist really is back for us all. Do me a favor, Drew. If you find Dio, kick his ass for me. He's really messing with my mojo."

"Scout's honor," Drew said. He loaded the cats back into the carrier, hugged Misty, and headed outside.

Bill followed him. "I don't have to open in the morning," he said. "Any chance I could crash at your place tonight?"

Drew pretended to think about it. "I think I have a spare room you could use."

"That's all I'm asking," Bill said. "Well, that and a few kisses."

Drew felt the grin pull up the corner of his lips. "Arrangements can be made. I'm sure of it."

Drew inhaled deeply through his nose, drawing the rich scent of brewing coffee into his nostrils. He kept his eyes closed, and a small smile danced on his lips. He'd missed this. No matter how late they'd stayed up, Bill was always awake at the crack of dawn. And if Bill was awake, that meant there'd be coffee and breakfast waiting for him downstairs.

He allowed himself to bask in the feelings of familiar comfort and love a little longer, before bounding out of bed and heading downstairs. Bill was at the kitchen counter, back towards the doorway. Two small kittens were doing their best to trip him up as he walked between the counter and the oven. Bill was clad only in a pair of boxers and an apron—another remnant of their previous life together.

Drew licked his lips and tried not to drool.

"See anything you like?" Bill asked, back still facing Drew.

"Oh yeah," Drew said. "There's definitely something here I like."

Bill turned around. He was holding a large, steaming cup of coffee and a plate with eggs Benedict, sausage links, and fried potatoes.

"Stop!" Drew said. "Don't move. This—I just need to drink it all in. My favorite breakfast foods, a large cup of coffee, and you...I'm not sure it gets better than this."

Bill laughed and set down the plate and cup. "Dig in. I'll join you in a minute."

Drew sat and grabbed the coffee. "This smells amazing."

"Eat!" Bill said. "You don't want it to get cold."

"If it does, I'll just hold the plate up to you and your hotness can warm it up again."

"You're ridiculous," Bill said, grinning.

"I blame you. I'm never ridiculous unless you're around. You're a bad influence."

"If I remember last night correctly, I think you were the bad influence. I was an innocent angel," Bill reminded him.

Drew laughed and tried to hide the blush that was threatening to spread up his neck and spill onto cheeks. He flicked his napkin at Bill. "Stop it. You're embarrassing me."

"Man as old as you? I would've thought you'd be nearly impossible to embarrass. You must have seen things."

Drew might have imagined the barest hint of bitterness flavoring Bill's teasing words, but he knew enough to not give it room to fester. He reached out and rested a hand on Bill's arm. "I have seen things. I've had many relationships, several serious."

Bill started to pull away and Drew grabbed his fingers and held on.

"Every relationship ended. The longest lasted fifteen years. I ended some, but more were ended by my partner. And I can tell you, that each relationship ended because I wasn't forthcoming enough about my past, or they believed I was making fun of them by pretending to have real powers, or I wouldn't reveal the reasons I never aged. The first thing I did every time was pick up the scraps of my broken heart— fewer scraps every time—and get the hell out of Dodge. I never stuck around. I didn't bide my time and hope that things would change. I never waited for anyone, no matter how much they meant to me.

"Oracle Bay may be home to me, one of the most powerful seats of oracular energy I've ever encountered, but I wouldn't have stayed for anyone else but you. I'll tell you anything you want to know about my past, but it won't change the truth about the present. You're the only man I've waited for; the only man I've hoped for. You're the love of my very long life, William Walters."

Bill pulled his hand out of Drew's, stood up, and pulled Drew up in front of him. He wrapped his arms around Drew's waist and hid his face against Drew's neck.

Drew ran his fingers through Bill's hair.

"I'm sorry," Bill said, voice choked with emotion. "I'm sorry I doubted you. Doubted us. You've always seemed too good to be true, and even when we were together before, I always assumed you had one foot out the door. It was almost a relief that you were so crazy and insisting that you be taken seriously as a crystal ball reader. It made it easy to use it as an excuse to walk away on my terms, before you inevitably broke my heart."

"That really sucks," Drew said.

"I'm a runner," Bill said, shrugging. "I don't trust anyone and believe that all good things come to an end sooner rather than later and usually in the most painful way imaginable. I'm working on it. My therapist is a very patient person."

Drew reached down and grasped Bill's shoulders. "Let's have breakfast. You were the one who didn't want it to get cold."

Bill sat down, surreptitiously wiping his eyes. "Thank you."

"For what?" Drew asked, spearing a bite of potato.

"For listening. For forgiving me. For wanting me."

"Promise me you won't run again. At least not without talking to me. Or your therapist." Drew tried to inject a teasing tone but fell short of the mark.

"I promise. I think you might be stuck with me for good," Bill said. He was more successful with this attempt at light-hearted banter.

"It is good," Drew said. "You promised me the next fifty years and I intend to collect on that. There's no backing out now." He pointed a finger towards Bill then leaned forward far enough to poke him in the chest.

"I don't think I could now," Bill said, suddenly serious again. "It was hard enough before when I honestly believed you were a little bit crazy and a whole lot lying to me. Now that I know the truth? What's there to walk away from?"

Drew pushed his plate back and stood up. "Come here."

Bill stood and walked into Drew's outstretched arms. Drew's arms twined around Bill's neck and Bill pulled him even closer until there was no space between them.

"Bill, you know I love you, right?" Drew asked, pulling back and tilting his head to look into the taller man's bottomless brown eyes.

"I do now. I love you, too, Drew Hardy. Or should I say, Solomon Paine?"

Drew laughed, pressed a kiss to Bill's lips, and said, "I'd rather you not say that name again. Legally speaking, I'm Andrew Hardy and have been for the last thirty years. I've had a lot of names over the years, but this is the combo I'm most comfortable with."

"I can't promise to never call you Solomon again, but I can at least swear not to mention it in mixed company. Do any of your friends know it? I'd like to know who I can team up with to tease you."

"Nobody alive today knows it. Well, as far as I'm aware. I do hang out with a bunch of psychics and seers. It's impossible to guess what they've picked up."

"I'll stick to Drew then."

"You'd better stick to me, 'cause I'm pretty stuck on you."

Bill rolled his eyes. "Did you have anything you needed to do this morning?"

"I'm meeting Ceri for lunch, but nothing until then. Why?"

"I don't think we've really covered the breadth and depth of reacquainting ourselves with each other, and it might be time to try again."

"Far be it from me to block such a worthy endeavor." Drew kissed Bill again, this time with intent, and they were both breathing faster when the kiss broke off.

"Wanna take this upstairs?" Bill asked, untying the apron and tossing it over the nearest chair.

"Absolutely," Drew replied. "After you."

Drew sat at his kitchen table after Bill had gone home to shower and take care of some errands. The gift basket sat in front of him. He hadn't really gone through it. He'd been approaching the gift baskets as a weird coincidence, and not as a clue to the murders in and of themselves. There was something about them—the timing was one thing, but there had to be something else.

He pulled everything out and lined up the items on the table. There was wine with Adriana's personal label on it. There were the cheeses and soaps from Joseph. He tilted his head at the cheese. They looked like what you would buy in the supermarket, complete with price tag. He picked up the phone.

"Hey Joseph, sorry to bother you, but when you donated cheese for the holiday baskets, you did your usual donation presentation, right? Wrapped in paper printed with your logo and tied with brown string?"

"Of course. Why?"

"The cheeses in my gift basket look like they came from the market," Drew explained. "They're wrapped in plastic and have price tags on them. I assumed they were past their best buy date when the basket arrived, so I didn't really even think about pulling them out, but I don't think they were from your original batch."

"I'll see what Misty put in our fridge," Joseph said. There was silence for a few moments, and then Joseph returned to the line. "There are supermarket cheeses in our fridge, too. You all definitely didn't get the specialty stuff I donated. Not that it isn't just as wonderful, of course. Anything else?"

Drew knew better than to take the note of impatience in Joseph's tone personally. He was a busy man and notorious for being grumpy. His relationship with Misty had mellowed him out a bit, but they hadn't been together long enough for him to slip into effusive friendliness. "That was everything. Thanks for your time."

"No problem. Later." Joseph disconnected the call before Drew could say goodbye.

Drew finished going through everything in the basket. Gift certificates to most of the eateries in town, although The Pour House was noticeably absent, a coupon for a fifty percent off your next haircut at Deja 'Do, a buy one get one free coupon for Title Wave, and charcuterie from Natalie Dale. Drew tapped the sausage against the side of the basket and thought about Natalie. He didn't know her well. No one really did. She lived outside of town, had her own slaughterhouse, and was rarely seen in Oracle Bay. It seemed unlikely that she'd arrange to kill two people she probably didn't even know, but he couldn't rule her out.

"You know what's weird," he said to Tuppence who'd hopped up on the table and was enthusiastically sniffing the summer sausage. "That baskets came for all the psychics and Andy at the same time, but Russell and Zeke received theirs later. Received theirs after I talked about them..."

He stood and rushed into the living room and grabbed his laptop. He opened the file with his interview notes from the last few days and scrolled down until he found what he was looking for.

Martha announced that Ryan's death was a murder and said she knew because she listened.

She tapped her ear. "I have ways to listen."

I asked if she'd bugged the police station and she got very excited and said I'd guessed her secret and that she'd been listening for years.

"Just to the cops?" Ceri asked.

"Oh no. I listen to everyone." Martha quickly qualified that by saying, "Only the cops and people I don't like."

Drew carried his laptop back to the kitchen and looked at the items in the basket. He knew there was something there he was missing but couldn't quite put his finger on it. In the meantime, he could go ask Adriana if she'd known about Martha's eavesdropping ways.

He sent a text to Ceri, letting her know where he was headed and why, grabbed his jacket, and took off.

DREW WALKED INTO COVINGTON WINE SHOPPE AND LOOKED AROUND. IT was completely empty. He thought about announcing himself when he heard raised voices from the back of the store. He walked towards the counter, grabbing a bottle of Champagne and setting it down. Then Drew leaned against the counter and prepared to eavesdrop.

"You need to get out of town before something happens to you, too!" Adriana yelled.

Drew raised his eyebrows. Was it concern or a threat? He had the hardest time reading that woman.

The reply was muffled enough Drew couldn't hear it.

"Well don't say I didn't warn you. You've been nothing but trouble. I can't prove it's your fault my sales have dropped, but I see you, interfering. It won't be my fault if you end up like Ryan and Martha."

Threat. Definitely a threat.

Drew shifted his feet slightly and his toe brushed up against something. There was a white triangle sticking out from under the counter. He bent down and yanked it; a note book with lined pages full of tiny script appeared. Footsteps echoed, so he shoved it in an inside jacket pocket without looking at it, then pushed his earbuds in his ears and looked at his phone.

"Oh. It's you," Adriana's disgruntled voice interrupted his audiobook.

Drew pulled out his earbuds and stowed them in his pocket next to the purloined notebook. "Hey, Adriana. I need a bottle of champagne. Is this one pretty good? I grabbed it at random, but you'd know better than I would. I'm celebrating and want something really good and biscuity."

Adriana's disdainful expression dropped away, and she pulled the bottle towards her and put on her glasses. "This one is a fantastic bottle, but I have another that will have better flavor and is at a slightly lower price point. Let me grab it for you."

She presented the other bottle for his inspection. "If you say it's better, I trust you implicitly," Drew said. "I'll take it."

She rang it up, and he presented a card.

"I have what might seem like an odd question," Drew said. "When Ceri and I were in here with you and Martha burst in to let us know Ryan's death was a murder, did Martha actually say she was bugging the police station and everyone else she didn't like?"

Adriana tilted her head to one side. "Huh. I don't remember her saying that. Are you sure you didn't misunderstand?"

"It's such an odd thing to have heard," Drew admitted. "I guess I could've misinterpreted what she meant when she said she was always listening."

"She was an odd one, poor dear," Adriana said. Nothing about her tone indicated she felt anything at all about Martha, much less that she was any sort of dear. "Best not to put too much stock in anything you think you may have heard. It doesn't matter now, anyway, does it? Poor thing was struck down in the prime of life and will never get a chance to eavesdrop on anyone again, if that's even what she was doing."

Drew took his bottle and smiled tightly at Adriana. "Thank you for this. Now that you have your screw topper, will you start doing classes? They'll be a huge hit."

"I'll be announcing the schedule soon. I hope to see you at one of my classes."

"I wouldn't miss it," Drew said. He left while he was still on her good side, if Adriana had one.

He spotted Ceri waiting for him at the end of the block and walked towards her. "Let's go somewhere we can sit," he said. "I found a clue."

"Oooh, very mysterious," she teased. "What is it?"

"I don't know yet," he admitted. "I did learn that Adriana either didn't hear what we did when Martha admitted to bugging the police station and possibly other businesses, or she's lying about it."

They started down the street, but before they'd gone far, movement caught Drew's eye. Someone was coming out of the back room of the wine shop. "Is that Dio?" he asked.

Ceri stopped dead in her tracks and squinted towards the figure. "That's Dio," she confirmed. "Let's get him!" She took off towards him, leaving Drew to back her play. He took a slightly different route towards the god, hoping to trap Dio between the two of them. If it was even possible for two mortals to catch a god who didn't want to be caught.

Dio saw Drew coming for him and backed up a few paces before turning to flee in the opposite direction. He ran smack into Ceri, who dove low at the last minute and took him out at the knees. "Gotcha!" she crowed. She pulled a length of soft nylon cord out of her purse and bound his hands.

"You are exceptionally good at this," Dio said, eying her appreciatively. "I think I've hung my hat on the wrong star."

"You're coming with us," Ceri said. "We have some questions for you."

"Of course," Dio said. "We can talk over wine."

"We are not having wine. We are going to The Pour House where we will have the added security of the proprietor to ensure you don't escape."

"Your fallen angel can't contain a god," Dio laughed.

"I can," Uni said.

All three of them jumped; Drew nearly lost his footing when his jump took him off the curb.

"I decided to stick around and see what happens to those sweet kittens you were so curious about," she said to Drew. "I've been following you."

"Ah," Drew said, unsure of how else to respond to an ancient goddess who was stalking him because she was interested in his cats. "We're going to the Pour House. We'd be honored if you joined us."

The four of them—two gods and two old seers—strode down Main Street and out to the edge of town. Zeke took one look at the company when they walked in and directed them to the back semi-private table that was almost always reserved for the psychics. "I'll get Andy," he said after taking their orders.

"Why are you still here?" Ceri demanded. "You were to leave. Your presence dulls our powers. Most of us cannot work at all now."

"Just wrapping up some loose ends," Dio said. "I've had a business relationship with Ms. Covington for a few years. I need to sever ties and was attempting to end that business relationship. She accused me of undercutting her and withholding inventory."

"You're her wine distributor?" Ceri asked.

He shrugged. "I have a lot of connections. I am only her European distributor."

"When are you leaving?" Drew asked. "I don't care about your business dealings. I care that you're still messing up the businesses of everyone else in town."

Dio's face took on a mournful cast. "I only discovered I had a daughter this week, and now you want me to abandon her?"

"Is she interested in a relationship with you?" Ceri asked.

"How am I to know when she refuses my calls?" Dio threw his arms out dramatically, nearly hitting Uni in the process.

"That is an answer in and of itself," Drew pointed out.

"It's not my fault I wasn't there," Dio protested. "I would've been a better father if I'd known I was one."

"You need to back off," Ceri said. "Start a long-distance correspondence. At some point, Sandy might want more. But not now. You're overwhelming her. It'd be better if you would go."

"Better for her or better for you?" Dio asked.

"Yes," Ceri said, smiling enigmatically.

Drew shook his head while they went back and forth and pulled out his phone to text Bill. "*FYI. At Pour House with Ceri and Dio. Ceri tied him up. Literally. Uni showed, too. See you later?*"

Seconds later, his phone beeped. "*Ugh. Tell him to get out. Dinner my place at 7? Bring your sleepover bag.*"

"*See you at 7. xo.*"

Drew returned his attention to the table in time to catch everyone staring at him, including Andy, who'd joined the group while he was distracted.

"Did you want to ask our captive about your cats?" Uni asked. "He has agreed to go a minimum of one hundred miles away to continue pursuit of a parental relationship with your friend the tarot card reader. Ceri, mistress of mirrors and scrying, is a good negotiator."

Drew shook himself and returned to the matter at hand. "Tell me about the kittens, Dio. Where did they come from and why did you give them to me?"

For the first time since Dio had returned to town, he looked more sheepish than anything else. He shrugged. "I remember you saying you liked cats but had never had your own. I was visiting Loki, and his cat had just had kittens. I think the father was one of Freya's."

"One of Freya's what?" Ceri asked, suspicion lacing her tone. She leaned forward, planted her elbows on the table, and stared Dio down. "Not one of Freya's chariot cats?"

"That's impossible," Drew said. "They'd be huge."

"Size is irrelevant," Dio said, waving his hand negligently and regaining his poise. "Her cats—indeed all cats—are the size they need to be at any given time. And yes, that was the impression I had. Drew's cats were sired by one of Freya's chariot cats and Loki's favorite pet."

"Oh my god," Drew muttered. "This is going to be bad."

"That is why they smelled different but not divine," Uni said, sounding altogether too pleased with herself. "I knew they were special."

"Imagine how much more mischievous than a regular cat they'll be," Andy said. "Their parents were a magical flying cat and the pampered pet of one of Europe's most notorious trickster gods."

Drew groaned and covered his face with his hands.

"Should I return them?" Dio asked. "I'm sure Loki could find another home for them."

"Just promise me they can't fly," Drew said.

"I'm sure Loki would've mentioned it if they could," Dio said, patting Drew's arm. "Don't worry about it."

Drew sat in the living room, too-divine-for-comfort kittens violently playing at his feet with a pair of catnip mice. Every once in a while, their hunting prowess went awry and one or the other snagged one of Drew's feet. He sighed deeply and shook his head at the beasties he'd been given. Obviously, he wasn't going to let Dio take them back. But kitten-proofing was taking on a whole new level —literally.

Drew had two hours before he was to meet Bill for dinner, and impatience was threatening to overwhelm him. He stood, pulled on his jacket, and paced.

He was being ridiculous. He took the jacket back off and slung it over the back of the couch. It made a harder thump than he was expecting, and that's when he remembered the notebook. He dug into the inside pocket and pulled it out. The inside cover bore the inscription, "Property of Martha Larson. Do not read. Top secret." It was written in purple in a loopy handwriting that further reinforced the middle school impressions. He fanned through the notebook—the single-sided entries alternated between purple and pink.

It looked more like a middle school diary than anything in which might be hidden the secrets leading to her death, but Drew shrugged and turned the page. Leave no clue unread! That was his motto. Or might be if he bothered to have one.

The first couple pages made up for the adolescent flavor of the cover. It detailed every bug she'd placed, precisely where they were, and when they'd been placed. There were additional notes for every change or replacement that had happened. The first entry was over five years old, and the most recent entry dated only three weeks earlier. None of the entries were for private residences, but the thought that she'd been so thorough made Drew doubt that any place was truly safe. He shuddered.

She'd listened to everything. Martha Larson had thousands of hours of taped conversations. Her entire life was consumed with knowing every last detail of everyone's lives in Oracle Bay. He read the first few entries closely, needing to know not only what she'd heard but how she'd interpreted it. After that, though, he skimmed, looking for his name or the names of his friends, Ryan, and Adriana. He'd found out too many secrets about the other residents of Oracle Bay. It was none of his business who was sleeping with who, who'd helped their kid cheat their way to a fifth-place finish in the one and only Oracle Bay Soapbox Derby, and who spent a little more money than was prudent on illegal drugs. As long as no one was getting hurt, these petty actions were meaningless.

It was fascinating what went on behind closed doors, but unless Drew wanted to lose himself in others' lives the way Martha had, it was better he stick to what was important. He paged forward, looking for more current events, but stopped when his own name jumped out at him.

It was Martha's recounting of the events leading up to his break-up with Bill. They'd had more arguments at Caffiend Dreams than he remembered. Martha had few kind words for Drew. She'd been on Bill's side—believed he was a delusional crackpot who'd taken a seemingly harmless hobby too far and was now ruining lives and relationships. It was old news, and resolved now, but it still cut him to the quick. That time had been painful enough, but to know that there'd been a witness to the most intimate moments of the implosion of their relationship twisted Drew's stomach in knots and had him hunched over trying to breathe through the pain.

He knew he shouldn't be reading this alone, but he didn't want anyone else to see this, to go through what he was going through. They all had trauma and grief, both public and private. To know that it'd been observed and written about by a woman who was barely more than an acquaintance wasn't something Drew wanted to inflict on anyone else, regardless of how much it might alleviate his own misery.

He flipped faster and faster, skipping huge chunks, looking for entries from the end of the last year. He slowed when he got to her notes about the apocalypse. They were confused, as one would expect. It was at this point she seemed to pick up that Andy was something more than just a brewmaster. There were too many details about what he and Ceri had been up to in his office at the Pour House. And an overall tone and commentary that seemed to imply the "so-called psychics" were running a secret drug cartel and using a lot of code words to get away with it. This was also her explanation for all the strange visitors in town. Martha seemed genuinely concerned at how many people were getting sucked into the web.

And then he found it. The entries from the night of Ryan's death.

Ryan, bless his soul, did his best to give that Mr. Hardy a piece of his mind. Tried to build a connection by saying his shop had been broken into, too. But that Mr. Hardy couldn't find a nice word for the old man and chased him out of his shop. I think I'll go offer a shoulder to Ryan, poor thing. He has enough to worry about, what with his son not wanting him to come live with them. What good are children if they won't take you when you're old?

...

I reviewed the tape of my time with Ryan, hoping there'd be a clue I missed. I've never felt so off in my life. Maybe those psychics put drugs in the wine we drank. It was Adriana's wine, from the basket. I'd delivered the basket myself the day before, and as far as I can tell, none of those druggies visited the bookstore in the meantime. Ryan said his shop hadn't actually been broken into. He just wanted Drew to feel guilty. We drank wine, and it was so good. I've never felt so amazing! But then Ryan poured himself a second glass, and a third, and...you know what happened next. I'll need to erase that tape. I tried to flirt with him! And so ineptly. It's embarrassing.

Drew paged forward and skimmed summaries of his conversations with Dio, Ceri, and Bill, as well as his interviews with the other Main Street business owners.

That Mr. Hardy has been nosing around a great deal. I want to believe he's the murderer, but I can't figure out how he's done it. He's always so smooth and snooty, you just know he's up to no good. And those eyes? How anyone can have such purely beautiful eyes and not be the devil is beyond me. He was surprised, though, when I told him Ryan was murdered. Not as surprised as I was to hear Adriana claim she'd bought the wine topper for classes and then had it stolen. Now that she's asked me to back her up, I will, of course. But she had me order it, then paid me cash for it, because she wanted it for a hobby and didn't want it on her business account.

Wasn't that interesting... That meant no one who wasn't an oracle had been targeted by Dio's pranks. Antonia'd had her tea set moved and replaced with cat figurines, but it hadn't been stolen. It was probably a twisted gesture of affection.

Drew flipped through a few more pages, pushed right past the argument Ceri and Andy had had, and hit the end of Martha's notes. Her last entry detailed Drew's interrogation at the Sleeping Inn.

The cops seem to believe Drew did it, and as much as I wish they were right, I don't think they are. He'd be more clever. And he would've killed me, too, to eliminate any witnesses. Also, if he were a murderer, would he be encouraging the cops to check for fingerprints? I wish I was cleverer. I'm sure I have all the clues here. All the "magic" people who think they're better than us lost items dear to them. Even people I didn't know were in the club, like Russell. It has to be related, right? Ugh. Maybe I should ask Adriana. She doesn't look down on me the way the others do. We're friends, and she is very clever. Plus, she owes me a favor for buying her machine.

The next entry was in a completely different handwriting and eschewed the purple and pink for no-nonsense black.

I don't know why I feel compelled to continue to enter notes. I guess it's useful to ensure I don't forget anything I learn. Martha may not have been particularly brilliant, but she was thorough. How she placed so many bugs so accurately and tracked them through the recording systems is truly astounding. I couldn't let it go, though. Not once I realized what was going on. When she mentioned hearing the police discuss Ryan's murder, I barely believed it. And now that I've seen her setup, I'm even more shocked.

I made a mistake by not sending baskets to the bad element in town. They noticed and have been singled out in other things as well. I will attempt to remedy things. Martha has a list. I don't know why Russell is on it, other than being 'other,' but perhaps he will feel included.

...

I've learned more, both from Martha's notes and my own auditory research. This psychics club seems to take themselves more seriously than they ought. And they count Zeke and Andy among their numbers, in addition to Russell. I'll send Zeke a basket as well and hope the baskets do their job and throw suspicion on Dio. He is a brilliant contact for my wines, but his pranks have gone too far and draw unnecessary attention to me. I need to get him out of town. I don't think I can get him to have a glass of wine. I'm beginning to lose hope that any of these ridiculous psychics will open one of my special bottles. They are destroying the dignity of this town. How can we ever be taken seriously as long as they are here with their pseudo-

science and puns? I am willing to forgive the other members of the town. Surely, once they see that silliness is dead in Oracle Bay, they can be convinced to rename their stores to something more fitting an upscale coastal tourist destination.

Bah! I am writing here like it's a diary and not using it for the cause it was intended. It is poor practice to write down one's plans and innermost thoughts. I will go back to monitoring the tapes and listening for sirens, letting me know I've succeeded. And I will also burn these last pages.

And that's where it ended. Drew wasn't sure what Adriana was hoping would happen when they drank the wine, but it didn't seem a good idea to find out. He pulled out his phone and called Ceri.

"Why are you calling me?" she asked. "Text is best."

"I needed to make sure everyone got the message. Do not drink the wine in the holiday gift basket. There's something wrong with it. Can you call Paska, Morgana, Andy and Zeke? I'll call Sandy, Misty, Jezebel, and Russell. And you, of course."

"Everyone's in town? Or just the late deliveries?"

"I think the late deliveries. And Ryan. I wanna get the notebook to the cops, but I don't want to go to the station and have to talk about everything while Adriana is listening. It'll give her time to cover-up further or get out of town. Besides, I don't know how long it'll take for them to act."

"Let's connect tomorrow. There's still something bothering me about this case," Ceri said. "But now, let's activate the phone tree."

Drew hung up and made the rest of his calls. No one had touched the wine—still wined out from Dio's extended stay—and now, no one would.

Drew breathed a sigh of relief and checked his watch. The last two hours had passed swiftly, and now he'd be hard-pressed to get to Bill's by seven. He texted his ETA to Bill, grabbed his jacket and the notebook, and headed out.

sixteen

Drew walked into Bill's house and was greeted with a glass of wine. He shied back. "Where'd you get this?" Drew asked.

"Picked it up in Long Beach earlier when I was down getting some groceries. Why?"

"I think the holiday gift basket wine is poisoned," Drew said. "At least the ones in the recent baskets. Yours is probably fine."

"This is a new development," Bill said. "Dinner will be ready in about a half hour. Wanna have our not-poisoned wine and discuss the case in the living room?"

"That sounds perfect. I have a dilemma, and I need some help figuring out what to do."

"Lay it on me. We'll figure it out together."

Drew outlined what he'd learned from Martha's surveillance log without going into too much detail about how much detail there really was. He knew he'd fill Bill in eventually, but he didn't want to get sidetracked again by the sheer violation of it all.

"You need to give it to the police," Bill said without hesitation when Drew was done. "Tell them everything. Give them the wine and have it tested."

"I know. My biggest hesitation is how. I don't want to walk in and tell them what I have. What if she's listening? It'd give her time to cover her tracks or get out of town. Also, these notebooks are full of personal information. Information the cops definitely don't need. I don't want to get anyone in trouble or give the police reason to pay extra attention to people who are otherwise innocent."

Bill sighed and scrubbed his hands through his hair. "Why can't everything just be easy? The cops are the good guys who will only extract the information necessary to catch the bad guys. Justice is served, and the heroes live happily ever after. Can you just hand over the wine and tell them to see if the same substance that killed Ryan and Martha is present in the wine Adriana gave you?"

"Then it'd be a storybook and not real life," Drew said. "Even if the cops aren't corrupt, they'd rationalize that they were compelled to act on the information they found. After all, crime doesn't solve itself, even when it's not hurting anyone. Things that weren't illegal would slip out somehow. Lives could be ruined because somebody likes gossip, and what I have here is the biggest rumor churner to show up in Oracle Bay in ages. I can't just drop it somewhere. It should be destroyed."

"But you can't!" Bill argued. "It has the proof that Adriana is guilty. Or at least enough circumstantial evidence to get a judge to sign off on a search warrant for her home and shop."

"Argh!" Drew yelled. "There has to be a solution!"

"Can you tear out the pages that don't talk about the events leading up to Ryan's and Martha's murders? Or sharpie them like a classified document?"

"It's tempting, but I don't think I could," Drew said slowly. "That's tampering with evidence and could get me in trouble—if I'm not already, that is. Plus, I don't know if I should be the one to judge what should and shouldn't be included. Plus, there are still the tapes that these transcriptions are based on. I'll have to give them the whole thing… I need a neutral place to hand it over, so Adriana doesn't hear."

"My concern is that you'll somehow still be implicated," Bill said. "The police already have a bullseye on your back. I don't want them to overlook the evidence and focus only on the fact that you're the one who presented it."

"Once they find Martha's equipment and Adriana's poison wine, they'll have to let me go," Drew said with a bravado he didn't feel.

"Now who's being hopelessly naïve? We will figure out how to get the journal to the cops without alerting Adriana and without incriminating you."

"What about dinner?" Drew asked.

"There's a few minutes left before it's ready. Let's get as much brainstorming done as we can now. I've no intention of giving you up for the whole evening. I've only just got you back. No one else is in danger tonight—everyone who might be a target knows not to drink the wine."

Drew huffed out a sigh. "You're right. I'd feel more comfortable if Adriana was behind bars—or her wine was."

"I drank a bottle of the wine I received, and nothing happened to me," Bill reminded him. "I wasn't a target."

Drew pulled out his phone and called Jezebel. "Where are you right now?"

"Kinda of a personal question, don't you think?" Jezebel scoffed.

Drew waited in silence.

"Fine," Jezebel huffed. "I'm at home in my basement. Do you need to know what I'm wearing, too?"

"Don't be ridiculous. Do you know if Gabrielle had any of the wine in her basket? Two of the other council members are dead and Misty has been targeted, too. If she hasn't, tell her to stay away from it."

"I'm fine with an apocalypse or a vengeful ex-boyfriend or even a possessed goat, but murder is a big nope for me. I'll call her. Do you know who did it yet?" Jezebel asked.

"Text her, don't call. Someone might hear the call if she's not at home. I think I know who the murderer is. Tomorrow, all shall be revealed. I hope." His voice rose in volume and deepened until Drew sounded more like a carnival barker than a small town, mild-mannered psychic. He did love a bit of drama every now then, especially when he was feeling a little secure and more than a little cocky.

"Well get on it. People are dying and I don't like the fact that someone is okay with it being me next." Jezebel did not sound dramatic. She sounded pissed off.

"I'd tell you more, but at the risk of sounding paranoid, someone could be listening." There hadn't been any evidence that any phone lines were tapped, but there wasn't any evidence otherwise.

"Yep. You sound paranoid. But I know you well enough to know that it's probably coming from a place of truth. I'll text Gabby. You get things done."

"Deal." Drew hung up and turned towards Bill. "I don't like this. Too much responsibility. It's been an age since I was a private investigator. I remember it being more thrilling and less gut-twisting. I was very glamorous."

"Need a drink and a roll in the hay to let go of your stress?" Bill teased.

"Sounds about right," Drew said, grabbing a pen and notepad and opening the log. He was already cross-eyed when Bill called him into dinner, and he had barely made a dent in his annotations.

"Do you wanna take turns?" Bill asked. "You look exhausted."

"I would love that, but I don't want anyone else to have to see the things I'm seeing."

"We're partners. Burdens shared are weights halved. Or something," Bill shrugged. "I'm terrible at remembering clichés."

"If you wouldn't mind, that would be wonderful," Drew sighed. "But when you need a break, I'll take my turn again."

"Sounds fair. Wine?"

Drew shuddered. "I can't believe I'm saying this, but not tonight."

"Fair enough," Bill said and got to work.

DREW WOKE UP RUBBING HIS EYES AND FEELING THE GRITTY SANDPAPER FEEL of not enough sleep. He stretched and his left arm hit empty pillow. He rolled onto one side. Bill was gone, but there was a note on the nightstand in front of the clock that read nine thirty-seven. He yawned, grabbed the note, and sat up.

"You didn't even move when I got up this morning, so I let you sleep. Come into the shop when you wake up for coffee and carefully constructed conversation. Love you."

Drew grinned, checked the location of the listening log, and got in the shower. The hot water did a lot towards making him feel awake and human again, and by the time he was dressed, a smile was playing on his lips. Today was going to be long and difficult, but Bill had come up with a brilliant plan to hand over the information to the cops and lure Adriana out at the same time, and Drew couldn't wait to watch it in action. Smart guys were so sexy.

It was pouring, so Drew drove the short distance into town, all the while chiding himself for his laziness. He stopped at home to feed the kittens and spend a few minutes playing with them, then grabbed an umbrella and walked down the street. He was already salivating over the thought of the caramel latte he was going to have but had to make a detour before his caffeine needs would be met.

Drew checked his watch. It was three minutes past eleven. Covington's Wine Shoppe would be open. He walked in and beamed at Adriana. "That champagne was marvelous! I can't get over how biscuity and light it was. Do you have any more bottles? I'm getting together with a group of friends tonight, and I have wine for dinner —everyone's bringing a bottle—but that champagne...it'd be perfect for dessert."

Adriana's eyes lit up. "Which friends are you entertaining? I do hope it's your little psychic group. If so, I'd be happy to sell you the champagne at your usual discount."

"I thought our discount had been canceled?" Drew asked.

She waved her hand in the air. "I do have a temper," Adriana admitted. "But I would not seriously do anything to jeopardize the continued patronage of my best clients. If you haven't already, you should drink the holiday gift basket wines. Everyone could bring one or two. There are several different wines that were included. The only thing they have in common was that they were made by me."

"Bill was telling me that the one he's opened so far was very good," Drew said. "I'm eager to try for myself."

"I know you'll love it. Now, let me get you that champagne."

Drew left the wine shop with four bottles of champagne and a lot of doubt about his life choices.

He texted everyone and let them know to keep the evening free, told them he'd tell them where to meet in an hour or so, and let them know to bring their holiday wine and to talk about it as often as seemed natural throughout the day.

Zeke and Russell offered pushback, of course, but this time it was Morgana who overrode them with a solid chunk of text.

"You might not want to practice your gifts in Oracle Bay, but you live here. Your gifts give you an advantage and put you at risk. Right now, you are at risk for reasons we don't understand. Someday we might all be at risk because of you. You don't ever have to put up a sign and sell yourself, but as long as you live here, you do have to participate in the important events in this town. And right now, the important event is us not getting murdered and a killer getting caught."

"Fine," was Russell's graceless reply.

"If you insist," Zeke said. *"I won't ever sell my talents, but I did accompany the nascent apocalypse, so I guess I owe you all one for winning."*

Drew grinned. Morgana was imposing, even over text. He'd never met anyone who could stand up to her. Paska was the only one who regularly tried, but he almost always backed down. Drew suspected the few times Morgana yielded were a ploy on her part to puff up Paska's ego. He'd love to know her story.

Drew walked into Caffiend Dreams and set the champagne on the nearest empty surface.

"Your coffee's up!" Bill called, placing a large, steaming latte on the counter next to a cranberry and cream cheese Danish.

"Thank you." Drew and Bill exchanged a smoldering smile before Drew turned back to the line of customers and took the next order.

"How'd you get served already?" a tourist asked, eyes narrowed in disapproval. "You just got here."

"I'll tell you my secret," Drew said, leaning in close. The tourist's mouth hung open slightly and he, in turn, leaned towards Drew. "Gotta sleep with the owner. It's the only way."

The tourist gasped and took a step back.

Ceri waltzed into the shop, eyed the table of champagne, and waved at Drew.

"Your mocha's on the counter, Ceri!" Bill called, setting down another coffee drink. "Do you want a chocolate croissant?"

"That sounds divine."

"Is she sleeping with him, too?" the tourist asked, eyes wide.

"I can't think of another way to explain it," Drew said, sighing. "And here I thought he had eyes only for me."

The man patted Drew's arm. "He's not worth it, then. You hold out for someone who'll put you first."

Drew grinned, caught Bill's eye, and nodded towards his new friend. Bill nodded back. That man would find his order was free when he got up to the counter.

Ceri and Drew slipped into their seats and sipped their beverages.

"Looking forward to tonight," she said. "Just wish we had a place big enough for everyone."

"There's so many more of us now," Drew said. "We need some serious space."

"What are Joseph and Bill gonna do while we're having our dinner meeting?"

"Karaoke, I think," Drew said. "They even convinced Vincent to join them. I almost wish I could skip out to watch that instead."

"Ha. Me, too," Ceri agreed. "But we'll have a great time. I'm excited to try the wine."

"I'm sure it's amazing," Drew said. "The champagne she recommended to me last night was out of this world."

Ceri stood up, grabbing her coffee. "I have a venue idea. Come with me."

"Right behind you," he said. "Just wanna say goodbye to Bill, first."

Drew hopped back in line and waited patiently for his turn to put in an order. He got a black coffee this time. When it was time to pay, he handed over his credit card and the notebook. Bill nodded, handed back the card, and gave Drew a cup.

Drew hoped it was enough—this and the other conversations that were happening. Adriana had been one of the first people to arrive on the scene and the last to leave when Ryan had died, and he'd seen her in the crowd when Martha's body was discovered. Of course, there'd been a lot of people present at both scenes, himself included, but it was something...

The trap was set. Now they just needed the cops.

DREW CAUGHT UP WITH CERI OUTSIDE. SHE WAS ALREADY THREE BLOCKS away and making good time. "Thanks for waiting," he said, breathing heavily.

"You're welcome," she replied.

"Do you think Andy will agree to this?"

"I don't know. I hope so. Otherwise we're gonna have to put a table in one of our shops, and I don't want to do that."

"You'd rather sacrifice Andy's space. His business?"

"Obviously," she said.

"You're terrible," Drew said.

"I will pay him. He must have a venue rental fee." Ceri smiled benignly. If Drew didn't know better, he'd say she looked innocent.

"He might. And he might not be excited about closing his entire bar for a private party with only a few hours' notice," Drew pointed out, holding back a grin. He liked Andy, but he was always going to be Team Ceri.

"He said he'd come tonight," Ceri said.

"I know you're being purposefully ridiculous, so I'm going to back off," Drew said, hands up in surrender. "He's your person, so you can do the ask."

Ceri stopped so suddenly Drew was a dozen steps ahead of her before he came to a halt. He turned around. She was smiling at him, but the glint in her eyes spelled trouble.

"I hope you know what you're doing, Ceridwen," Drew said. "He's a fallen angel, and—"

"And what? I'm merely a long-lived mortal?" she scoffed.

"No. You're the woman who holds his heart and his soul. And if you're honest with yourself, you'll see—"

"I'll see nothing," she said. "Except maybe someone who was a little hard up after too many years alone." She started walking again, this time faster than before.

Drew knew when to stop talking—most of the time—so he shut up and walked the rest of the way to the Pour House in silence.

The lunch crowd was starting to fill up the place already. Ceri caught Brandy's eye, shrugged and nodded, and said, "We'll head to our table."

"Do you want a drink?" Brandy asked.

"Soda water for me," Ceri said.

"Same," Drew echoed. "No food right now. We just came from Caffiend Dreams."

"I'll send the boss over with your fancy water," Brandy said, rolling her eyes. "I don't know if it's better when I pour you free beers all night or when you take up space to drink free water."

Drew grinned. "If you like this, you're gonna love what's coming next."

Brandy's brows lowered over her eyes, and she pointed at them. "If you bring any more of your weird friends with boundary issues in, you will be permanently banned, Drew Hardy. I don't care what Andy says."

"I usually say that you're the best general manager in the world," Andy said as he walked behind the bar and started pouring beers. "I'll meet you all at the table in a minute."

"We don't want beers," Ceri said as Andy started loading a tray with beer and soda water.

"Maybe they're all for me," Andy said. "It's been a weird few weeks and I have a feeling that I'm not going to like whatever you're going to say next. So maybe I'm having beer for lunch today."

"Valid life choice," Drew said. "Especially if you have the metabolism of a hummingbird and can burn through it in no time flat."

They walked to the back table. Ceri sat in the back corner and patted the seat next to her while looking at Drew. He wrinkled his nose at her but sat down anyway. Andy handed over the waters, lined up all three beers in the corner opposite Ceri, and sat down. "Let me know if you change your mind," he said. "You have a good ten minutes before I start on the second one. But in the meantime, why don't you tell me why you're here and what you want."

Ceri took a notebook out of her purse. "We wanted to ask you about using the Pour House for tonight's dinner." She passed the notebook to Drew, who glanced down at it before sliding it over to Andy. "Group text."

Ceri already had her phone out, and Drew and Andy weren't far behind.

"You want to use the Pour House tonight?" Andy asked, eyebrows lifting into his hairline. "Just this semi-private table, right?"

"No. The whole thing, of course," Ceri said. "It's a special night."

Drew's phone vibrated.

Ceri: "*This place, particularly this corner, is bugged. Anything we say will be overheard. Tonight is a trap, and we need your help.*"

"That's very short notice to ask me to close down the bar for a private event, Ceri. You know I'd love to accommodate you, but I am running a business."

Andy: "*Seriously? It's bugged & you want to meet here?*"

"I'll pay your venue rental fee," Ceri said.

"You're the only one of us who has a big enough space for us all to eat together," Drew chimed in.

Ceri: "*Did you miss the part where it's a trap?*"

Drew: "*Having someone listening is both the feature and the bug.*"

Andy leaned back, covered his face with one hand, and refused to look at Drew.

Ceri sent a rude gif.

Drew: "*My work here is done.*"

"Let me think about it a minute. What time would you need it empty?" Andy asked.

Drew and Ceri exchanged glances.

"Seven?" Drew asked. "Would that be okay?"

"I'll need to run the times by Brandy to figure out the best time to close, but that should be fine. Will you need the kitchen and bar?"

"I thought we could just order in," Drew said. "And we all have a bottle to pass and share, not to mention the champagne I have. I'd love to throw it in the fridge, though, if you agree and it's okay."

Andy sighed dramatically. "Fine. You can have the place."

Andy: "*I don't know what your plan is, but it is not going to work.*"

Ceri: "*Wanna bet, old man?*"

Andy: "*Absolutely. If it works and I'm wrong, I'll close down the bar next weekend and host the best damn Oracle Bay Masquerade Ball anyone has ever seen.*"

"Are you serious right now?" Ceri blurted out, then snapped her jaw closed and grinned tightly.

"Super serious," Andy replied. "The place is yours tonight."

Ceri: "*And if you're right, and the trap doesn't work?*"

Andy: "*You have to tell me why you broke things off between us. No hedging. No half-truths. No matter what the reason is, I'll walk away after and never bring it up again. It's not a ploy to lure you back into a relationship. I just want to know.*"

Drew put down his phone. The conversation had definitely moved out of group text territory. He looked around the room, desperately trying to avoid looking at either Andy or Ceri and spotted the last person he wanted to see.

Dio saw him watching, waved once, and walked across the room and sat down. "Hey guys!" he said. "Miss me?"

"Not even a tiny bit," Drew said. "Weren't you supposed to be out of town?"

"I forgot something and had to come back," Dio said. He sat down next to Andy, snagged one of the beers, and gave it a delicate sniff. "How can you drink this stuff?" he asked. "It smells like bitterness and rotten bread."

"It most certainly does not," Andy said. He straightened in his chair, and his chest puffed out visibly.

"Hey guys, we don't need to get into a beer versus wine conversation here," Ceri said. "Dio, did you find what you'd left behind? Are you leaving now? Your presence makes things...difficult for us."

"Why are you being coy?" Dio asked.

Ceri huffed under her breath, grabbed the notebook back from Andy, and wrote in big block letters, *The booth is bugged. Shut up.* Out loud, she said, "No one's being coy. Just expressing our dislike."

"Fine. I'm back in Oracle Bay because I forgot something. I'm here at your beer hall because I ran into the coffee man and he asked me to come by and talk to Drew and Ceri. Seemed to think I'd be able to help with an event you're planning tonight. I can only assume he meant you need me to provide the wine."

"Oh no, we're set," Drew said. "We all got wine as holiday gifts, so we're going to do a bottle share."

"Huh," Dio said. His head was swinging slowly side to side and was tilted a bit. "Gotcha!" he exclaimed, clapping his hand over the base of the wall sconce. He'd had to lean most of his body across the table to reach, causing everyone else to grab their drinks to keep them steady.

"What are you doing?" Andy demanded.

"Disabling the bug," Dio said.

"You can do that?" Ceri asked. "Are you sure it's disabled?"

"We needed that!" Drew yelled.

"It's temporary," Dio admitted. "It'll probably be back online in ten minutes. Making things that are supposed to work fail temporarily and things that aren't supposed to work function is one of my favorite tricks."

"Tricks... Are you a trickster?" Drew asked.

Dio buffed his fingernails on his jacket. "Says so on Wikipedia. What more could you want?"

A slow grin spread across Drew's face. "I have a job for you."

seventeen

The crowd that gathered at the Pour House was a mix of nerves and excitement. Drew wasn't quite sure anyone knew the entirety of the plan except for the four conspirators who'd finished the plan in this very bar hours earlier.

Misty arrived with pizzas for everyone, and the wine bottles were arranged on a table near the bar, far away from any food or actual beverages. "I got a phone call from a blocked number on my way here," she said. "Warning me to stay away from the Pour House tonight, if I knew what was good for me. Whoever it was swore there was going to be a drug bust."

"That's weird," Drew said. "The voice didn't sound familiar at all?

"It sounded disguised. I wonder if there's an app for that?"

"There's an app for everything," Morgana said, walking up behind them.

Russell and Paska walked in last, about twenty minutes after the agreed upon start time. "Oh good! You're finally here!" Ceri said. "Grab a slice and we can get this business meeting going."

Russell glared at her, then at his cousin Misty, and then at everyone else for good measure. "I don't like this," he said. "I don't want this life."

"I know," Drew said. "But I don't think you have a choice."

Russell huffed. He put down a backpack and pulled a box out. There was a clear table next to the one they were eating at, and he put his Ouija board there.

"I'll pour wine for everyone while Russell prepares, shall I?" Ceri asked.

"I'll help," Jezebel said.

Drew watched Russell sit at the table in front of the Ouija board while Ceri and Jezebel handed out wine from the wineskin Dio had provided them.

"Do you need anything?" Drew asked Russell.

"No. Yes. A drink, and the person who knew the departed the best."

"That's probably me," Misty said. "Between the events I help manage, my role as first property manager and then owner of the main street businesses, and the fact that we were all on the city council together, I can't imagine anyone else here knew them better than me?" She looked around, eyes wide and pleading for someone else to volunteer.

"Come sit next to me, then. I'll explain what's going to happen," Russell began. "I have items that belonged to each of our murder victims. I will take them out of my bag, one at a time, place them next to the board. Then, we will put our fingers on the planchette, and I will open the gates that separate us from the dead. It might take a few moments to sort through the spirits desperate for a chat, there are an awful lot here considering the peaceful small-town vibe Oracle Bay rocks. Once we find our first person, you can ask them the questions. In my experience, they'll quickly give up on the planchette and effort of spelling out their answers and either use me as a vessel or pull enough strength from me to vocalize. Try not to scream. That usually alarms the spirits."

"I'm going to need another glass of wine," Jezebel said. "I was not ready for energy sucking dead people."

"We all are tested," Morgana reminded her. "But I agree. More wine is in order. That first glass was remarkably good and went down so easily. If it was not for the seriousness of the endeavor, I might almost say I felt giddy."

"Whoa," Sandy said, a giggle escaping at the end. "Now I have seen everything. We'll have to order a dozen more bottles of this wine if it makes Morgana almost giddy."

Andy refilled everyone's glass. For a moment, the only sounds were pouring, clinking, and laughter.

"Are you ready, Misty?" Russell asked.

"As I'll ever be. I'm having a very hard time taking you seriously, you know," she said.

"That's okay. I'm having a difficult time taking myself seriously right now. I hope that doesn't interfere with what I'm doing." He opened the knapsack at his feet and pulled out a book. "This one was in Ryan's private collection. It was given to me earlier today by an interested party who assured me it was Ryan's most prized possession."

"You said possession," Ceri gasped, laughing. "And you're going to raise the dead."

The room erupted in laughter until Russell waved his hands and quieted them down. "As I was saying... This book goes here." He placed it on the table next to the board. "And now, place your fingers on the planchette."

Misty stifled her giggles and put her fingers on the planchette. Russell followed suit.

"I will open the door between the living and the dead, now," he said. "Try not to laugh."

His request elicited another round of giggles, followed by several people saying, "Shh...shh."

When everything was quiet, Russell closed his eyes and said, "You are welcome now. You can stay until I close the door, and then you'll return to the other side of the veil. I am looking for the recently departed soul Ryan Kowalski. If you are here, come signal on the spirit board."

"That's it?" Morgana asked, all sounds of humor gone from her voice. "It sounds very informal, doesn't it?"

"It's always worked for me," Russell shrugged. "Now we wait."

It wasn't long before the planchette was moving. Misty's eyes were wide as she watched the letters be chosen. "Hi. George. I George. Message."

"I'm sorry George," Russell said. "Maybe next time. Today I need to speak to Ryan."

The planchette careened around the board. "W-H-A-T D-O Y-O-U W-A-N-T?"

"Tell us about the vandalism to Title Wave the night you died and everything you remember leading up to your death."

There was a pause, and for a moment Drew thought Ryan might've taken off. Then the planchette moved again. "T-O-O M-A-N-Y Q-U-E-S-T-I-O-N-S."

"You can use me to speak through if it's easier," Russell offered. The pained grimace on his face belied the sincerity of his offer. Seconds later, his spine stiffened, his eyes widened, and he rolled his neck and popped his jaw.

"I feel so young!" Ryan's voice crowed from Russell's mouth. "I never thought I'd feel like this again."

"Can you answer my questions?" Misty asked.

Russell/Ryan heaved a long-suffering sigh. "Fine. There was nothing wrong with my shop. I lied. Are you happy now?"

"Why would you do that?" Misty asked.

"I wanted to prove to that insufferable psychic that he's not that special. As for my death, I don't remember much of anything. I was cleaning up the store, so it was ready for the perspective buyer the next day and decided to have some wine. Martha showed up and offered to help. She was always showing up where she didn't belong.

I gave her a glass of wine, poured myself another, and put her to work. That's it."

"Thank you, Ryan," Russell's voice said. "Is there anything else you'd like to tell us before you go?"

After a few moments of silence, Russell said, "He's gone. Keep your fingers on the planchette, Misty. I'm going to change Ryan's item for Martha's. He put the signed first edition of Infinite Jest back in the bag and pulled out a one-foot-tall angel figurine. After situating it next to the board, he placed his fingers back on the planchette. "Martha? Are you there? We'd love to talk."

A breeze blew through the bar, blowing around the napkins and whipping up people's hair.

"Martha, if that's you, come talk to us through the spirit board," Russell commanded. The lightness of his touch on the planchette didn't change, but his knuckles turned white with strain.

"I don't like the board," Martha said. Her voice, while perfectly familiar, sounded distant and hollow and cold. "I'd rather talk like this. What do you want from me?"

"I want to know how you died," Misty said. "We are trying to solve your murder."

"I knew I was being murdered!" Martha exclaimed. A translucent figure took shape and hovered over the Ouija board. "At first, I felt so happy. I couldn't stop laughing." Someone giggled nervously in the background. "But then, it was too much. My head was too full, and I couldn't stop. I had to move, but I wanted to be still. I got itchy. I knew who'd done this to me. I didn't make the connection with Ryan, but now I was sure. I tried to find her. I was looking for her, but I had trouble breathing and needed to lay down. That's the last thing I remember."

"Who did it?" Misty asked. "Who was it?"

"Adriana, of course. She poisoned the wine." The spirit looked at the wine glasses in everyone's hands and the empty bottles near the bar. "Yours is poisoned, too. You're all going to die."

"Don't be silly," Paska slurred. "It's just going to be a nap time, and everything will be beautiful. I want to sleep outside so I can watch the stars through my eyelids."

"See you on the other side, creepy man," Martha said. "I'm bored now. Can I go?"

"Do you want revenge?" Misty asked.

The figure paused. "Revenge on whom?"

"The one who did this to you, of course."

Another pause. "How?"

"Just hang out a bit, invisibly. You'll figure out what to do."

"Sure. Might be fun."

The Ouija board snapped closed, flinging the planchette away and nearly catching Misty's and Russell's fingers.

Misty giggled, but the laughter turned into a hiccupping sob. "What are we doing?" she whispered.

"Napping," Russell said. "That's what Paska said to do, and he's my mentor now."

"I should call Joseph," she slurred.

"He's singing karaoke with Bill and Vincent," Drew reminded her. "We can just sit down for a minute and then they'll come get us." He looked around the room. He, Misty, and Russell were the only people not lying down or slumped over. "Sitting looks nice."

Twenty minutes later, which was about nineteen minutes too long, the front door slammed open and the crash reverberated through the bar.

"Yesss…" a low voice hissed. "This is better than I could've imagined."

Drew cracked open his eyes from his position under the Ouija table. Adriana stood in the doorway. The darkness of her outfit bled into the night so that it appeared she was a floating head. He shuddered before he could stop himself, then closed his eyes and hoped she hadn't noticed.

Adriana walked around the bar, looking at each person and occasionally nudging someone with a shoe. "I couldn't have planned this better."

Drew opened his eyes again. She was standing over the open pizza boxes sprinkling something on them, then did the same to all the unfinished slices at the table.

Adriana walked to the center of the room, spun around, and cackled. She pulled a bottle of wine out of her bag, pulled the cork out with her teeth, and spat the cork out. She took a swig right from the bottle. Drew crossed his fingers under his body and hoped she'd start the big confession monologue that all villains were supposed to give when they thought they'd won.

"Shame about you, Misty," Adriana said, walking over to Misty's prone body. "You were the only one I really needed. If you'd just had your wine at home, you'd be fine. You should've listened to my warning. The rest of you, though. You're the kind of people that hold this town back." She paused by Russell. "Well, not you, really. I don't know how you got mixed up in this. You were always so polite and really knew a lot about wine. Shame you had to fall in with a bad crowd."

She walked to each body and stared for a minute. She didn't speak again, though, until she got to Zeke's. "You're even more of an enigma than Russell. I probably should've left you out of it, but when I heard you were associated with this lot, I had no choice. Ryan was right all along."

Adriana stopped at the planchette that'd been tossed aside when Martha flounced off the Ouija board. She bent over and picked it up. When she straightened and looked up, a glowing translucent figure stood before her. Adriana yelped and jumped back several paces, stumbling over Paska's still figure.

"Hi Adriana," Martha said. "Miss me?"

"What?" Adriana looked around. "Is this some kind of joke?"

"You tell me. I thought we were friends."

Adriana leaned forward and extended her hand so slowly Drew

didn't think she'd reach the apparition before morning. Finally, her hand slid through the wispy form. Adriana pulled back much faster than she'd reached forward. "Ugh. It's...cold."

"I bring the chill from beyond the veil," Martha intoned. "Just kidding. I don't know why I feel cold to you. You're the first person who's tried to touch me since."

"I don't know what kind of trick this is, but it's in poor taste," Adriana hissed. "I've seen what I came to see, and now I'm leaving."

"Before you even hear what proof they have of what you did?"

"What kind of proof could this lot have? Every one of them, almost without exception, is at best a delusional fool, and at worst an idiotic tool of either the devil or the New Age."

Drew opened his eyes all the way, certain Adriana wouldn't be looking at him any time soon and regarded her quizzically. *The New Age?* He'd been aware that Big Crystal was pretty popular among upper middle-class white women with nothing better to do but peddle ineffective and often harmful cures in the name of healing and getting back to nature and cultural appropriation, but he hadn't known The New Age was recruiting idiots to tell fortunes. He hoped his recruitment check came in soon.

"They got me here, didn't they?" Martha asked. "And they found the notebook."

"Damnit!" Adriana swore. "Where?"

"That wasn't part of my briefing. Drew found it and read it and handed it over to the cops."

Drew closed his eyes again, just in time. Adriana marched over to him, pulled her leg back, and kicked him in the stomach as hard as she could. Nausea welled up, and it took every ounce of self-control to stay still and silent and not give in to PTSD.

"He said he was there for Champagne. I should've known," Adriana snarled. "He only drinks Prosecco from other stores."

"I didn't tell you this when I was alive, but you need to get a grip," Martha said.

"Get a grip? Get a grip?" Adriana screamed. "I spent my entire adult life making Covington's Wine Shoppe a success, and then punsters and psychics move in to invalidate my efforts. It started with those weird ones, Morticia and Pascal, or whatever their names are. And then Misty grew up and bought into it—her aunt was a bad influence, and I'd hoped that insanity would die out when she left town. And then the others slowly came in, but when that last one, the one that looks so young and sweet, came to town, she brought chaos. And that chaos was centered on the lunatics."

Drew opened his eyes again, still breathing through the pain of her kick, and watched Adriana melt down. If all was going well, this was almost over.

"But you didn't try to murder them right away," Martha said. "You killed Ryan. And me. You'd obviously laced the wine with enough fentanyl to kill a horse, but it doesn't make sense that Ryan would be the first target. If you wanted to stack the City Council with more like-minded folks, it would've made more sense to kill Gabrielle or Misty." Her form wavered between near transparence and near solidity.

"Ryan needed to die. He was about to sell his bookstore, and you're the one who told me the buyer wanted to keep the business name and open another, equally abhorrent business." Adriana stretched out her arm and pointed at Martha, wagging her finger.

"But killing him didn't change that," Martha pointed out. "The same person is still going to take over the space and will probably end up with the business, too. And you know Misty encouraged them to consider puns for the name of their enterprises."

"I will find a way to make sure that doesn't happen," Adriana said. The longer she spoke, the less Adriana sounded like the level-headed shop owner Drew was familiar with. Mostly level-headed. Actually, he was beginning to believe the level head was a front and this seething irrational anger was the true Adriana. She was pacing now, lightly treading a bar table sized square on the floor in front of Martha's form.

"How?" Martha asked.

"I will give every new Main Street business owner a welcome bottle of wine until I find one that's acceptable." Adriana stopped moving for a second and turned to face the sea of scattered psychics. "If it worked on them, it'll keep working." She resumed pacing.

"I know I'm not very smart," Martha said. "Lord knows, you told me that often enough, but don't you think the cops will eventually figure it out?"

"They haven't yet," Adriana said, smugness radiating from her body.

Misty gasped, and Adriana's head whipped around. Drew closed his eyes, not wanting anything to give them away.

"Did you hear something?" Adriana asked. It sounded like she'd stopped moving.

"Nothing," Martha said. "So, this wasn't your first wine rodeo?"

"This was the best. No one suspected the wine."

"I know how you did it, and now I know why you killed Ryan, but what about me? I helped you. You could've bought my silence if that's what you needed." Martha's voice sounded plaintive. Drew'd never liked Martha much, but it still tugged at his heartstrings to hear the sadness in her voice.

"You were about to tell the police to dust for prints," Adriana said. "I had to do something."

"I wish you'd tried blackmail," Martha said.

"Blackmail wasn't as fun as showing up at your place, pretending we were friends, and then giving you a bottle of wine. I know your weakness. I knew the minute I left your place that you'd open the wine."

"That's not fair," Martha said.

"Isn't it, Martha?" Adriana asked. "Because you thought we were friends, so you let me in. Into your house and into your life. It was worth killing you just so I would never have to listen to you slur through your bitter, gossipy complaints again."

A palpable silence fell over the bar.

"You're horrible," Martha said. "I was on the fence about helping you get caught. I thought maybe it'd been an accident, that you hadn't meant to kill me. But you deserve whatever you get from here on out, you joyless, miserable hag. I have only one more question. How? How did you tamper with the wine without anyone knowing?"

Drew did a mental fist pump. She'd remembered.

"It was so easy. I pretended I was looking into wine making classes—like I'd ever do anything so horrific," Adriana shuddered. "I steamed off the old wine labels and removed the tops. Then I put in the fentanyl, used my screw topper to put on new tops, applied new labels, and called it good. Whenever everyone else's stuff was going missing, I took that opportunity to misplace the screw topper as well, as a few people, namely you, knew I had it."

"Wow. That is so much premeditation," Martha breathed. "I hope it's enough." She looked around. "I am exhausted, and I'm fading. Either I need a vessel, or a way back."

Russell climbed to his feet. "The doorway opens for you, Martha. Thank you for your service. If you ever have need of me again, I owe you one."

The apparition folded slightly, like it was bowing at the waist. Martha's ghost beelined for Russell, dove into and through him, then disappeared.

"What?" Adriana exclaimed. "You're...dead."

The doors of the Pour House burst open and four cops, followed distantly by Dio, burst in.

"Freeze!" Chad yelled.

Adriana did not freeze. She turned and ran towards the back doors that led out onto the patio.

Ceri, who'd been slumped in a booth for close to an hour at this point, straightened up, stuck out her foot, and tripped the fleeing suspect.

Adriana hit the ground with a loud thump that vibrated the table and knocked down a pizza.

"No one touch the pizza!" Kyle yelled. "It's evidence!"

"She sprinkled mushrooms on all the food," Drew said. "It's a fair bet they weren't chanterelles."

Chad had walked forward and handcuffed Adriana.

"Thank you for confessing," he said. "I don't know why you did it, other than finding the bodies of the people you thought you'd murdered, but we all enjoyed your conversation with the person pretending to be one of your victims."

"It wasn't one of them," Adriana said. "Martha was here!"

"It was me," Ceri said, stepping forward. "I've always had a gift for mimicry." She said the last in Kyle's voice, and other than being slightly more tenor than he was, it was spot on.

"But the ghost!" Adriana yelled.

"I didn't see anything," Drew said. "But I was lying on the floor, pretending to be dead. I expect the bruise on my stomach from where you kicked me will be spectacular."

"There was an apparition! Martha appeared!" Adriana insisted.

"You may be right, ma'am," Roger said. "We have the recording and will listen to it critically with the DA as we build the case against you. If there is a spirit involved, we will do our best to ensure they take the stand. Otherwise, we will have to go with Ms...." He looked at Ceri. "I don't know your last name."

She sighed. "Kenny. Ceridwen Kenny."

"Right," Roger said. "Ms. Kenny will testify that she played the part."

"It's not fair!" Adriana said. "It's all lies."

"Lies you told yourself," Roger said, helping Adriana to her feet. "We'll have a search warrant for your shop, and if the search doesn't turn up the screw top machine, the labels you created, and a whole lot of fentanyl, we'll talk. We also have the bottles here—unopened. We'll check for fingerprints, of course, as well as the presence of drugs. And we've pulled out the evidence found at Ryan's murder and are looking at that wine bottle, as well as any at Martha's home as well. Plus, we have the notebook Martha kept and the notes you added. It's a lovely mix of circumstantial and hard evidence, and I look forward to seeing you in court. Now, if you don't mind, it's time to get going."

He read Adriana her rights as he led her out of the bar.

The rest of the psychics had gotten up and were rubbing aching muscles and looking around.

"Well, you were right," Andy said. "It worked. I owe you a ball."

"I love a good masquerade," Ceri said. "Especially when I'm not in charge of the planning."

<h1 style="text-align:center">*eighteen*</h1>

"Are you ready yet?" Bill called up the stairs.

"Five more minutes," Drew replied.

"You're already gorgeous," Bill said. "You don't need five more minutes."

"Fine. I'm coming down." Drew started down the staircase. He was wearing a black suit, impeccably tailored for his trim frame, a black vest with red and gold embroidery, and a red tie. Dangling from his hand was a mask with devil horns detailed in red and gold.

"I am…" Bill said, staring up at Drew where he'd stopped halfway down. Bill was in a burgundy suit. His burgundy vest was identical to Drew's, only the embroidery was gold and black. He was wearing a black tie and had a black half-mask with cat ears outlined in gold.

"You are speechless?" Drew asked.

"I am so lucky," Bill said. "You look magnificent."

"As do you. I almost want to skip this altogether and stay in."

"Ceri would never forgive you," Bill said. "This masquerade ball was her idea."

"Sinners and saints," Drew laughed. "If only everyone knew the truth."

"I can't believe she pulled it together on such short notice," Bill said.

"She and Brandy could rule the world if they wanted to," Drew said. "Any of them could, really. Are you ready?" He held out his hand and smiled when Bill took it.

"Always ready for you."

"Mew!"

Drew looked down. Tuppence and Hercule were sitting at his feet, tiny faces tilted up, and eyes full of innocent earnestness.

"No kittens at the party," Drew said. "Sorry. It's a human only affair."

"Mew," Tuppence said, ears drooping. How she managed to look even more sad and pathetic was a mystery known only to young mammals.

"Sorry. But I did get you a special treat!" Drew walked into the kitchen, followed closely by the cats who managed to sound like an entire herd of elephants when they ran, and opened the pantry. He had a bag of cat treats, and he doled out three per kitten before putting the bag back on the highest shelf.

"Now we can go," Drew said. "I can't wait to dance with you."

DREW AND BILL WALKED INTO THE POUR HOUSE. IT'D BEEN TRANSFORMED in the few days since they'd been there. Red and white lights twinkled on the ceiling, tables had been moved out of the center of the room, and a buffet table was set up against one end.

Ceri ran over to them, hair streaming behind her. She was wearing a form-fitting ivory gown with intricate gold beadwork and a short cape that evoked feathers. Her mask was the same color as her dress and covered in feathers and gold beads.

"You look amazing, Ceri!" Bill said.

"How'd you know it was me?" she teased.

"How could anyone think that this gorgeous red hair belongs to anyone else?" Andy asked, striding up and handing Drew and Bill beers.

Drew watched as Ceri bit her lip and considered Andy. He was dressed in a shiny red suit over a black shirt. His black mask had red sequin flames in the corner, and he smelled a little like sulfur.

"Hard night?" Drew asked. "Do you have any scorch marks that need patching up?"

"I know that you enjoy mocking those you care about, but if you could not right now, that'd be grand," Andy bit back. "I don't have any scorch marks on this suit, and I'd like to keep it that way. Spontaneous combustion puts a real damper on a party, and if I ruin Ceri's party, I don't know how I'll ever get her to talk to me again."

"I talk to you," she said. "I've done nothing but talk to you the last few days."

"Party planning talk only," Andy said, turning to face her.

"Hey, you two," Bill said. "I don't mean to be critical, but maybe one or both of you should head outside to calm down. Andy's doing a real good impression of the Hunchback of Notre Dame right now. I don't know what that means, but I don't think it's part of his costume."

"You're right," Andy said, taking a deep breath. He stood up straighter, and Andy and Bill watched as the bulge on his back shrank and disappeared. "I'll take a walk and catch up with you later." He took long steps across the still mostly empty dance floor, walked out onto the back deck, and disappeared into the darkness.

"I hope walking is all he does," Ceri said.

"You wanna talk about what's going on here?" Drew asked. "A month ago, you two were hot and heavy. Now you're both awkward and angry."

Ceri sighed. "It's no big deal, really. We had a fling, as you know. It was never supposed to be anything more. But he wanted things I wasn't prepared to give, so I called it off."

"And then you convinced him to shut down the bar for the night so you could throw the town a party?" Drew asked. "I think he's got the friends part down."

Ceri hung her head. "You think I'm using him, don't you?"

"It's really none of my business how you handle things with Andy," Drew said. "I shouldn't have said anything. If you want to talk, I'm here for you, but I don't want to be the kind of friend who passes judgment on my bestie. I want you to be happy, and if pulling back from what you had with him makes you happy, then I support you fully. You don't owe him anything."

"Thank you," Ceri said. "That is exactly what I needed to hear." She straightened her spine and glided towards the bar. The new staff were tending the bar. Brandy and Zeke both had the night off to enjoy the festivities, although Brandy was spending more time doing circuits of the room to make sure everything was in order than enjoying herself.

Drew pulled Bill over to the back corner where two chairs had opened up. "Wanna go under the bleachers and make out?" he asked.

"I always got caught by the parent chaperone every time I tried to get fresh with someone at a school dance," Bill confessed.

"I think we're safe here." Drew kissed him.

"Safe as houses," Dio agreed.

"Damnit!" Drew yelled, startling several nearby people. "Sorry, everyone. Spilled my beer." He faced Dio. "What are you doing here? I thought you were leaving town?"

"Sandy invited me to the dance. Her mom and step-dad had to go back to Seattle, and Sandy through it might be a nice time for us to get to know each other." Dio was in a greenish-black suit that shimmered between the two colors depending on how the light hit it. He had a dark green vest, a black tie with ivy leaf detail, and his mask looked like it was made out of green vines. "Wine?" he offered.

Glasses appeared in Bill's and Drew's hands. They stared down at it, lips pursed.

"Don't worry. It's safe to drink. Unlike the bottle that woman sent home with me when she ran me out of town. I drank it after I helped you guys out with that little crime business you had going on. I have never been so sick in my life. Well, at first, it was wonderful. I almost understood why you mortals chase your dragons instead of drinking the good stuff. But then, oh… I have had hangovers before, although they usually disappear as soon as I remember I'm a god. But whatever was in that wine was worse than any epic hangover I could create after a three-month festival of debauchery. I came back to give her a piece of my mind and make sure Sandy had my number and found her in jail. Adriana, not Sandy. I'd hate to be the person who put my daughter in jail."

"If you turn into an overbearing, overprotective father this late in the game, I will ban you from my life and find a way to ban you from this town," Sandy said. "Sorry Drew. I meant to give you a heads up that he'd be here, but it all happened so fast."

"It's not a big deal," Drew said. "I don't want to see a lot of him, at least not right now, but he's your dad. You deserve that time."

"And, I was a great help, wasn't I?" Dio asked, batting his eyelashes towards Drew. "What would've you done if you hadn't had me to trick the cops into showing up at Martha's and breaking in to save that poor screaming person they never actually found? It was mere coincidence that the incriminating notebook—well, incriminating of Martha and Adriana—was found right outside her secret room that had mysteriously unlocked itself."

"Fine. You're a genius, and we're all grateful," Drew said.

Dio beamed. "That's all I've ever wanted."

A song ended, and something new started. Etta James started singing, and Bill stood up. "They're playing our song. Dance with me?"

"There is nothing I'd rather do," Drew said. He shoved his wine glass into Dio's hands and followed Bill onto the dance floor. He slid into Bill's arms and looked up at him. His breath caught in his throat when he saw the look in Bill's eyes. Bill's lips quirked up in a soft smile that spread across his face to his eyes until he seemed almost as effervescent as the champagne they'd been drinking. Slowly, Bill's gaze grew more serious. His eyes widened and his smile faded into a lip-biting intensity that raised Drew's heart rate and temperature.

Drew stretched up on tiptoe, trying to lure Bill down into a kiss.

Bill resisted, although one hand slid from Drew's waist to curve possessively around his hips. "Do you know how amazing you are?" Bill asked. "You're everything I could've wanted, and to have you here, in my arms in front of all our friends... It's something I didn't even dare to dream would happen."

Drew reached a hand up and caressed Bill's face. "I've looked for you for almost two hundred years. Everything I've done before was a dress rehearsal for you. Thank you for everything. For loving me as I am." He stretched up and kissed Bill, barely brushing their lips together. He felt the tears spring to his eyes. He pulled back and settled into their dance stance again. "I love you, Bill."

"I love you right back, Drew. To the moon and back, forever."

It was very late. The ball was over, and almost everyone had gone. Drew and Bill had tried to help Andy clean up, but he shooed them away. As they left, Drew saw Ceri sitting in a shadowed corner. He waved at her, and she made a rude gesture in return.

"Where do you want to walk to?" Bill asked. "My house or yours?"

"Mine. I have hungry mouths to feed," Drew said.

"So responsible," Bill teased. "You'd be an amazing dad."

Drew froze for a second, then willed his feet forward. "Not sure what you meant by that," he said. "I can't have children."

"You can't?" Bill asked. "Why not? You never mentioned this before. Is it because you're too old? Are...things...defunct?"

Drew rolled his eyes. "No. Everything is in proper working order. It's just..."

"Oh. My. God." Bill stopped and clapped both hands over his

mouth. "Are you...are you..." he gritted his teeth, leaned away from Drew, and then finished his question. "Are you gay?"

"You are such a jerk, Bill," Drew said.

"Does that mean you're not? Because that is going to put a huge damper on the rest of my life plans."

Drew grabbed Bill's hand, pulled him in close, and kissed him.

"Being a father was never something I thought about," Drew admitted. "It wasn't a practical possibility until recently, and there's always the fear that I would outlive any child I had."

"I am mostly teasing," Bill said. "Mostly. We can talk about it later. I don't want to rush things."

"You are rushing," Drew said. "I know the proper order of things. There's a whole rhyme about trees and kissing. Love and marriage definitely come before the baby carriage."

They started walking again, hand-in-hand.

"So, marriage, huh?" Bill asked.

"You're relentless," Drew said. "What's your hurry? We've only just reunited."

"My hurry is you. You've seen so much, *loved* so much. And you've suffered so much loss. You're almost two hundred years older than me, and I will die before you do. We have fifty, sixty years max together, and then I'll be gone, and you'll be alone again. I don't want to waste time on protocols and formalities and spacing out the next steps. I want to dive in headfirst and get on with the rest of our lives. I want to live as furiously and gloriously as we can in the time we have together. I don't want you to look back and regret a single second. I want you to remember me when I'm gone and smile because we had the best damn life anyone could ever have."

Drew stopped walking and pulled Bill close. He reached his hands up to cup his face and whispered, "Every day we are together is the best day of my life. I love you, Bill."

"I love you too, Solomon Drew."

Their lips met and the cool mist ubiquitous on the coast in

winter did nothing to cool their passions. Steam rose from their bodies as the moisture hit them.

"Come live with me?" Bill asked.

"Can I bring my cats?" Drew murmured against Bill's lips.

"I wouldn't have it any other way."

They kissed again, then joined hands and walked home.

"Can you hand me my sunglasses?" Drew asked.

"Only if you rub sunscreen on my back," Bill replied.

"Oh no! An opportunity to get my hands on you? Whatever shall I do?"

Bill laughed and handed over the sunglasses, then plopped down on the towel while Drew squeezed cold sunscreen on his back. Goosebumps rippled over his skin, and he shivered.

Drew rubbed in the sunscreen, all the while keeping an eye on the pale sandy beach and dark blue water of the tropical Pacific. He and Bill were in Puerto Vallarta to celebrate their reunion and Bill's first vacation in four years.

"What are you thinking?" Drew asked.

"I wasn't," Bill replied. "Not until you brought it up, anyway."

"I don't want to leave tomorrow," Drew admitted. "It's weird being away from Oracle Bay for so long, but I love having you all to myself. I like staying up late with you and sleeping late with you."

"And eating tacos with me?" Bill asked.

"I do love the tacos, and there is some surprisingly good beer here," Drew said. "Andy will be so jealous."

"Will he?" Bill asked.

"I don't see why not," Drew replied. "Heat and new microbrews sound right up his alley."

"I think he's getting his share now. He's right over there." Bill pointed.

Drew rolled over and followed Bill's finger. Andy was standing at the edge of the sand with a bottle of Mexican lager sweating in his hand.

"Should we...go talk to him?" Bill asked.

"Probably," Drew said. "Although this violates my no contact clause. We'll be back in two days. Couldn't they have waited until then?"

"Maybe he's not here for you," Bill suggested.

Andy straightened up, waved, and walked towards them.

"Sure. Maybe not." Drew sighed and stood up, brushing the sand off his body. "Andy! What brings you here, and how on earth did you find us?"

"I'm here because of Ceridwen," Andy said. "And I found you because everyone you know is a psychic." The *idiot* went unspoken.

"Where is she?" Drew asked. "Is she okay?"

"She's back in Oracle Bay, and no, she is not okay. We need to go."

Bill held up his hand. "Slow down a minute. We are on the last full day of our vacation. We have reservations at a very nice restaurant tonight. I had a plan. We'll be home day after tomorrow, can't it wait?"

"No," Andy said. "Your plan will need to be postponed."

"What's wrong with her, and why do you need me?" Drew asked.

Andy shrugged and slumped. There were dark circles under his eyes that hadn't been there two weeks before. "She's comatose. She came to me before it happened and said she hadn't been sleeping, and she'd stopped seeing customers."

"Why'd she come to you and not me or Misty or Sandy?" Drew asked. "You guys haven't been seeing each other for months."

Andy looked down at the sand and scuffed his feet before raising his head to meet Drew's eyes. "She thought it was something to do with me, remnants from when she scried me."

"How long has she been unconscious?" Drew's piercing gaze wouldn't let Andy off the hook.

"Two days. She came to see me, reassured me that she'd be fine until you got back, then collapsed in my arms. I fl-took her to the hospital and called Misty. No one—not the doctors, not your psychic friends—could figure out what was wrong. The only consensus all parties came to was that she's safe for the time being, and you're the one who will fix this."

"And did they say they needed him immediately?" Bill asked. "Or did you let your worry overtake you and run down here to force Drew to go home early because you're in love with her?"

"Time could be running out," Andy shouted, earning startled looks from nearby sunbathers.

"I'll check the flights," Drew said, phone already in his hand. After a few moments of browsing and a phone call with his travel agent, Drew looked at the other two men. "When's your return flight, Andy?"

"Um, I don't know. I bought a ticket here, not back."

"You bought a one-way ticket on your urgent mission to find me and return home with me?" Drew said.

"I don't use airplanes very often. This was the first time."

"Why now?" Bill asked.

"It's a long flight, and I'm exhausted, okay?" Andy snapped. "I thought it would be faster."

"Okay, okay," Drew said. "Not a problem. We can find flights for everyone. There isn't another flight out tonight. The next available flight is at nine o'clock in the morning. I'll call my travel agent back and move Bill's and my flight up several hours and book you on the same flight. Does that sound good?"

"Fine," Andy grumbled.

Drew made the changes, then picked up their beach stuff. "You can walk back to our hotel with us and see if they have a room for you. I'm going to shower and get changed, because from the sound of it, I have a fancy dinner and a plan to look forward to tonight."

"We're wasting time," Andy muttered.

"There's nothing else I can do," Drew said. "We'll leave on the next flight we can and get back to town a good twelve hours earlier than planned."

"You sound angry," Andy observed.

"I am upset," Drew said. "Someone should've called me when Ceri wouldn't wake up, or when they realized I was the key to helping her, but that didn't happen. So that makes me angry. And then you show up less than twenty-four hours before my vacation is due to end and that's also upsetting."

"We've tried calling," Andy said. "But all our calls and texts and Facebook messages and emails went unanswered."

Drew ducked his head and screwed up his face. "I disconnected from all my social media apps and removed everything from my phone, then blocked everyone but Ceri. She was my emergency contact."

"Let's just go," Andy sighed. "I am eager to try this fancy dinner, since I'm stuck here."

"Sorry, old man," Bill said. "This is a dinner for two. There's a hotel bar with food and decent beer that should get you through. See you at the airport in the morning."

Andy glared at Bill, and Drew was a little afraid the stare would burn a hole in his boyfriend's chest. "Back off, Andy," he said. "You're starting to smoke and the odor around here is getting a little sulfurous."

Andy turned his glare to Drew. "I will leave, but you will be sorry you spoke to me like that," he said, his voice an otherworldly growl that pushed shivers down Drew's spine. Andy turned to leave, and as he did, his silvery gray wings popped out, raising screams among the nearby beachgoers. He leapt into the air, then flew off over the ocean and disappeared.

"Wow," Bill said. "That was different."

"Let's get out of here before anyone remembers we were with him," Drew said. "I don't want to be questioned."

"You know, before we do that, can we pause for a moment?"

"If we must," Drew said through gritted teeth. They were starting to draw a crowd. He turned back to look at Bill. He wasn't where he'd been a moment before.

"Down here," Bill said.

Drew looked down. Bill was on the sand in front of him on one knee. "Wha—"

"I was going to do it at dinner, but now seems perfect. Drew Hardy, you've been the love of my life since the moment we met and the years we spent apart only reinforced my love for you. Will you make me the happiest man on earth and be my husband?"

"Oh my god." Drew's jaw dropped and he clapped one hand over his open mouth. "Now?"

"Well, the cupid I hired showed up a little early, and I didn't want my money wasted," Bill said, a wide grin plastered across his face.

Drew laughed. "Of course, I'll marry you, Bill. Nothing would make me happier. Sorry your cupid was kind of a dud."

Bill shrugged. "It's all worth it, since you said yes." He pulled a ring box out of his pocket and opened it. The beaten silver ring was adorned with a simple blue crystal, the exact same shade as Drew's crystal ball.

"It's beautiful," Drew said, pulling the ring out and putting it on his finger.

Bill stood and kissed him, long and hard, while the crowd cheered and laughed about the cupid.

"We're gonna live happily ever after," Drew said. "As soon as we save Ceri."

"Let's get started then. I have some champagne in the hotel."

"You are the perfect man, Bill Walters."

"I know, Solomon Drew Hardy."

They clasped hands and walked down the beach, the setting sun a fiery aura dimmed only by their love.

· · ★ ★ ★ ★ ★ ★ ★ · ·

READY FOR CERI & ANDY'S STORY? CLICK HERE TO GET HELL AND HIGH Water!

want more amy cissell?

And why wouldn't you?

Love it, hate it, somewhere in between? Please leave a review for Belle of the Ball at Goodreads, Bookbub, or your favorite online retailer.

Links to all retails sites are at:
https://books2read.com/BelleoftheBall

Reviews are always appreciated & allow me to keep writing what you love!

Sign up for Cissell's Epistles at https://amycissell.com for new release updates, exclusive content, and a bevy of book recommendations! (You'll also get to choose a free book as a thank you for hanging out!)

Come hang out in my Facebook Reader Group - the Amyzonians can always use another shenaniganator. (It's a word. Promise.)

https://www.facebook.com/groups/amycissellauthor/

Join my patreon - https://www.patreon.com/ACissellWrites - for early access to books, free copies of my digital books, free paperbacks, and access to my entire back catalog!

* * * ★ ★ ★ ★ ★ ★ ★ * * *

hell and high water

Ceridwen Kenny stood outside The Pour House, Oracle Bay's local brewpub, and pursed her lips, trying to slow her breathing. The season was turning; winter storms were giving way to spring squalls, and the cold wind whipped her long red hair across her face until only her blue eyes, a few patches of pale white skin, and the tips of her pointy ears shone through.

She didn't want to be here. It'd be different if she was meeting the rest of the psychics to discuss their local businesses, or the latest mystery, or which supernatural creature had shown up this week. Having someone else there as a buffer made a world of difference. She couldn't count on Brandy, the brewpub's business manager, or Zeke, the pub's head bartender, newly appointed assistant manager, and part-time prophet of the Lord.

She shook her head. She was a grown-ass woman, fast approaching her fourth century of life, and she wasn't afraid of anyone or anything. Not even the arrogant, ridiculous fallen angel who owned the place and whatever he'd done to her that was making her fall apart.

Ceri took a deep breath, let it out, and allowed her gaze to drift from the front of the bar to the Pacific Ocean. The grey waves were curling into the shore but breaking too quickly for the few surfers, braving the cold water and colder air. She glanced at her phone. She'd left home an hour and a half ago, and even considering that it'd taken an hour to walk from her place to the bar, she'd still burned almost thirty minutes doing...nothing.

It was out of character, but she couldn't deny what was going on. She was procrastinating, and she was avoiding. Just because they'd spent the better part of two months in each other's beds didn't mean they couldn't have a friendly, cordial relationship, and the fact that she'd ended things when he wanted more and she didn't was no reason to expect him to turn down the request she was dreading making.

She pushed the door open and strode in. Her temper was already flaring, even though he hadn't done anything. Yet. He'd invaded her mind, her dreams, and her habits—she seldom slept, she'd removed the mirrors from her house, and was now the kind of person who avoided confrontation instead of facing it head on—and that was enough.

Felicity, Oracle Bay newcomer—there'd been a lot of those after the near-apocalypse—and one of the Pour House's newest servers looked up from where she was putting away clean glassware behind the bar and waved. She was always cheerful, almost to the point of annoyance. She was a white woman with long, dark brown hair that was caught back in a clip decorated with miniature violets that sparkled when she moved.

Zeke was on the floor talking to a white woman dressed completely in black and shrouding her face with her black hoodie. She was sitting alone—one of the few people who'd shown up for the early afternoon opening time on a Tuesday in March—and probably intimidating the crap out of the other customers. Ceri had heard him complain more than once about having to be anywhere besides behind the bar on the rare occasions he graced the rest of the psychics with his prophetic presence.

Ceri pulled her attention away from the woman—focusing on a stranger was just one more way to delay—and paused, not sure what to do now that she was here. Asking for Andy seemed weird. Presumptuous? Ridiculous at best.

"He's in his office," Brandy said from her place at the end of the bar where she was poring over her laptop. She looked at Ceri and grinned, amusement dancing in her hazel eyes.

"Who?" Ceri asked, then rolled her eyes at herself. Only two people had offices, and one of them was talking to her right now.

Brandy didn't even try to hide her smirk. "Oh, honey. I don't know what is going on between the two of you, but whatever it is, you need to get it straightened out. It's making you stupid. I say that with friendship and love."

"Sure thing, Brandy. You're definitely not calling me out because you want your boss to pull it together and brew some new award-winning beers. It's friendship."

Brandy winked at Ceri. "I really love running this bar, so I was telling the truth. Mostly."

"Is he busy?"

"Never too busy for you. It's a standing order. The boss's only order, actually. You're allowed unfettered access to anywhere and anything at the Pour House. You want to examine the books? I'll log you into the accounting software and glare at you from the other side of the bar."

"Just Andy's office for now. I'll let you know if I need to check your math later."

"Have fun, but don't scare the clientele."

"Pinky promise," Ceri said, letting the grin that had been threatening to sneak out during her conversation creep across her face.

Ceri strode over to the stairs, then stomped up to the second floor. His office door was closed, as usual, so she raised her hand to knock.

The door opened before her hand dropped. Andy stood in the

doorway, mere inches from her. She was conscious of his closeness, his body heat, and his scent—wood smoke, leather, and peat.

"What do you want?" he snapped. Silver wings popped open behind him, sending sparks into the air that flitted down to singe his shirt. The scent of sulfur intertwined with the other smoky smells that made up Andras Sterling, fallen angel, former Grand Marquis of Hell, and current owner of the best brewpub on Washington State's Long Beach peninsula.

Ceri cringed inwardly. He was already angry with her, and all she'd done was show up. Her eyes drifted from the sparks flying off his wings to his body, then up to his face. Andy was white with lightly tanned skin, tall and broad-shouldered, had grey eyes like the sea after a storm, and silver hair that contrasted sharply with his unlined, ageless face. He was, in a word, beautiful.

Ceri's breath hitched, and she blushed when Andy's lips curled in a sardonic smile. Dammit. He affected her, and she wished he didn't know how much.

"Well?" he prompted. "Did you come all the way over here just to admire me, or did you have something to say?" Andy tapped his foot, and the sulfur smell intensified. Sparks flew with each tap of his toe, and she watched, mesmerized and afraid to say what she'd come there to say.

"I am tired of games, Ceridwen," he said. The silver-grey wings that had torn through his shirt drooped, the tips brushing against the floor. "You said it was over between us, that it was an apocalyptic fling you never meant to last longer than the final battle. And yet, you keep seeking me out, raising my hopes, and my well..." His voice trailed off, and he arched an eyebrow at her with a smirk. "Say what you want and leave."

Shame heated her skin and pushed a lump into her throat. She'd treated him poorly, and that was no lie. She hadn't said anything that wasn't true, but she hadn't approached it with kindness, trusting that the several millennia of experience and life he had behind him meant he didn't need kindness.

"I'm sorry."

"Save it," Andy ground out. "Get to the point and get out."

Ceri bit her lip. She knew she had to tell him, to ask for his help, but admitting she needed him after walking away was almost too much. A small wave of dizziness pushed through her hesitation. "Our connection didn't sever," she said, the words coming so fast they tumbled over each other in their effort to be free. "When I scried you and was pulled into you, into all of you, the visions and the memories stayed longer than with anyone else I've ever read."

Andy took a step back, and the sparks died in the air; no more appeared to take their places. He motioned towards one of the two chairs facing each other near the window, and she sat.

"I told everyone the aftereffects would fade eventually because that's what always happens. But they didn't. Not only is it still incredibly taxing to use my skills for anyone else, half the time I see you instead of them. I'll be scrying Joe's future as a senior accountant before he goes for the big promotion he's too scared to apply for, and then he's burning in hell while demons torture him. While *you* torture him." She didn't add that every time she glanced in a mirror without purpose, flames leapt to the surface and consumed her mind with nightmares of being the one Andy was torturing.

Andy reached forward as if to grab the hands that were shaking in Ceri's lap but stopped himself. She didn't like to be touched without invitation, and she'd revoked his invitation.

"And the dreams," she continued. Her voice broke, and she curled in on herself. Looking at her hands twisting in her lap, she could no longer maintain the confident façade she'd been wearing for months. "I can't tell if I'm dreaming your memories, or if it's my brain taking bits of everything I've learned and mixing it into something new."

"What makes you think we're still connected, and it's not just your brain having trouble handling everything it downloaded?"

"I can still see your present and your future, and it changes based on what—" she'd almost said, "what I do," which was not what she wanted to convey. "Based on what you do," she finished clumsily. "I know where you are and what you're doing. I know how your decision to brew a salted caramel porter will affect sales and what awards it will win.

"And if that wasn't bad enough, I can never turn it off. It's draining me. Every day, things are a little more difficult, and the parts of me that are *me* are a little more faded. The parts that are you are stronger. I'm tired. I haven't worked in six weeks because I can't risk getting pulled into a hell I can't control and can't escape. It took me an hour to make the twenty-minute walk here, and I'm drenched with sweat from the effort."

Andy's wings flared out and curved around him. The rotten egg odor of his anger diminished. "What can I do? What should I do? I never meant..."

Ceri smiled sadly. "I know. Neither of us did. I didn't realize at first. It wasn't until..." She trailed off. The symptoms hadn't intensified until she stopped spending nights, and a few afternoons, and some unforgettable mornings, with Andy. "Can we try something? Hold my hand?" She reached out to him. He took her hand and pulled her closer to him.

"Does it help? The contact?" Concern reverberated through his voice, and he placed his other hand on her upper arm. Wood smoke and leather once again were his dominant scents.

"A bit," she admitted. "But not enough. Andy, it's killing me. I don't know how much longer..."

"I will stay here and hold you until we figure out how to fix this. You're going to be fine. I did this, and I will find a way to make it right."

"You're gonna hold me and figure out how to fix me at the same time?" Ceri laughed. "That's some multitasking. Besides, I'm still fine. Just tired. We have time to figure this out. At the rate things have been deteriorating, I'd estimate I have at least four to five months before it gets really bad. I wouldn't have waited until the end to come to you, no matter how stubborn I am."

"We'll figure this out together, and whenever you need relief, my body is yours." He winced. "That isn't what I meant. I mean that, too, but…"

"I know. Thank you. It doesn't change things, and I don't want it to get weird."

"Ceri, in the last year, we've seen magical goats turn into goddesses, had an apocalypse, and gotten drunk with a wine god, and that barely scratches the surface. It's already weird."

"You know what I meant."

He sighed regretfully and retracted his wings. "I know. Have you told your friends?"

She shook her head. "Not yet. Everyone's so busy, and Drew was preparing for his and Bill's first long vacation. I'm waiting for them to get back, so I don't have to tell the story more than once."

"And then find another excuse? Misty is getting ready for the grand opening of two new businesses, or Sandy is headed out of town to visit Dionysus for some father daughter time, or the Autumn Bazaar is only five months away…"

Ceri wrinkled her nose at him. Maybe procrastination wasn't as foreign a trait as she wanted to believe. "Rude. But true. I'll tell them as soon as Drew returns. He should be back in three days."

"In the meantime, you should get plenty of rest. I'll drive you home."

"Fine. I'll let you do that, but only because I'm really tired." Ceri's eyelids drooped a bit, but she mustered a smile. "Let's go. I haven't been sleeping well at night, but maybe I can manage a nap. If it's not asking too much, perhaps you can lie down with me?" She held her breath; asking that question was harder than it should've been knowing how much it would help, and if he said no…

"Anything. Always. There's nothing I wouldn't do."

"Thank you." Ceri stood up and smiled at Andy and stepped back, breaking their physical contact. The smile slid off her face. Flames leapt into her mind, pulling her into hell. The blood drained from her face, and she gasped for the air that wouldn't quite fill her lungs. The world turned grey, and her knees buckled.

Andy's arms were around her before she hit the ground. The hell-fire shrank back, but it didn't bring the relief she'd felt from his touch moments before. Shivers wracked her body, and only the heat from his kept her teeth from chattering. Her heart raced, and the pressure she hoped was panic and not a heart attack landed on her chest, making it even harder to breathe. The grey in her vision was quickly darkening, and she closed her eyes. The sound of his wings snapping out kept her on this side of consciousness, and his roar of anger forced her eyes open. He launched himself upwards, one fist raised to break the ceiling before it could break them, and flew through the roof of his pub into the late morning sky.

"Brandy is gonna be mad you broke the roof," Ceri coughed out. Her strength drained from her body, leaving her limp in his arms. The sun blazed down at her, filling her field of vision with bright white light—too bright to look at—then the darkness pulled her down.

One-click Hell and High Water now!

PSYCHICS OF
ORACLE BAY
BOOK 5
Hell and
High Water
USA TODAY BESTSELLING AUTHOR
AMY CISSELL

raising a demon
MIDLIFE MAGIC IN EDEN VALLEY #1

Raising a Demon is the first book in Midlife Magic in Eden Valley, a magical new paranormal women's fiction series. Eden Valley & Oracle Bay are in the same universe, and there are some crossover characters and cameos!

Being a single mother has its challenges, but Evie never imagined that "the talk" would involve Ouija boards and pentagrams.

Evelyn Addams is forty-three and fabulous. She has a great kid, fantastic friends, and doesn't need a man to complete her. But when she catches ten-year-old Lily summoning a demon to ask for birthday wishes—and the demon who turns up is Evie's summer fling from eleven years ago—her comfortable life is shattered.

Reuniting with an old flame is tricky enough but finding out he grows horns and a tail makes a romantic reconnection downright complicated. And when Lily is kidnapped by her newfound grandfather, the last shred of her old life is destroyed, and everything goes to hell.

Will Evie and her friends rescue Lily from hell before the lights go out and the lost souls come out to play? And can she ignore past and Luc's family complications to take a second chance on love and learn how to raise a demon's daughter? Get your copy of Raising a Demon today!

http://www.books2read.com/raisingademon

acknowledgments

All my love to the Amyzonians—my Facebook reader group—you guys are fantastic. Thanks for liking and sharing my posts, reading and reviewing, staying engaged with me, and voting on all my weird polls.

Thank you to my editor Suzanne Lahna. Working with you was such an amazing experience. Thanks for caring about Bill & Drew's story and working so hard to make it better.

Christopher—my proofreader, formatter, business partner, and even more importantly, husband and bestest encourager—I could never do this without you.

There is no way to talk about the people who support and lift me up without mentioning Liana. My best girl, favorite kid, most challenging person I know, and greatest love. Maybe someday I'll let you read more than the dedication and acknowledgments. Love you to the moon and the stars and back.

Last and certainly least, the cats. There are so many of you now, but as is now tradition (twice is tradition, right?) I'll thank you in order of your general likability and lack of asshattery as of December 2019. 1) Darwin (age 14), you've been the number one cat in my heart for almost 15 years, but your move inside and subsequent near-constant yowling has put your ranking in danger. 2) Frank the Tank (age 5). You haven't chewed through any of my undergarments lately and you're good-looking and even tempered (and quiet), so you're inching your way to number one territory. Keep it up! 3) Mr. Sterling (age 11). You've really improved in the last six months. Much less pee and barf to clean up. Good job! 4) Rupurrt Giles (age 2). You are an enthusiastic asshole with nearly boundless energy and a love for being the cattiest cat to ever cat. You, sir, are the worst.

Amy can be found on most social media channels @acissellwrites. Come visit her website at amycissell.com for blogs & books! (autographed copies, if you want!)

Amy Cissell is a USA Today Bestselling Author of urban fantasy and paranormal romance novels. She lives in Portland, OR with her husband, her haunted house-obsessed daughter, their three cats, and the murder of crows she's conspiring to turn into her vengeful army.

When she's not working or writing, she's sleeping because that's all she has time to do! There are few things Amy loves more than a well-timed pun, a good book, a glass of wine, and time at the Oregon Coast.

Although she reads anything and everything, her first love is fantasy. Eleven-year-old Amy discovered fantasy when she 'borrowed' her father's copy of The Hobbit and an enduring love affair (mostly with dragons) was born.

facebook.com/acissellwrites

instagram.com/acissellwrites

bookbub.com/authors/amy-cissell

goodreads.com/acissellwrites

tiktok.com/@acissellwrites

patreon.com/ACissellWrites

Valley of Angels (November 2021)

Guardian of Eden (February 2022)

Eden Valley World Novellas

Match Made in Hell (June 2021)

Hell's Bells (December 2021)

Fall From Grace (January 2022)

Devil May Care (February 2022)

Box Sets

Welcome to Eden Valley (Novellas 1-4)

Vamps in the Vineyard

Here to Slay (September 2022)

Vamps in the Vineyard Novellas

(newsletter subscribers only)

Stakes and Stems (September 2023)

Slay Bells Ring (January 2023)

Contemporary/Urban Fantasy

An Eleanor Morgan Fantasy Adventure

(complete series)

The Cardinal Gate (February 2017)

The Waning Moon (June 2017)

The Ruby Blade (October 2017)

The Broken World (March 2018)

The Lost Child (June 2019)

The Iron River (May 2020)

The Dark Throne (February 2021)

Box Sets (ebook only)

Eleanor Morgan Books 1-4

Eleanor Morgan Books 5-7

Ghosts of Valhalla

As Yet Untitled (late 2023)

www.ingramcontent.com/pod-product-compliance
Lightning Source LLC
Chambersburg PA
CBHW070445200726
48293CB00007B/2127